THE NIGHT HAS CLAWS

THE NIGHT HAS CLAWS

KAT KRUGER

The Magdeburg Trilogy
Book Two

FIERCE INK PRESS

The Night Has Claws
Copyright © 2013 by Kat Kruger
All rights reserved

Published by Fierce Ink Press Co-Op Ltd.
www.fierceinkpress.com

First edition, 2013

Library and Archives Canada Cataloguing in Publication information is available upon request.

ISBN 978-0-9917937-5-4 (paperback)
Also available in electronic format

Edited by Allister Thompson
Cover design by Angela Goddard

The text type was set in Didot.

To my husband.

For the werewolves,
not-so-mad science
and wordsmithing.

"*He alone to whom creation belongs can change the form of things. And it would be a shameful thing for a man, to whom all the beasts of the earth are subject, to be clothed in the form of a beast.*"
— Henri Boguet, *Discours des Sorciers*, translated into English as *An Examen of Witches* by E. Allen Ashwin

A. FORMIDABLE

Formidable: *adjective*. Inspiring fear or respect through being impressively large, powerful, intense or capable.

I swallow down even the idea of crying. One day I might drown in all the misery I've had to push down since I was bitten, but not today. Not when there's a horrible corpse bleeding at my feet. I let out a weird noise at the sight of Boadicea's body. Killing her wasn't part of the plan.

Connor puts his hand on my shoulder and I wish I had a little bottle labeled "drink me" so I could just shrink into oblivion like Alice in Wonderland. It's unfair. All of it. We turned his life upside-down and now he's throwing me this pity party.

"Don't make this harder than it needs to be," I say and instantly regret the cliché.

I can't even look at him because I'll flake out if I do. There's no time for him to stick around and feel sorry for me. No time for long goodbyes like in a movie. He needs to walk away so I can finish my job, and he can tell the pack about whatever just went down.

His hand slides away, fingertips pulling down against the

sleeve of my hoodie like waves at low tide sucking back the shore, and I wish a piece of me could be carried off with him. A good cry is what I need at this exact moment. I would totally love to just scream — the way I used to when I was six years old for the sake of no reason at all — until my throat gets hoarse enough that it kills. The way strep throat feels, all scratchy and hurty and too mind-numbingly painful to even breathe. That's what I want, desperately. That's what I *need* more than anything. Then the tears could just flow as freely and naturally as breathing. But I can't do that right now because of him.

My voice is barely functional when I say "I'm sorry" to no one in particular. I dig into the soil of the withered flowerbed with my bare hands while trying not to look at her. In a painting she'd look fab: pale skin, strawberry blonde hair spread out like a fan, nude chiffon blouse all airy and frou-frou. Up close and personal it's a different story. The blood is the worst part of it, not seeping enough into the dry earth, so it's pooling beneath her body. I try to work fast.

Grit builds beneath my fingernails. I can't see it underneath my polish — a dark but sparkly shade of purple that I picked more for the name than anything, *Formidable!*, as if a coat of toxic lacquer could give me superpowers — but I feel the dirt there. That's not exactly even relevant right now. I should say something else so he doesn't think I'm a completely heartless B.

"You don't know what they're capable of," I say without looking up, reminding him of that scientist Henri Boguet and his henchmen.

He doesn't answer. He must hate me. He has to think I'm a monster. I glance back to gauge the look on his face but he's gone. Screw him! It's not like I meant for it to happen. This meeting had all the makings of a trap. As *if* I was supposed to know she grew a conscience!

I do my best to cover the body. Seconds or minutes or even an hour goes by, but then I feel his hand on my shoulder again and relief washes over me. I turn expecting to see his brown eyes and mess of chestnut hair but instead it's blue-eyed Josh. The disappointment on my face is something he should be used to by now but it's like he keeps expecting me to somehow un-remember what he did to me.

Josh glances between me and the mound of earth, and he can't hide his disbelief. Sitting back on my heels I'll admit it's pathetic. Even in the faded light I can see her outline beneath the dirt, looking like a kid on a beach who asked to be covered in sand. It won't fool anybody but he doesn't have to point out with his disapproving look how ridiculous I am. Before he can say anything I come to my own defense.

"Let's see *you* do better with the grave-digging, Dr. Frankenstein."

"We've got bigger issues," he says.

The sound of shattering stone makes me straighten up, full attention. Tombstones and mausoleums surround us here in Père Lachaise Cemetery but there aren't a whole lot of things in the natural world that can destroy granite and marble, not without the sounds of machines too.

"Did Connor make it out of here?" I ask.

Josh hesitates in that annoying way of his when he doesn't want to be the bearer of bad news. Like I'm made of glass or something and so über fragile that it'd break me just to hear what he has to say. It makes me completely crazy and sometimes I want to punch his face so the words spill out of his mouth. Somehow he always manages to stutter the message out before it gets to that point, though. He shakes his head.

I take off down the cobblestone path. To hell with the half-buried body. The Hounds will take care of it later. Whatever is going on has something to do with Boguet and those asshats he has working for him. The asshats in question, Trajan and Attila, have been useful for their black market antivenin but that also makes them shifty as all hell. And maybe Boadicea wasn't about to off Connor at the precise moment when I shot her but she wasn't exactly on the up-and-up either.

One moment Josh is trailing behind me, the next he's in the lead. Damn him for being so athletic. Ahead of us I see some of the Hounds from Josh's hostel who have shifted already. Our living arrangements are covered by the Hounds. Brother Christopher, a white-robed monk who oversees the hostel, leads the boys. In this form, the claw marks on his scarred face are mostly filled in with fur. A blessing for his curse.

Boguet has also transformed into the half-beast, half-man creature of my nightmares. I know it's him because of the old-man tweed suit he always wears, now stretched and torn from the transformation. The elbow patches are a dead giveaway. He stands near two majestic wolves, which makes his misshapen form even more hideous by comparison. I recognize Connor as a wolf even though there are striking similarities between him and Arden. It's the eyes; they never lie. There's so much blood, I can't tell whose it is.

Tombstones are overturned around them. It's like some unnatural force tore through this part of the cemetery, leaving a swath of destruction in its wake. Even Boguet himself is bleeding from a gash in his ribs, which says either Connor or Arden was able to stand his ground as a man before transforming into a wolf. Trajan and Attila are nowhere to be seen and that stacks the odds in our favor for winning this fight.

As Josh shifts to join the others, I quickly strip down to just my leggings and T-shirt. Enough outfits get ruined from the change every month without me having to try. I really hate this part — when the animal *literally* crawls up from under my skin. The pull of the full moon makes it easier. Not that it's easy.

Since being bitten I've wondered what it's like to be a born werewolf, like Arden and Amara, and if the shift is the same slow torture for them as it is for us. When I watched Connor transform last night, it killed me a little. Everything about his change was chilling, peaceful, beautiful. Like watching a sculpture come to life.

I stifle the scream that wants to escape my lungs as my body turns into the terrible monster that will probably have to do ugly things tonight. Like the born, the shift for the bitten happens in only a few seconds but the time it takes could stretch into infinity for all the pain we go through. It's like everything that's on the inside of us gets rearranged to make room for the wolf: bones, organs, everything.

The awful sound of sinews tearing and bones cracking accompanies the change like some twisted symphony. It's a noise I dread whenever I brace for the throes of sheer agony that will flood my body. After the transformation I join the others in the fight, together in a line of six. Like the tattoo on my ankle, it's the number of the beast. They growl in unison without me. I find it hard enough to keep a hold on the real me without openly embracing my inner wolf.

As we approach, it looks like Arden is unconscious and Connor repositions himself over his body. Our eyes meet briefly. Lips curled back from his teeth and ears pressed flat against his head, Connor trembles. I doubt he knows it's me. He didn't when he shifted for the first time last night. He was pure animal then.

I know the words that will come next. Everything is a ritual to the Hounds. But I'm surprised when Brother Christopher isn't the one who says them. For the first time he lets Josh have this honor. And I don't like it. It feels like some kind of initiation.

"By the hands of the Hounds of God, we cast thee back into darkness," Josh says.

When he speaks his voice rasps from being not-quite-human, not-quite-wolf, and I despise the sound. It makes my skin crawl even more than seeing him like this. And the holier-than-thou air about him. There's no darkness that's blacker than our fate. No place we can send Boguet that makes up for anything that goes down after we're bitten. There's *nothing* worse than surviving a bite. Nothing. I'm not onside with him, but at least he's done something. He created an antivenin. Science, though, *that's* the devil's handiwork in their books.

Boguet is crazy-mad. Whatever his reasons, he has it in for Connor and Arden in a big way. Lucky for them, the Hounds are stepping up to save their asses. Boguet makes a quick lunge toward us but we surround him easily. I'd claw his eyes out if I knew for sure that any of the blood spilled was Connor's, but I don't so I just stand my ground and let the others fight it out. There will be epic stories told after all of this is over, but they can be heroes. Me? Not interested.

Somehow Boguet manages to break through our circle. He turns his attention back to the wolves — wolf. Who knows why but Arden has turned back into a hot mess of a man now, naked and lying face down against the cobblestone pathway. Bloody, disheveled and barely conscious.

As Boguet turns his attention toward them I race past the others to take up a defensive stance between the two sides, but I can't get there in time. The mad scientist is only a few feet away when Josh heaves up a fallen tombstone like it weighs nothing and shatters it across Boguet's back. Huge fragments of marble splinter and fly apart in every direction. Arden lets out a warning cry, too late, as a massive chunk catches Connor in the back of the skull and knocks him out cold.

I wish I could say time freezes or speeds up. But it

doesn't. Things just happen at a regular pace while I stand dumbly in place. The others surround Boguet's fallen form. He's captured, but he's not. We still have to shift back in order to claim that victory. Putting him in shackles needs human hands and the full moon makes going back to that form insanely hard. Nothing about being bitten is easy. Like, ever.

The others stand in their circle around him chanting their prayer. It's supposed to help. The sound of it snaps me back to reality. Brother Christopher motions for me to join them but I won't and he knows it. Josh told me once that the chant is a prayer of confession. Like what we are is a sin that can be absolved. I stride past them and over to the true-born werewolves. Kneeling down next to them, I look for signs of life. They fell facing each other and both are unconscious now. Arden's hand lingers at the fur of Connor's throat where a gold ring hangs from a matching chain.

Time passes as I sit on my haunches and stare. Eventually we all shift back one by one. There's no real method to it. It doesn't matter how old you are or how long ago you were bitten. It's different for everyone — controlling the monster, pushing it back down. And even if you think you've mastered the beast, it rises up to surprise you every once in a while. Like it did that night when Josh bit me. Since then Connor Lewis was the only normal thing in my life.

Not was. *Is*.

I hope.

He made me feel like a normal girl but only because he

had no clue about the monster within me. Maybe I *am* selfish for wanting him to be alive for that reason alone, but I can't help it. His eyes flicker open. My hand dives into the fur of his neck. It's stupid and reckless and freaks him out. He scrambles unsteadily to his paws but slips on the pool of blood beneath him and collapses against Arden's unmoving body. I can see the fear in his glassy eyes. I want him to know everything is okay. Words are useless now, though.

His nostrils flare and I wish for the animal stink of me to be covered up. As we take each other in, the others work quickly. Boguet has already been restrained and is being ushered out of sight. Those remaining check Arden for a pulse, then, I guess finding none, they seal his corpse in a black body bag and carry him away. It's time to go. Connor's fading out fast. Gently, I reach out and stroke the short fur of his muzzle and I hope he understands.

The cemetery groundskeeper, who's part of Arden's pack, lets us out through a side entrance. The more I see of the born werewolves, the more I see the differences between them and humans. Even though he looks like the stereotype of a blue-collar worker in his long-sleeved cotton shirt and heavy overalls, there's no denying the wolfiness of his features. As he holds open the door for us, he pulls out a cellphone and dials. Aquila, their pack leader, will hear about what went down here. That's good. Someone needs to look after Connor.

Josh is on the other side in the driver's seat of my Jeep, which he backed in close to the metal gate. He hands me my hoodie and Keds while the others, having retrieved Boadicea's body from its makeshift grave, load two body bags behind our seats. I put the hoodie on over my stretched and torn T-shirt and leggings, followed by my socks and shoes, focusing all my attention on the simple task of dressing myself. Or I try to. Otherwise I'd gag. Here I am about to chauffeur two dead people to their ultimate destination. Josh wordlessly slides over to shotgun and as Brother Christopher covers the bags with camouflage netting, I hop into the driver's seat. His sedan with blacked out windows idles nearby. When it pulls away I follow.

We don't say a word to each other, Josh and I. There was a time when I wanted to fill in all the silences. When he did too. It makes me super sad to remember that there was a time when he was crushing on me so hard that he talked for hours about nothing and everything all at the same time.

The silence is unnatural. I've always lived for words, since I was a kid. I would devour languages, collect every new word the way other kids collected LEGO or stickers. Once there was a time when I lived for the warm embrace of imperfect little sentences flowing from Josh's beautiful mouth. He gave up his entire world for me.

"You alright?" he asks.

I haven't been alright for months and I don't want to talk about it.

"Maddy?"

When he ended things between us I made a bunch of cruel promises to myself. This kind of reticence between us was one of them. I didn't want his pity or to see those sad blue eyes look at me full of regret. And I *definitely* didn't want to become his pet project on his road to redemption. He wasn't supposed to love me. Ever. But he did and he ruined everything.

"You had no choice," he says.

"Stop talking."

I grip the steering wheel, hard. Hot, stupid tears start to roll down my face. Nothing he can say will make things right with us. Like it or not, he's friend-zoned in ways that are beyond both of our control. He wants so desperately for me to forgive him, but once he bit me there was no way he could contain the aftermath. It was like that oil spill in the Gulf of Mexico. An accident waiting to happen, and once it did no amount of golf balls in the world could plug it up. He didn't mean to destroy my life, but it was only a matter of time. He polluted everything. Now we're suffocating, sinking, not able to come up out of the darkness for air because we don't even know which direction we're facing anymore. We're smothered in that black night.

Every bit of me longs for a comforting hand on my shoulder. A connection to another human being. Someone to make me feel like everything's *actually* going to be okay in the end. Josh and I lost what we used to have together. And I hate myself for sometimes still wanting it.

I park behind the sedan on the side of the road at Vincennes Park. Before the others can see me, I wipe away the remains of my tears from my face with the backs of my hands then leap out of the Jeep and wait for them to unload the bodies. I'm done. I just want to walk away. But I have to suffer through a little more before I can leave.

We march into the forest until we're greeted by Madame Lefèvre, the woman who runs my boarding house, and four of the older girls. While we were en route, they dug two shallow graves here in the middle of nowhere. The school-marm wears thin black leather gloves and an outfit that should only ever be seen in one place: horseback riding in the English countryside.

Being bitten messes a person up.

She tries so hard to set an example, especially for the younger girls. I don't see the point. It's certifiably insane the way she insists on teaching us manners and etiquette and how to be 'proper' young ladies. *Please*. All the pretty bows and curtsies in the world can't hide the fact that we're all monsters. And we can't be trusted.

Josh takes hold of my hand and instinctively I resist, but he doesn't let go. Instead he pulls me into the circle forming around Arden and Boadicea, who lie side by side, each in their own open grave. Everyone in the circle bows their heads except for me. I just stare at the corpses. Arden's hands have been strategically placed to cover his man parts. Next to him Boadicea looks like a blushing bride in the bright moonlight. Brother Christopher leads the prayer for the dead, even though the words are really meant for the living.

"Remember, O Lord, our God of spirits and of all flesh, those whom we have remembered and those whom we have not remembered, those of the true faith; give them rest in the land of the living, in Your kingdom, in the delight of Paradise, in the bosom of our Holy Father, from whence pain and sorrow and sighing have fled away, where the light of Your face visits them and always shines upon them."

The Hounds around me chant, "Peace be with them."

Death and dying were all I thought about for the first month after being bitten. I remember getting goosebumps reading through an ancient book from the library while in recovery: "*I see him there at the oars of his little boat in the lake, the ferryman of the dead, Kharon, with his hand upon the oar, and he calls me now.*"

I fish coins from the pocket of my hoodie and hand them to Josh. It's our little secret. You're supposed to place pennies on the eyes of the dead as a fee for entering the afterlife. Not that I believe in anything after this life. I carry them around for him — for the ritual of it — so he won't worry so much about my soul after I'm gone. I imagine my spirit just flickering out like a candle. The essence of me gone forever. Two pennies don't exactly add up to the amount I owe for taking someone's life, but maybe Captain Death can put the rest on credit for me.

Josh places the coins over Arden's eyes and I want to curse at him. They were meant for Boadicea. Before I can fix his mistake, he pulls out coins of his own and places them on her eyes. Something catches in my throat and a surge of unwanted emotion rolls over me unexpectedly. He never told me he'd started carrying pennies too. The last thing I want is to have a meltdown here in front of all these Hounds, so I turn away as two of the guys begin to shovel dirt over the bodies.

Madame Lefèvre gathers the girls like a flock of sheep,

shepherding us back home. Instead of joining them, I head back to my Jeep. For a second I just sit plunked down behind the steering wheel again. An image of Connor comes to mind, lying there in the cemetery, waking up alone and confused. Pulling out my phone from my hoodie pocket, I see that it's almost lost its charge. I quickly map our GPS coordinates then share it with the message: *Arden's here.*

I just really hope he understands.

I may be cursed.

I may be a monster.

But I never meant for any of this to happen.

1. UNKNOWN BROTHER

I wake at the hospital. It takes me a second to remember where I am and how I got here. Last night I drove here in the car of a dead girl after a fight in a graveyard. I thought Arden died. But he didn't. He was buried alive. Imagining what went down isn't hard to do. I can list on one hand the number of movies I've seen in which people have been put to the ground prematurely. The idea has always freaked me out even if there are worse ways to go. All the same, slowly running out of air would come with a terror I've never known. In our everyday lives breathing comes naturally, without any thought: inhale, exhale, repeat until death. Six feet underground, all that changes. Every breath becomes an enemy closing in and there is no escape. Suffocation is the endgame. In Arden's case, he was lucky for the shallow grave that allowed him to dig his way out, broken arm and all. Here I am in the hazy aftermath, awake but in the fog of sleep and wakefulness. I must have dozed off in the chair by Arden's bed where he now lies beneath the thin sheets, motionless except for the faint pulse of life rising and falling with his every breath. The color has returned to his face and someone has washed off all the dirt that he was covered in. He looks surprisingly peaceful and in good health considering he was on the brink of death just a few hours ago.

Stretching out in the chair, I let out a loud and unrestrained yawn without thinking. His eyes flutter open to the noise. They glow golden amber in the bright sunlight that floods the room, and all I see in them is the wolf that he once was. The one he can never be again. I lean forward in the chair, unsure of what to say. Our relationship has been tenuous at best, to say the least. Since day one he's been impossibly rude to me. I've been nothing but a problem for him, waiting to unravel. After what happened last night, I don't know what to make of our situation. Arden lets out an incomprehensible noise, unable to get any words out, not that he was ever one for saying much. I pour him a glass of water from a small pitcher by his bedside and he takes a long, quenching swig then sets the glass down next to him.

When he finally speaks, all he says is, "*Pourqoui?*"

Why? Why did I save him? His voice is brittle, like an autumn leaf left out to dry. It's another reminder of how human he is, how fragile. I can't shake the sting of betrayal in his eyes.

I swallow hard and respond in French. "Roul said that mercy has a human heart. What was I supposed to do?"

"This is no mercy," he tells me flatly. "You should've listened to me."

Listened. Right. Arden had asked me to kill him. That I remember as clearly as though he just said the words. I want to feel sorry for him, but I just can't. I can't overlook his callous disregard for both the death that he's been spared and the life he's been given. Maybe it's not ideal — life just isn't — but it's something. And it sure as hell beats dying in the middle of the woods from hypothermia. I preferred him when he was unconscious.

"Look, if you want to off yourself, that's on you but I wasn't about to stand by and let you die out there."

I brace myself. This is usually the part where he gets up in my grill to assert his dominance and where I want to feel my fist connect with his face. Instead he looks away, out the window and across the city. There's nothing about this scenario that's right.

He speaks quietly, as though to himself. "I *did* die out there."

Rising from my seat, I push the chair back angrily enough that it tips over behind me. "What do you want, Arden? A standing O for wallowing in self-pity?"

Although I know it's uncalled for, my emotions have been a little out of control around the full moon. I guess being a new werewolf does that to you. There's not much I know about my new condition but I am aware that shifting can be brought on by extreme emotions, anger being one of them, so I force myself to calm down. The last thing I need is to turn into a wolf in the middle of a hospital. Arden's eyes are back on me with a slight look of bemusement. He scans the clothes I'm wearing — his clothes — borrowed after the fight with Boguet. I probably look ridiculous dressed in his stylish black outfit that's meant for someone far more *Esquire* than me. At least I broke through his spell of melancholy.

"I don't want this life, Connor."

We both know there's no changing the cards we've been dealt. We were both recently bitten, but with completely different outcomes. Me, I became the wolf I never knew I was meant to be. And him, well, he was 'cured' against his will from being the wolf he always was. Behind me, I can hear others entering the room. It's a doctor, the same one who saved Arden's life. The life he doesn't want. She's brought a nurse with her who picks up and rights the chair behind me.

I switch to English and say quickly to Arden, "This *is* your life now."

The doctor whose name — no joke — is Dr. Moreau (as in *The Island Of*) speaks to us in French and the nurse translates for her in passable English. Even though we understand everything the doctor is saying, I don't interrupt and Arden has the sense to play along. That or he doesn't care, which is probably more likely. The ruse of only being able to speak English was how I avoided not having to explain everything that brought us here last night. Truth is, I wouldn't even have known where to begin. Even after thinking about it for so many hours, my brain still whirs in an attempt to piece together a believable story. There are too many ways this hospital stint could go wrong if I have to talk about what actually happened. How would I omit the part involving people who turn into wolves or wolf-human hybrids?

Near as I can tell the doctor is giving Arden a clean bill of health, save the broken arm. We're told that he'll need to take antibiotics to prevent infection. They stress the importance of this by talking to me directly as though between the two of us I'm somehow the one who's more together. And it's no wonder, because to look at him Arden gives the impression that he's bored by all this talk. Even the word 'amputation' doesn't affect his demeanor. Before he's discharged, we're given some forms to sign and handed a prescription for the antibiotics and the name of an over-the-counter painkiller. Just as they're about to leave, the doctor ends with a translated address to Arden specifically.

"I did not see a reason to involve the police, but you are fortunate that your brother acted so quickly."

Brothers. Another lie I was forced to tell. I can feel his gaze on me again, but this time I don't meet his eyes. I'm just thankful he went along with the charade and hasn't said anything to compromise my story. I tell him, after the pair leaves the room, "I've got a change of clothes in the car for you."

Stepping out before he can press any questions on me, I lope down the corridors of the hospital in search of a way out. There's an antiseptic scent that fails to cover up other human odors: vomit, blood and even death. Smells that I never would have noticed in my former life. This is *my* life now. I'm glad when I step outside into the crisp November air. Shoving my hands into the pockets of a borrowed gray wool coat — the only article of clothing that survived Arden's emergency room visit — I walk across the parking lot to where I parked Boadicea's car last night. Opening the trunk, I reach for my backpack and pull the zipper. Tightness squeezes my heart when I see the gun laid on top of the change of clothes. Lowering my head, I press my brow against the cool metal of the trunk's lid. Boadicea — Brigid — said she was a ghost, but I didn't believe her. Ghosts don't bleed. I very distinctly remember the red pool of it flowing from her heart after Madison fired this gun.

A chilling breath blows into my ear from behind like a phantom presence. As I close my eyes to block out the memory, warm tears stream down my face. I need to hold it together. At least until I get Arden sorted out. Pushing the heels of my hands into my eyes, I wipe away the moisture, gently lay the gun aside and pull the clothes out of my backpack. With an aggressive slam of the trunk, I return to Arden's room and hand him my clothes. By the expression on his face it must be obvious that I've been crying so I turn away quickly and tell him, "I'll wait out in the hall."

I lean back against the hallway wall between rooms and stare at the yellowed vinyl at my feet. Every hospital in the world must have flooring just like this. Eventually the door clicks open and Arden emerges from the room wearing my *American Idiot* T-shirt and jeans. It would have called too much attention to us if we switched outfits here. Our clothes fit each other despite the obvious differences in style. He fills out my T-shirt with lean muscles while his shirt is loose around my lanky frame. Otherwise, he *could* pass as a relation. All the same, to me it's weird knowing we're wearing each other's clothes. Pushing off the wall, I pass him the wool coat. Since being bitten, I've operated at a higher body temperature. As we walk to the parking lot, it's quiet between us. Even though we've developed a relationship of uneasy silence, it feels different now in light of our recent reversal of fortunes. After all, just a couple months ago I was the weak human trying to make it in a world full of werewolves.

After I start the car, the vents blast hot air at us so I turn the climate control down to a more comfortable temperature. As I drive away, I can't help thinking that in daylight the hospital looks even more like a château. While waiting for word on Arden last night I did a web search on my iPhone and discovered the place used to be an insane asylum, mostly for the wealthy. I glance back in the rearview mirror at the French formal garden that's well maintained even in the fall, all perfect symmetry out here in the midst of all the chaos inside. I don't know what to expect at the flat. I suspect Amara will be long gone and for a brief moment I'm outraged on his behalf. Werewolves are supposed to mate for life. Whatever Amara saw in him, despondent or not, it's still there beneath the surface. Not the wolf, but everything else. The midday traffic is heavy on Avenue de Saint-Maurice and as I merge into it I see Arden pull something from his coat pocket. In his palm are two copper pennies, flecked with dirt across their embossed surfaces.

He speaks in a hushed tone. "Where did these come from?"

"I found them last night at your, um ... I mean ... at the grave."

His fingers close tightly around the pennies and he stares down at his fist.

"What are they for?" I ask.

Pulling his clenched hand close to his chest, Arden stares out the passenger side window where a single hand-print of caked dirt reminds me of last night's escapade. "Eye pennies. An old human superstition. To pay your way into the afterlife."

I once saw that in a movie too. Coins for the dead. The Greeks used to put them in the mouths or on the eyes of the deceased to pay the ferryman Kharon's fee to cross the River Styx into Hades. Arden was naked when I found him, so the coins must have been buried with him by the Hounds, who thought he was dead. I shudder to think about it. With a grimace I know it's no small blessing that it was, at least, a shallow grave.

We're quiet for the rest of the drive, which is just as well because I never realized how congested Paris traffic was until I got into the driver's seat of the car. Usually, I'm either on foot, on bike or underground on the Métro. Like any major city, the pressure to be places causes a certain level of road rage. At one point, a bus tries to cross about six lines of traffic at the Place de la Nation roundabout. It's only when we get to our neighborhood in the 11th arrondisse-ment that I ease my tense grip on the steering wheel. I park the car around the corner from Arden's butcher shop and our apartment above it. We stand together on the tiny land-ing looking at an envelope taped to the edge of the frame. He pulls it down and just stares at it. It takes me a second to figure out he can't open it with one hand, but he's too stubborn to ask for my help.

"Here," I say, taking it from him.

Inside is a key to the apartment and a note. Handing the note and envelope over without looking at it, I unlock the door and step inside to give him a moment to read. When I glance back, Arden crumples the paper and tosses it at his feet in the hallway. He takes the key from my hand and heads straight for his bedroom. I can take a hint.

All the same, I follow on his heels and offer, "If you need anything..."

"I don't," he says curtly.

"Yeah, but if you do..."

"I won't."

The bedroom door slams in my face. I walk back across the room to close the front door but pause when I see the crumpled note. It isn't for me to read but I do anyway. I pick it up and smooth out the crinkles. In elegant cursive script are the words, "*Requiescat in pace et in amore.*" It's a Latin phrase. I know the first part as RIP from cartoon headstones and *amore* doesn't take a genius to figure out. "Rest in peace and in love." I don't have to recognize the handwriting to know it's from Amara, which means she knows he's alive despite the fact that she left him out in the woods to die. Everything about werewolf society is messed up to me. It leaves Arden alone in the world after a lifetime of living with a pack. The people he loved the most, the ones who should have stood by him no matter what, have turned their backs on him. I crush the paper in my fist and toss it to the worn floorboards where it belongs. It's complete garbage.

2. RIVER STYX

At the first opportunity, I shower and switch into my own clothes to try to regain the feeling of being in my own skin again. What I want is to get back to my life, whatever that means now that I'm a werewolf. I would love to sleep but if I stop moving I'll have to think about last night, last week and everything that's gone down since this school semester started in Paris. And I just can't face that yet. Just the idea of heading to school and sitting in class is absurd so I decide to bag up my dirty clothes and grab a bite to eat at a neighborhood laundromat café. The place is empty except for the lone employee who leans behind a shiny Formica bar, engrossed in a book. A massive column of washers and dryers divides the room, four machines wide on each side, and beyond that is a lounge of sorts. The walls are painted bright red and blue while all the furnishings are bright white. After putting in a load of laundry, I buy a coffee and sandwich then take a seat on an uncomfortable plastic chair at one of several café tables. As plush as they look, I don't trust myself on one of the couches because I'd pass out from exhaustion for sure. Even still, the white noise of the machine is enough to put me in a trance so I put in my EarPods and stream a local metal station.

While I do feel bad for Arden, living with him is going to be the worst. I can't even begin to imagine it. Maybe if his arm wasn't in a cast, things could return to something that resembles the status quo. In the state that he's in, though, he's probably going to need my help and I doubt his ego will allow asking for it. He normally spends most of his time either working downstairs in his butcher shop or out who-knows-where with who-knows-who. But how's he going to operate his business now that everyone has abandoned him? Not to mention the danger Arden's in, keeping me around while I'm on the most-wanted list of the four-hundred-year-old human he bit. My guess is that Boguet isn't done with me and that before Boadicea died she was trying to warn me of his plans. Madison took off with the answers before I even had a second to formulate the questions.

After I'm done folding and sorting clothes I bring them back to the flat and keep myself busy by washing a sink full of dirty dishes and general tidying up. I'm completely exhausted. I crash on my own bed enveloped in the downy soft-and-perfumed scent of clean sheets, and sleep is welcomed instantly. I sleep straight through until morning and when I get up my mind instantly goes to a plan of attack for the day. There are things I need to find out, people I need to track down, and I have no idea where to begin. Arden is still in his bedroom. I gently knock on his door and when there's no answer I decide to check in on him. Quietly pushing the door open, I poke my head in through the crack of the doorway and see that he's still fast asleep. Even at rest he looks uncomfortable as a human. It's dispiriting to see him this way, looking so vulnerable. Is this how he saw me at one point? Weak, unable to defend myself ... prey? I suddenly feel uncomfortable watching him.

I head out on my bike and leave Arden to sleep off being human. The first logical place to start my search is at school, where I assume Madison and Josh will be. When I get there, everything is so unnervingly normal that it makes me feel out of place and I consider turning back. My life has become anything but average and this environment makes it more achingly obvious to me. I have questions, though, and some of the few people who can answer them may be here. The kids who mill around the front of the building begin to stare at me as I lock up my bike, like somehow they know what I've become. For a second it panics me but then I remember that the last time I saw any of them was at the mash-up party on Friday night. That's when Josh clocked me for trying to kiss Madison in full view of an entire auditorium of students. It seems like a lifetime ago. The rumor mill must have been working overtime this weekend filling in the blanks. Under their watchful gazes, I make my way inside while trying to keep a lookout for the only two friends I've made here.

I peek into our psych classroom where the lesson is already underway, but all three of our seats are empty. It occurs to me that they may not return to school at all. Maybe now that they've captured Henri Boguet they'll be shipped off to some other city to fake friendships, all in the name of maintaining some semblance of justice in the werewolf world. It's almost lunchtime and I want to get out of here before the other kids have a chance to ask me any questions. I'll next have to try Madison's boarding house all the way across town. First I walk by our usual haunt J'm Sushi just for good measure, peering through the glass facing of the brightly colored building in the hopes of seeing Madison's cherry-red hair. There's no sign of her, or Josh for that matter, but memories of a simpler life from just days ago begin to stir. I grab a bite to eat at Starbucks instead and sit alone with a latté and sandwich. It brings to mind the first day of this semester when I headed back to the school courtyard with my lunch instead of hanging out here. I'd wanted to stretch my comfort zone, make new friends, reinvent myself. Well, mission accomplished.

What if it's dangerous for me to be out at all? For one thing, any number of triggers might make me unsafe for human interaction, not the least of which are full moons. When I look around at the café full of people just going about their regular lives, it's alarming to think that I could transform at random in their midst. In reality, I've had zero control over it so far. I start to feel a little nauseous. The clatter of dishes. The hiss of the espresso machine. The sheer volume of noise that humans can produce in such a confined space. Not to mention the intense fusion of odors that seem so strong in my nostrils and the artificial lighting that bothers my eyes. I feel trapped all at once and sense the animal caged within me rattling my very bones. It shakes me to the core.

I thrust myself up onto my feet, abandoning my meal,

and walk with purpose toward the door. *This is not going to happen.* I repeat the thought several times. *Everything will surely be okay once I get outside. I just have to make it out that door. One foot in front of the other.* Once I reach fresh air the anxiety lifts a little so I keep moving with no destination in mind. I've got to hold my human self together. A car swishes by, honking insanely loudly, and calls my attention to how fast my heart is beating. I spin away from the noise and crash into a pedestrian on the sidewalk. I try to mutter an apology as I stumble across the concrete, dodging other passersby. This is too much. There are so many people here out on the street. What am I supposed to do?

Monceau Park. It's where I ran to the last time I felt this way. Granted, Madison was there to help. I can't even know for sure if we made it inside the gates because I blacked out, but this time I have to get through the crisis on my own. Sticking close to buildings and dodging down less traveled alleyways, I manage to get to the park. There are still lots of people around but I spot a free bench and speed up in order to collapse onto it. I need to just take a few breaths and regain my composure. Tears stream down my face, my skin is covered in sweat and my hands shake so visibly that I have to clasp them together in front of me. Although the smells and sounds of the city have been replaced by those of a more natural environment, I can't say for sure if this is any better. Quieter at least but when I close my eyes to think about the scent of autumn leaves and how they would feel crunching beneath my paws—

"*Monsieur, pourquoi êtes-vous si triste?*" a tiny voice asks.

My eyes blink open in alarm. I see a small pair of shiny black shoes and white-stockinged feet on the gravel path before me. Slowly, I raise my eyes to take in the figure of a little girl dressed in a red duffel coat. I wholly expect her to say, "*My, what big eyes you have.*"

"I'm ... not sad," I manage to tell her in French, my voice raw from the strain. "I'm just ... not ... feeling well."

"Do you want something to feel better?"

I nod, unable to get out any more words. As much as I'd like to wipe the dampness from my face, I don't trust myself to even move just yet. I watch as she digs a hand deeply into a pocket while I internally recite the alphabet backwards. It's a trick I recall learning from Roul. When the kid finally finds what she was searching for, she proudly holds up a sticker in front of my face. It's decorated with Winnie the Pooh. I gaze at it for an inordinate amount of time, the cartoon image bringing back memories of childhood. She peels off the adhesive, places it onto the back of my left hand and I actually start to feel better.

"Clara!" a woman calls out from across the lawn.

Then the little girl runs off, leaving me alone on the bench with her little present. Swallowing hard, I shakily touch the sticker. Somehow it prevented me from shifting in broad daylight, in the middle of a public park. I wait a few more minutes to ensure I've regained complete control before getting up and walking away. That does it. Finding Madison will have to wait for another day. I don't trust myself on the Métro, a subterranean tin can full of potential prey. The only reason I return to school premises is to grab my bike for the ride home. It dawns on me that I'll need Arden to call the school to inform them that I've come down with something and won't be in for the rest of the day. Maybe the rest of the week. Asking him for even this one small favor might not be easy. On the best of days he really couldn't care less about me and my state of affairs, but he was way too complacent about everything yesterday, and without Amara around I don't know what to expect from him. Hopefully the pain meds will have a positive effect on his personality.

After making my way up the stairs I notice the crumpled paper is still in the hallway where I left it. Inside, there are no signs of life. I try to pick up any indication of his presence in the flat.

"Arden?"

My voice resonates. Maybe he's too doped up to hear me. I push open his bedroom door to see that he's lying on top of the sheets still wearing my clothes. His eyes are open and turned up to the ceiling. A wave of anxiety washes over me. He's usually so guarded and protective about his space. Maybe that was mostly the wolf in him, though they couldn't be all animal, those instincts. Surely his personality couldn't have changed *that* drastically. A couple days worth of stubble has grown and his lips are parched again. Even his face has taken on a wasted pallor. He's breathing but he has yet to acknowledge my presence in any way. He stirs ever so slightly and I let out a sigh of relief.

"I thought you were dead," I tell him, unable to mask my annoyance.

He continues his ceiling-staring vigil. I take a quick scan around the room for signs of prescription bottles but find nothing. Just the two copper pennies on the nightstand as reminders of his near-death experience.

"Did you pick up your antibiotics?"

"No," he says in a dry voice.

"And the painkiller?"

He merely shakes his head.

"Aren't you in a lot of agony?"

"Yes."

In frustration, I run my hands through my hair. What the hell am I supposed to do with him? He's clearly not in a right state of mind. His behavior is disturbing to say the least. Maybe he doesn't understand what he's doing.

"You heard the doctor, right? If you don't take your meds the fractured bone could get infected. You could lose your whole arm."

It seems like my words have finally gotten through to him because he turns his gaze toward me. Then he says, "Bite me."

I lose it. "Piss off, Arden! I'm trying to be a decent—"

Human being is how I wanted to end that sentence. The words would ring hollow now so I stop short.

"No," he insists. "*Bite* me."

I'm about to lip off but he explains himself.

"I want my life back. If you bite me, I'll get it."

I shake my head. "No. No way. The only reason I'm home right now is because I almost lost control out there. I don't know how to shift. Or not shift. It just happens."

"I'll teach you," he offers.

It gives me pause. How else am I going to learn? I don't know the first thing about being a werewolf but I imagine transformation is kind of the cornerstone for all future understanding. Then again, there's no telling what might happen when I shift.

"I'm not going to bite you," I say, crossing my arms in the hope that I come off as firm in my decision. "It's ridiculous."

He props himself up on the elbow of his good arm, glaring. "You owe it to me."

This is not untrue. Arden wouldn't be in this position if it weren't for me — or my DNA at the very least. After all, even though it happened without my consent, the cure was based on my mutated genes. Maybe I owe him at least an effort to reverse the effects.

"How do we know it'll even work?" I counter. "What if this cure is permanent? Has that even crossed your mind? Or what if you turn into a bitten?"

That last question causes a flicker of hesitation to cross his face, but it passes.

"There's one way to find out."

I just stare at him. He's a wreck. Barely the shadow of the man I met in September. The desperation of his plan speaks volumes to his frame of mind. The Arden I knew then would never have let himself get into this state.

"Is it really that abysmal, Arden? Being human?"

"I have nothing."

I would love to argue the point and prove him wrong. But

how can I? Amara, his soul mate of who knows how many years, is gone. With her, every friend and family member has vanished from his life. Dr. Moreau only skimmed over the recovery process: eight to ten weeks for the cast to come off and several more months for rehab. That's if he takes the antibiotics and doesn't lose his arm. In his current mental state, that's a big if.

"Fine. What do I need to do?"

"Undress."

"This is crazy," I say, tossing my jacket to the floor and pulling off my T-shirt.

I glance over to see if he's watching, too embarrassed to strip down completely naked in front of him, but his eyes are closed now. The fingers of his good hand paw at the sheets, like he's visualizing what he must have done thousands of times before. Slipping out of the rest of my clothes I crouch down, hoping posture has something to do with the shift.

"Close your eyes."

I follow his instructions.

"What's your last memory? As a wolf."

Lying in a pool of your blood, I want to say, but I dig deeper, sensing that particular recollection will do me no good. The two times I've shifted so far have been entirely out of my control, like a switch flipped in my body. The first time was like a waking dream. Or nightmare. It was during the night of the full moon. The other time also happened without my conscious effort but I was slightly more aware of what was going on. At least I had a fragment more control over my thoughts. That seems to be the better memory to work from in this scenario.

"At the cemetery, fighting off Boguet," I finally reply.

"Go back to that."

Pulling the thought from my mind, I remember Boguet, the wolf-man, sinking his venomous teeth into Wolf Arden before discarding him like a rag doll. I transformed in a moment between fear and some sense of daring.

"Think wolf; be wolf."

I take myself deeper into the memory. Monochromatic vision. A heightened sense of smell and hearing. The feel of all four paws on the cobblestone path. A yelp of anguish. Wolf Arden needed my help. The way he does now. And then it just happened.

"Good," he says.

I open my eyes as a wolf, and all my senses are overwhelmed except for my vision, which is filtered in hues of blue-gray. He props himself up on the bed and looks me up and down. Something about the urgency in the way that he gestures for me to come to him makes me uneasy. This space is too closed in and filled with the scent of other wolves. They're not here, but he is. And he's not a wolf. The anxiety of being confined with him sets me pacing along the hardwood floor. His movements are startling. But then he goes very still and speaks even slower, repeating the same word in a hushed voice. It takes all my concentration to fill in the blanks until I understand.

"Co-con-on-nor-con-nor — Connor."

That's me. Connor. Connor Lewis. My head is swamped by a sensory overload as I try to swim through a flood of smells and sounds that my human self is mostly unaware of. Shaking it off, I push down my hesitation and leap up on the bed next to Arden. Now that I'm so close to him, I take in more unpleasant human scents: sweat and tears. Before I can reconsider, he extends his right forearm. You'd think it would come natural, biting into flesh as a predator, but I'm beginning to recognize that I'm not pure wolf in this form. As I wrap my teeth around his flesh, the human in me is beyond disgusted by the idea of sinking my fangs into him enough to draw blood that I can't bite down.

Like his old self, he lets out a growl of frustration and slips his arm out of my mouth. His good hand reaches around my neck and grabs a fistful of fur. With a yank, Arden flips me onto my back and up against his torso until I'm in a chokehold. A savage instinct switches on in me as I fight against his grip. Paws flailing and body twisting, I snarl at him. My teeth gnash at the air, hopeful of grabbing on to something. When he finally releases me, I bite down on the first thing I can: his upper arm. The taste of copper flows into my mouth. That's when I feel it, the sensation that Boguet talked about. A blood-lust taking control over whatever humanity I have in me, letting the animal in me dominate. Perhaps sensing it too, Arden begins to struggle, but I just clamp down harder, tearing at his flesh.

"*Arrêtes!*" he yells. "Connor, stop!"

It triggers my human brain. Releasing his arm, I scramble upright and off the bed. I lope off toward the door, watching as he cradles his arm against his chest, blood soaking onto the duvet and the borrowed T-shirt. It only takes a few seconds for things to go terribly wrong. His eyes roll back until I only see the whites. He clutches at his heart and his breathing becomes much more rapid. Then he's retching and dry heaving as the rest of his body spasms.

I wait.

And I wait.

But nothing else happens.

When he finally goes still enough to look over at me there's anguish in his eyes. The strength fades from them as his head lolls sideways and onto a pillow. Neither of us thought this scenario through, each in our desperation to make things right. Pacing back and forth in a frenzy, all I can think is: human. Human. I have to get back to my human form. But the only one who can tell me how to do that is unconscious.

In the form of a wolf, I feel trapped. Trapped in the animal body. Trapped in the room. The scent of fresh blood gnaws at me, and I stalk back and forth by the foot of the bed. I have no sense of time but after a while I'm able to collect some of my human thoughts. Me pacing around indefinitely will do neither of us any good and only serve to wear thin the hardwood floor. What I need to do is get back to my other form. I grasp onto the same logic I used to shift into a wolf. Think human; be human. It's unsurprisingly easier said than done. When you've got four paws, a muzzle and a thick furry hide, the memory of what it's like to be in your own skin becomes conflicted, to say the least. I have to dig deep to pull it out of me. I notice the Winnie the Pooh sticker clinging to the fur on the top of my paw and

I'm brought back to the TV glow of childhood memories. In a blink I see my human hand beneath the sticker and the world looks the way I remember it.

When I get to his side, Arden doesn't look any better. I feel for a pulse, expecting none, yet it's there rapidly beating. His skin is hot to the touch. My mind stalls. Last year in school we were given basic CPR training but none of what I can draw on is relevant at the moment. Treating a werewolf bite isn't exactly a standard medical problem. In order to stop the blood flow I grab my shirt from the floor and tie it around his arm where I bit him. He gasps for air and it underscores my need to act fast. I pull a card from my backpack: *Rodolfus de Aquila, CEO, Fenrir Pharmaceuticals*. Arden might never be a wolf again but at least he might be able to take advantage of their biochemistry to counter whatever is going on in his body. The pack leader picks up after three rings.

"*Salve*," he greets, not in French, but he tends to carry Latin phrases with him.

Before he can say anything else I spew out the details of what just happened. I provide no commentary on how immensely stupid this risk was or how completely idiotic I was for having agreed to my part in it.

"It's sepsis," he tells me calmly.

"In English."

"Blood poisoning," Roul explains. "This *cure* has somehow shut down access to the gene that allows us to transform, and his body can no longer assimilate the venom. He's the same as the majority of humans now and the bite will be fatal. At this point, his only chance for survival would require an antivenin that Fenrir doesn't produce. Only Boguet Biotech does."

But Boguet's been captured. It's not like he'd help me out anyway, since Arden was the one who bit him.

"It shouldn't take long for him to pass."

He says it like it's a good thing. Like I shouldn't care that I may have just killed someone. Somehow, now more than ever, I feel like my humanity is at stake.

"I have the antivenin," I realize aloud and hang up on the pack leader of the Paris werewolves.

3. HOW TO SAVE A LIFE

I tear through my backpack tossing out books and pens. Hope rises at the sight of something bright yellow, but it turns out to be a highlighter. There it is! It's in the EpiPen that Madison left with me for just such an occasion, in the front pouch where she had placed it for easy access. By this point Arden has gone horribly still and I'm afraid I might be too late. Removing the cap, I inject the antivenin into his arm, close to the bite mark, then I step back, hoping, waiting, anticipating what will happen next. I hang my hope on his next movement. If he does nothing it will mean I've killed him.

Suddenly realizing I'm naked, I slip back into my jeans. I have to be honest with myself and consider the worst-case scenario — what needs to be done if he doesn't pull through. I'll have to bury him in the same spot where we found him, I suppose. The grave is in the woods near the wolf exhibit of the zoo at Vincennes Park. He might like to be close to them even if they aren't wild. I walk over to the nightstand, touching the copper pennies, considering whether I'll take them with me. I'm not a superstitious person but maybe I should be. Arden takes in a long shud-

40

dering breath that makes me jump. He coughs and splutters. Is this it? Are these his final moments? His good hand grabs at the sheets, pulling them toward him. And then he raises his head, glaring with all the hate he has reserved for me.

"Why ... can't ... you let me ... die?"

I have to choke back my relief. We stare at each other for a long while. As I pocket the copper pennies, I try not to shake. A mix of relief and anger swirls through me. Arden is the first to break his gaze. He lays his head down, closing his eyes, probably exhausted.

"I'm a werewolf, Arden," I tell him, suppressing emotion, "not a grim reaper."

Striding out and slamming the door behind me, I make it into the living room before letting out a howl of frustration. I'd leave right away but I'm too riled up and know that's not a good idea. I can't bear to have him judging me with those amber eyes. And for what? For not letting him die? I wish there was something in the room I could throw. Instead, I kick at the Persian rug in the middle of the floor. The tassels wind up getting caught on my bare toes so I flail about until I slip up and fall flat on my ass. Sitting there on the verge of screaming and/or punching out at something, I sense my mood isn't just due to the werewolf adrenaline flowing through my veins in the aftermath of what happened with Arden. I can feel hunger gnawing at me and it hits me that I haven't actually eaten since the laundromat yesterday afternoon. I push myself up off the floor and rummage through the kitchen. One thing I've learned about werewolves is that they have tendencies toward a raw food diet, which means

I'm out of luck in my search for anything processed. In the fridge there's some kind of vegetation that's seen better days but aside from that there's just a whole skinned rabbit staring at me like something out of a horror movie. I'm hungry enough that I consider cooking it. How, though, is the question. I'd have to Google it. As I make my way to my bedroom for my laptop, there's a knock on the door.

Lately, I have misgivings about who's on the other side in these scenarios. For the past few months it's always been a werewolf. Everybody I know in the city is one. Sure enough, staring back at me through the peephole is Roul. I open the door, taking Arden's usual protective stance within the frame while Roul stands expressionless before me. From front on he's a paradox. He wears a deep blue coat over a gray three-piece suit and his hair is combed neatly to the side. Half his face is covered by a tattoo of a snarling wolf's head that I know descends below the collar of his dress shirt to depict the rest of the animal along his entire right side. From this point of view he reminds me of Two-Face from *Batman*, only with Roul what you see is what you get. There's no unstable lunatic struggling for supremacy within him. At least, not that I've seen.

"What are you doing here?"

He pauses before answering, giving me the once-over the way I just did with him. I must look like hell. Not as awful as Arden, but I'm shirtless, sockless, possibly covered in blood. Werewolves, or Parisian ones at the very least, tend to be a little more put-together.

"I didn't expect you to let him live," he says but there's

no reproach in his voice.

"I couldn't just leave him to freeze to death."

He's shaking his head, and it's clear that I've misread his meaning. "I didn't expect that either."

I get it. His version of mercy means a swift death. That gun he gave me wasn't just for my protection. When I don't speak, he continues.

"Cruelty is something I've become intimately acquainted with in my lifetime," he informs me, looking into my eyes. "And sometimes it wears a mask of compassion."

Remorse taints my voice when I say, as much for my benefit as his, "I didn't do it to be cruel."

"Exactly my point," he agrees. "There's no point dwelling on it. It's done. Whatever happens next is up to him."

It makes me think about what I said at the hospital. I regret being so flip when telling Arden it was on him if he wanted to off himself. That's his choice now: living as a human. Or not. Roul pulls a small container from his pocket. It rattles as he tries to hand me the plastic bottle but I don't take it readily.

"What are those?"

"Pills," he replies. "As you once pointed out, I'm a drug dealer."

"And I'm supposed to do *what* with them?"

He smiles gently. "They'll help his broken arm heal faster. It's a regenerative drug, reverse engineered from our biochemistry for human use."

It's impossible for me to mask my surprise. "How did you know about his arm? What, do you have a werewolf working at the hospital too?"

He takes my anger in stride and without reaction. "Not at all. I simply picked up the phone and called after I saw you had no intention of heeding my request. If he follows the instructions, the bones will mend quickly and the cast can be removed in about two weeks."

If he follows instructions. It's more likely that I'm going to have to administer them, given his current condition. I take the bottle to examine the label for the basics. He has to take one pill a day. Everything aside, this is the first kind gesture Roul's exhibited since he discovered one of his pack members turned human. Unfortunately, the drugs will pose a different problem.

"How exactly am I supposed to explain this to his doctor?"

"I'll arrange to have a medical practitioner remove the cast."

He seems to have an answer for everything.

"Do you have something for the pain?"

With a shake of his head he replies, "Whatever his doctor prescribed should be sufficient. Although our pain threshold is quite high, we suffer just as humans do."

I scoff. "You think you know what it's like? Really? He's a wreck. And not just because of the broken bones."

He grimaces. "Don't judge what you don't understand, Connor."

"Help me work through it then."

There's a long pause. Long enough that I think he's not going to answer me at all. But then he does, and he's unexpectedly wistful. "Losing a mate is like losing a part of yourself. There's no cure for it, no drug to ease the agony of it. For the rest of your years, there will always be a place within you that feels ... hollow. What haunts your unguarded moments and chases your living memories most is the knowledge that this void in your life will never again be filled. So, yes, broken bones may heal but there are other injuries that can leave lasting scars. Ones that no one else sees but yourself." His eyes scan mine before he finishes with, "Does that about cover it?"

By the way that his tone has changed, it's obvious that he speaks from experience. Guilt stabs me in the gut as I remember him telling me about losing his mate at the hands of Boguet about four hundred years ago. It's hard to imagine carrying that loss with you for so long.

"In this case, Amara's mate isn't exactly dead," I say. "He's just human."

"Semantics to us," he responds in his usual no-nonsense tone. "Besides, it's not a choice she's afforded. We're bound by rules, not the least of which are enforced by your friends, the Hounds—"

"I told you before, they're not my friends."

With an arched eyebrow, he asks, "Are you so certain?"

"I *had* friends who I just learned are part of that cult or whatever it is, but they've disappeared."

He thrusts his hands into his trouser pockets and stands back with an amused look. "Have they now?"

I squint at him, suspicious of his meaning. "What?"

"The Hounds don't just disappear," he tells me. "They

watch our every move and I can guarantee they're not done with you."

"What do you—" I start, somewhat alarmed but then catch on to what he's doing. "We were talking about Arden."

Roul takes a thoughtful pause. "We don't mingle with humans. We can't. Arden, for all intents and purposes, died two nights ago."

"Why bother integrating into human society at all if you're going to be snobs about it?"

"Survival," he states. "The spaces we inhabited shrank as human populations grew. I was living here long before this place became the city of Paris. And just so we're clear, we don't exclude humans from our lives out of some sense of elitism. It's for a common protection."

"And the Hounds? Why do you exclude them too? They're the bitten, the cursed, the ostracized. Why *wouldn't* they organize against you?"

"Your sense of outrage over civil rights is misguided," he informs me. "Would you have us embrace our oppressors?"

We've veered off topic and onto werewolf politics again.

"There are always exceptions to rules," I insist. "Arden was born one of you and has never known anything else. Don't you think that counts for anything? Does Amara even know that he's alive?"

He nods. It's a succinct gesture that I question immediately. Amara doesn't have a cellphone. Between the time I hung up on him and the time it took for him to drive here, not more than fifteen minutes could have passed. How could he have let her know so quickly?

"Is she staying with you?"

"Yes," he answers just as tersely.

There are a lot of things I don't know about being a werewolf — things I might not want to know — but my limited database includes the fact that werewolves mate for life. Arden made that abundantly clear when he got all up in my grill after Amara fell asleep with me that one time. It was just a show of force, of course. I was always a non-threat. A whelp compared to the pack at large. But Rodolfus de Aquila is another matter altogether. He's Arden's rival in many ways already: the one who took leadership over of the pack after Arden's father was killed, the one who defies their conventions. And now, to pour salt on his wounds, Roul has just added co-habitation with Arden's ex-girlfriend.

With a shake of my head, I ask, "Are you kidding me?"

"I have obligations to my pack. Ones that go beyond the social niceties of human moral code. Arden of all people knows that."

"Doesn't she care that he's alive?"

"It doesn't matter," Roul explains. "An intimate relationship is no longer a possibility for them. Trust me, humans and werewolves aren't meant to live together in that way."

How can he be so callous toward Arden if he knows how painful it is to go through this ordeal? He was with a human at some point. That much I know already. Although I'm a direct descendant of his, the rest of my human ancestors were never aware of the truth. My mutated DNA is the result of some secret love affair that happened centuries ago between my great-great-great-super-great-grandmother and the man standing in front of me. I can only guess that she was the one Boguet killed.

"That's a strange sense of loyalty," I remark.

"My allegiance lies with my pack. That's something you'll need to come to terms with if you want to survive in this world as part of my pack."

As much as I've always been a fine, upstanding teenager — one who's never crossed the law or even come close to breaking the limited rules that have been imposed on my life — I'm not a fan of being told I have no options. There are always choices. Not all of them are good ones, but they're choices nonetheless. If pack loyalty means sticking together at the expense of others, I want no part of it.

"No," I tell him. "I don't think so."

His gunmetal gray eyes flicker past me for a flash of second. "Lone wolves don't make it very far."

"I'd just as soon take my chances on my own than turn my back on someone just because he's not a werewolf," I say. "So I'm not leaving Arden to fend for himself."

He lets out a sigh in the frustrated kind of way that my dad does when he's given up the fight. I expect him to drop negotiations and just lay down the law. But he doesn't.

"I won't force your hand until I have to," he says instead. "As far as everyone in your human life is concerned, Arden will remain your legal guardian for now. But you can't return to school. Not until you've got your shifting under control. After that, it's up to you whether you want to go back. I've sent the necessary medical documentation to your school and Amara has informed them that you'll be absent until further notice."

"And what exactly have I come down with?"

"Mono," he replies.

The kissing disease. As if the rumor mill doesn't have enough ammunition after the whole incident at the dance. Not that my high school reputation means anything anymore. What does it matter what any of those kids think now that I've got a werewolf's lifespan ahead of me?

"This arrangement may have a time limit," he warns me. "Once the Hounds have a say in it, I don't imagine they'll approve even if they consider your unique circumstances."

Not knowing what else to say, I shrug. Roul turns to leave, then pauses. Looking past me as he speaks, he measures out his words carefully.

"I don't imagine you understand the consequences of what you've done, but he deserves a better end than this."

He says the words like he had no part in it, and it fills me with intense rage. I slam the door and spin around on my heels, intending to head to my room, but I freeze in my tracks. Arden stands across the room propped against a wall, just staring at me.

"What?" I ask, hostile.

In a quiet voice he responds, "You'll need to be a better wolf."

"Yeah, well, you'll need to learn to be a better human."

Reaching into the back pocket of the borrowed jeans, he

pulls out a small square of paper and holds it out to me. "I'll need something for the pain first."

B. WU-WEI

Wu-wei: *noun*. Non-action, or letting things take their natural course.

For the record, werewolves are a bunch of dumbasses. Connor should be locked away indefinitely. He was *this* close to losing it at Monceau Park. I'd been looking for him all over the city so we could talk about what exactly went down. I drove right back to the cemetery after we buried Arden and Boadicea, but didn't see any signs of the pack coming to Connor's rescue. Then I went to check in on him at his apartment thinking maybe they brought him back home, but nobody answered when I rang the doorbell. Granted, it *was* about three in the morning by the time I got there, but I was totally prepared to be yelled at just to know he was safe. Being told off by pack werewolves would have just been practice for when I'd catch hell from Madame Lefèvre after I got back to the boarding house.

When I randomly saw Connor duck into the park I thought it was a lucky break, but after witnessing his near-meltdown I let go of the idea of talking to him just then. It's not like I could've stepped in and done anything about it. A wolf loose in a public park can be explained, but the thing that *I* would have had to turn into in order to stop him? Um, reality check. That could *never* happen. Not in a million years. Avoiding biting humans may be the Golden Rule among the Hounds, but exposing ourselves TMZ-style takes the silver medal. Those people in the park, starting with that little girl, would have all been toast. The lucky ones, anyway.

Someone needs to have the awkward conversation with Connor. It's the kind of sit-down chat that Aquila should have had with him already as his pack leader. "*What you're feeling is perfectly normal. You'll want to maul other living creatures, but you have to control those urges...*" I'm assuming that Aquila actually found him at the cemetery and eventually brought him home. If not, then at least Amara would have said something when Connor made it back to their apartment. She's technically his legal guardian so she *must* have given him some pointers about self-control. Even if she was an emotional train-wreck after hearing about Arden dying — unlikely! — she should have pulled herself together enough to make sure he didn't leave the apartment. Like I said, werewolves = dumbasses.

My phone vibrates where it's charging on the bedside table. I switched it to mute because I *so* didn't want to have to deal with Josh right now. If he saw what I did at the park today, he'd flip. That buzzing noise is more irritating than the barking ringtone I set for him. I should just turn it off. But it's *just* out of arm's reach and I'm totally not budging from the comfort of this fuzzy pink throw rug for the off chance that it's not actually Josh. Finally it goes to voice mail.

I dump the contents of Boadicea's Louis Vuitton tote bag in front of me and it's like I just died and got a swag bag in designer heaven: silk Burberry scarf in a classic check pattern, a snakeskin-print Vivienne Westwood wallet, large Jackie O-style Gucci sunglasses, Chloé eau de toilette. She was such a posh girly-girl. The kind who belonged in Connor's world. He totally denies it but he doesn't exactly come from nothing. Perspective. He doesn't get it, how lucky he is in every way. Connor might hate the fact that he's so different, but whatever it is that makes him different is exactly what saved him from this whole cursed existence.

It's only a matter of time before the pack has him cut all ties with us. Or the Hounds. It doesn't even matter, things being as messed up as they are, me being as messed up as I am. I might as well put the space between us now. Still, it's killing me to know what it is that makes him more special than the rest of us humans.

Madame Lefèvre has the USB drive that I swiped off Boadicea. I wasn't about to play interference with evidence after she tore a strip off me. She can't be that mad at me after I delivered that info. Now that Boguet is behind bars, whatever happens is on him and whatever form of justice the Hounds decide to unleash is out of my hands. That doesn't mean I didn't copy the contents of the flash drive onto my laptop first. I'm not totally naive. Living with the Hounds has taught me one thing: nobody's completely on the up-and-up. Most people can't even be honest with themselves so I'm not exactly going to trust that they'll be truthful with me.

Boadicea, though. I need to figure out what her deal was. For her to hand all this classified info over to Connor doesn't make any sense. I don't think he's in Aquila's pocket so I doubt it's corporate espionage. I don't even understand half of what's in the folder. A lot of stuff about DNA. The words on their own make sense to me but strung together, I have no clue. Whatever Boguet was up to, it was bad-ass enough to catch the attention of the Hounds.

As I riffle through all Boadicea's pretty things, there's really only one item I hoped to find in her purse: a gun. It's a relief to see it now. She could have easily been reaching for the weapon when she pulled the USB stick out instead. Before that night I'd never fired a gun, let alone killed someone. There's no undoing what I did but at least I know now that she was actually dangerous. I didn't just make that part up.

I open up her wallet and pull out all the plastic. Platinum credit cards up the yin yang. How much stuff could I buy before these get cancelled? The definition of the word 'gauche' comes up with a line drawing of me right beside it. *Keep it classy, Madison.* Still ... dead girl don't care, right?

I strike gold again when I pull out the electronic key card: Boguet Biotechnology. The logo is a bore: a clean font, his name written in a warm orange on the first line, the second line done in a cool businesslike gray with the letter "i" replaced by a stylized double helix. Nobody would ever suspect what was going on behind the lab doors and all those shady shifters he genetically modified to do his dirty work. Maybe someone should find out. I pocket the card and bookmark that thought.

While pulling on a hoodie I walk over to my nightstand and pick up my phone. There are three text messages and a missed call. All from the wrong boy. What's a girl gotta do to get a hold of Connor Lewis, anyway?

4. SOMEBODY THAT I USED TO KNOW

I do my best to properly bandage up Arden's arm where I bit him, finding some gauze in the bathroom medicine cabinet and sterilizing the wounds with soap and water. Despite being in such close proximity to each other, we awkwardly try to avoid making eye contact. It's clear that he's in a lot of physical pain, not just from the bite but from the broken bones beneath the cast as well. His eyes are damp and he can't suppress a small yelp of anguish when I knock into the plaster. If he'd ever been in any kind of pain before, he never would have let me see it. Now all I see is how fragile he is.

"Sorry," I say while tying off the gauze as gently as possible.

He bites his lower lip and I avert my gaze. Despite the quiet that comes with an absence of neighbors or other flatmates, my ears pick up the steady hum of the fridge. How did I not hear that before? I notice so much more now. There's no such thing as absolute silence. Not anymore. Except maybe for Arden. Did he lose all his heightened senses with the cure? Now doesn't exactly feel like the right time to talk to him about it. He can barely sit up straight at the kitchen table.

Sitting back in the chair, he asks almost in a whisper, "Why'd you do it?"

"What do you mean?" I step back to give him the wide berth he requires for personal space. "Bite you? You're the one who—"

"No." He slowly shakes his head. "Why'd you ... save me?"

What am I supposed to say? I shrug.

"When you bit me, there were only supposed to be two options," he continues, staring at the tabletop. "I didn't think you'd care either way."

I know better than to try to flatter him. Legal guardian or not, my little white lie at the hospital about him being family seems closer to the truth to me now than anything. He's like that annoying older brother I never had: effortlessly stylish, ruthlessly tormenting, lording his proxy powers of parental control over my every move. Yet a brother nonetheless. All the time that I thought he was being arrogant and overbearing just for the hell of it, he'd actually been looking out for me in his own way.

"It's not about that," I explain. "It's simple human compassion. It's about doing the right thing. Or trying to. And before you go off your head, I didn't think you really wanted to die from hypothermia, buck naked out in the woods. Besides ... I wouldn't have been able to live with myself if I'd just walked away."

He focuses on a deep crack in the surface of the wooden table. I can tell he's fading out. Eventually he closes his eyes and I fold the note with the name of the painkiller into my wallet. My phone buzzes. It's a text from Madison.

WRU@? A sigh of relief escapes me tinged with frustration at her poor timing. My thumb hovers over the keypad of my iPhone as I think of a response. She's not exactly in my good books just now, but I also need to talk to her. I doubt Arden will allow her to set foot in here — his disdain for the Hounds runs deep — but I don't trust myself to be out in the real world for more than a few minutes.

"I'll be back in a bit, alright?" I say.

He grunts from his seat, clutching at the edge of it with his good hand. Pale and probably feverish, it's all he can do to support himself. I can't even begin to imagine the pain that he's endured so far. The nearest pharmacy is only a few blocks away, so it'll be a quick trip, which is doubly good not just because it will save him from even a minute more of agony. The last thing I want is a repeat of this afternoon's near-shift experience at the coffee shop.

When I swing open the downstairs door, mid-text, I get a whiff of a familiar scent and a girl's voice calls out before it completely registers. I jump back, startled, and catch sight of her leaning back against the building's stone facade. Madison's cherry-red hair flows loosely around the shoulders of her simple black hoodie, highlighting the word printed in the middle: *Meh*.

As she pushes off the wall, she says, "Freak out much?"

"I wasn't expecting you," I respond, regaining my composure.

"Clearly."

"What are you doing here?"

I stash my phone in my back pocket as she stares at me. Her silence is unnerving, made even more so by the way her hawk-like eyes search mine, like they're mining for something deeper. Something I should protect.

Finally, she remarks, "I thought you'd be more of a mess."

My jaw clenches. "I am."

"You don't look it."

"Looks can be deceiving," I tell her as I walk away. "You should know."

She walks by my side, staking claim to her part of the narrow sidewalk so that oncomers have to weave onto the street and into traffic in order to pass us. My pace is faster than usual, partly to minimize my time out in the real world and partly to keep our conversation brief. I'm still not sure how I can trust her. My last conscious memory of her involves a gun and a dead girl. That's something that a person can't shake easily.

"What's that supposed to mean?" she asks with snark in her voice.

"You're a smart girl, Madison, figure it out."

"Don't be an ass, Connor."

I walk on, seething in silence. What can I say to her that she won't refute with more questionable stories and/or lies anyway? Whatever she has left to tell me can only be in favor of the Hounds. I never would have pegged Madison as the religious type, but I never would have thought of her as a cold-blooded killer either. We continue toward the pharmacy for a while without speaking. The mid-afternoon traffic swooshes by, underscoring the dead air between us. Although the sidewalk widens out when we turn a corner, a line of motorcycles — all sporty European models — takes up the extra space. Between the bikes and Madison's refusal to budge from her charted course, oncoming pedestrians are crowded out again. I'm not used to being so obviously on her radar. For the most part, she's the one who calls the shots or marches off on her own when others aren't playing by her rules. The last thing I'd expect would be for her to tail me on a mundane errand. She's obviously not willing to broach the subject yet, but the fact that she's quiet and watchful makes me uneasy. Madison Dallaire is a lot of things, none of which are synonymous with 'reserved.'

"I was looking for you today," I say.

"And?" she presses impatiently.

Not wanting to get into my near-shift experience at the park, I just say, "You weren't in class. I almost thought you were gone for good."

Her eyebrows pinch and she scrunches her nose like her pet dog just rolled in dead squirrel. "I cut classes, Drama! Like you've never done that before?"

"Of course, I have. You just — there are a lot of things I need to figure out."

"I can help, you know."

We stop at my destination. When she casts her head upward, her eyes reflect the flashing green neon cross sign that is the symbol of pharmacies across the city. Something about that color brings to mind Boadicea. Her emerald eyes.

I have to look away.

"What are we doing here?"

"I'm picking up meds."

"You know you don't need them anymore. Whatever it was you were taking."

"They're not for—"

I stop mid-sentence because she must not know about Arden, being alive, that is.

"You didn't answer my question," I say. "What are *you* doing here?"

"Checking in on you."

"For you or for your job?"

She looks mad — more so than usual — but I don't have any guilt left in me. In fact, I'm short on a lot of emotions at the moment. I don't know what she expected. For us to go back to the way things were? Out of everyone I've met since moving to Paris, she was the one person I thought was straight-up with me, even if her delivery always left something to be desired. Her involvement with the Hounds has called into question the motives behind everything that led up to this point.

"Take your time, Madison. Let me know when you've come up with the right answer."

Instead of putting up a fight, she lets me walk through the automated entry without a word. I take a deep breath and make my way slowly to the counter as the glass doors slide quietly behind me, leaving her outside. Right now, I'm glad for it. All I wanted was to get this one simple task done as quickly as possible and now she's out there waiting to drag it out. After I hand the doctor's note to the pharmacist, I glance back. She is texting while standing by the tall window outside the entrance. Who is she texting? A few days ago I wouldn't have questioned something so trivial, but what am I supposed to think now? Our entire relationship since that first day of school has been a ruse.

I pay for the box of Nurofen and turn back to the door. During the short time it takes to complete the transaction some guy has approached Madison, his intentions clear even from this point of view. He leans persistently into her personal space, hitting on her. Good luck. Although he looks more her type than Josh ever did, the fact of the matter is she hasn't had eyes for anyone, not that I've seen anyway. That is, with exception to the night of the mash-up party when we almost kissed. I've chalked that up to the combination of a full moon and werewolf pheromones. By the time I step outside Madison is already flashing him dagger eyes. I stand by her side and it seems to register with the guy that I might be the reason why she's not accepting his advances. He peers over at me, sizing me up. There's no comparison. He's got the cool hairstyle and piercings to match. But I'm the one standing comfortably in place next to Madison, wearing a shabby fall jacket and even shabbier jeans. All I can do is shrug. *C'est la vie.* With a shrug of his own, he steps away and slowly disappears down the street with the expression of a wounded animal.

"It's not a sport, you know," I note, still feeling kind of good about the whole situation. "Shooting down guys like that."

Instead of coming back with a witty response, she asks, "Where have you been? I stopped by your place after what went down but you weren't there."

"I've been cleaning up your mess."

"Excuse me?" she says testily.

Leaning toward her, I tell her quietly, "Arden's alive."

She looks genuinely shocked. "We buried him."

"You can imagine what that does to mess a guy up."

For a second she kind of squirms like she's uncomfortable in her own skin, but it doesn't take long for her to recover. "He's a tough guy."

"He's human now."

Her hazel eyes widen again.

"It was Boguet and his cure." I wait for a response. "Are you seriously telling me you don't know that already?"

"Um, how exactly would I?"

"How about that flash drive you stole, for starters?"

"Don't be such a diva," she says. "I didn't steal it. It's evidence. Boguet's in custody and about to stand trial."

"By your *cult*."

"It's not a cult, Connor. They're the capital 'L' Law. They make the rules we live by and enforce them too."

Suddenly Roul's comment about the Hounds being oppressors makes a lot more sense to me. They're more than just a group of religious fanatics.

"So what's the punishment for trying to wipe out the werewolf population?"

She shakes her head. "It's sort of a precedent-setting case."

Everything in my life is precedent-setting these days. We turn to walk back toward my flat as I take in this new bit of information. At least Henri Boguet is safely behind bars. Arden was likely the first victim of the field testing for his so-called cure. The ubiquitous *they* probably didn't bank on someone like Boguet waiting four hundred years to dish out his cold plate of revenge on the wolf who bit him. Whether his biotechnology firm is still operating during his absence is another question altogether. Was everything he did really just the vengeful act of one man, or are there bigger plans in motion? Is the rest of the pack in danger? Or are they safe while the mad scientist sits in werewolf prison? If Madison turned the flash drive over to the Hounds without looking at or understanding what was on it, she wouldn't have any answers. Judging by her reaction to Arden's newfound human condition, I'd say that's exactly the case. Then again, she may very well be playing with me. If the Hounds are some kind of werewolf government, wouldn't that make her a spy?

She lets out a huffy sigh. "Look, I'm trying to figure things out too, alright? Just because I'm with the Hounds doesn't mean I'm *with* them, you know?"

Even as I'm forming a follow-up question, Madison manages to cut me off. "You shouldn't even be out here."

Before I realize what I'm saying, I blurt out, "Hey, do you have another one of those antivenin EpiPens? I—"

In an instant, she stops me in my tracks, forcing a palm over my mouth while clutching my shirt with her other hand to keep me close. It's a ridiculous sight, I'm sure, given how small she is compared to me. Her sneak attack catches me off guard, and I have to pause to process what's going on. My pulse quickens not just from the surprise, but also a little from her touch and sweet vanilla scent.

"I don't want to hear that you bit someone," she says urgently.

I remember our conversation about how the Hounds view biting. It's punishable by death. She's protecting me. Her body is pressed firmly against me now and to prolong the moment I toy with the idea of faking her out. I part my lips and pretend to speak through her fingers pressed against my lips. I'm starting to enjoy this a little and I'll admit it's as much for the intimacy as it is to turn the tables. For once I let her be the one to worry about consequences. But then the dampness in her eyes comes unbidden.

"Connor, please," she whispers.

Guilt weighs on me and I wrap my hand around the one covering my mouth. Even though she resists I pull it away as gently as possible given her surprising strength. Before I can say a word, her hands go up to the sides of her head and she digs the heels into her ears to block out any sound. Legally she's an adult, having emancipated herself from her parents when she turned seventeen. After she was bitten, no doubt. To look at her now, she's just a girl who's frightened of a few words. I place my hands on hers, lean my forehead against hers and wait it out. I won't fight her. I *can't* fight her. Not when she's disarming me with those eyes. A cool breeze sends her hair swirling around us.

"You can't undo the words once you say them," she

finally tells me.

"I know," I reply as our hands move in unison away from her head.

It was never my intention to admit to biting anyone but I'll keep that information to myself. Madison must sense my deception because she withdraws her hands from mine and thrusts them into her hoodie pockets. She turns to walk away again. When I catch up to her she hands me an EpiPen, which I promptly stash away in my jacket.

"A bite is a bite," she says. "Even with the antivenin, being bitten leaves a scar that you can't ever walk away from."

It brings to mind that kid I bit in kindergarten. There's no doubt in my mind that I damaged him for life. Not just physically either. When I look at the hand where Amara bit me, I can barely call it a scar.

She catches me staring at the faint lines on the back of my hand, imperceptible to the human eye. "Who bit you?"

Despite my mixed feelings about Amara, I'm not about to answer that question. If she is some kind of a spy I don't want to play any part in the role of executioner. Judging from her reaction just a moment ago, I'm starting to doubt that's what she is.

"Why can't you let that go?"

"Because, like you said, it's my job."

"Well, I'm not friends with your job," I say, fully aware that her snark has rubbed off on me.

She crosses her arms. "Fine."

I know it's anything but fine by her. At the same time, I

don't really care just now.

"You're going to have to come clean at some point."

My eyes scan the streetscape and the bare tree limbs shivering in the autumn air. Exposed and stripped down. Even though the chill doesn't bother me, out of habit I pull up the collar of my jacket.

"And if I don't?"

"This isn't a joke."

"Who says I'm joking? I didn't sign up for this, Madison."

"And you think *I* did?"

"No, I — look, neither one of us did. But I don't see how that means I have no choice in the matter. If I want to keep it to myself, that's on me."

"Here's what you need to wrap your head around, Connor," she says, taking her no-nonsense tone. "Whoever bit you took everything away from you. *Everything.* You don't get to just walk out here in the real world. Not without thinking you could go off like a loaded gun and kill someone. Or worse. The fundamental takeaway here is that you don't get to be the person you used to be. And you *definitely* don't get to be the person you wanted to be. All that is gone. The one who took it all away from you is the one who bit you. Someone ended your life. The Hounds will end theirs. Without exception."

If I was someone else, someone who'd had a life, I could imagine being pretty pissed about losing it all. With everything that's gone down in the past few days, I haven't really had the chance to process what being a werewolf will really mean in the long run. Now that I turn the idea around in my head I'm oddly at peace with it. I had nothing before I was bitten. No real friends to speak of, certainly no girlfriend and not much of anything going for me, really. Maybe for someone like Madison, being bitten was more devastating. Besides the near-death experience, of course. I didn't know her then but she once had a family, a boyfriend who was clearly head-over-heels for her, and who knows what dreams of hers were waiting to be fulfilled? Now that girl is hidden away behind Splat hair color and constantly changing eyebrow rings. This afternoon it happens to be a serpent with the head poking out on one side and the tail on the other.

"What about Josh?" I ask. "He's a pretty clear example of an exception to the rule. I mean, he bit you but the Hounds let him live. And isn't he the one who led the charge against Boguet at the cemetery?"

We pause outside the street level door that leads up to my flat.

"Don't..." Her voice trails off as she avoids eye contact. "Let's not go there."

"It works both ways, Madison."

She turns away, to leave I think, but I don't want our conversation to end.

"Wait," I say.

The branches of a nearby tree wave in the wind and the last of the still-clinging foliage breaks off and flutters away. Finding an honest moment with Madison is like capturing one of those leaves once it's caught in a breeze.

"Does all of this get easier? Being a werewolf, I mean."

She doesn't hesitate to answer. "No, it does not. But ... I'll try to help."

I tilt back my head and let out a long sigh. Above us Arden is waiting for me. I should get up there and relieve him of his pain.

As if reading my mind, Madison says, "You seriously shouldn't be out here."

As I reach for the door she takes the chance to slip something into my palm.

"What's this?" I ask, taking possession of a manila envelope.

In a wry tone, she informs me, "You've been served."

I've watched enough TV law dramas to know what those words mean. It's a subpoena for me to appear in court and testify. My frustration with her can't be contained and it comes out in an angry huff. Every time I start to trust Madison, her association with the Hounds keeps sticking daggers into my back. Without thinking, I crush the paper in my hand.

"Why didn't you just give this to me at the start?"

"Because I didn't want you to get all ragey on me," she replies, staring at my closed fist.

"I don't—"

"Just chill, already, Connor," she says gently. "You were going to be called to testify anyway. Would you rather it was some random stranger here instead of me? You need to calm down."

Although I won't admit it out loud, she's right. Being

summoned to werewolf court is unexpected enough. I don't know how I would have reacted had a stranger delivered the news. I stare at the simple lettering on the front of Madison's hoodie. *Meh.* As with most of her outfits and accessories I get a sense that she's wearing it ironically. What would happen to me if I chose to not show up? Would the Hounds track me down, drag me into court as an unwilling participant, somehow punish me if I refused to testify? And why do they want me there anyway? It's not like I really know anything.

With a sigh of defeat I ask, "Do I need a lawyer or something?"

"No, you're just a witness. The prosecutor is going to want to talk to you, though, so you should tell your pack leader."

"I don't have a pack leader."

"What about..."

I shake my head. She gives me the once-over like she's trying to figure out if I'm for real or maybe if I've lost my mind altogether. Whatever her assessment, for once she keeps it to herself. And I'm glad because the last thing I need right now is to second-guess myself and my decision to live outside the pack. Instead of saying anything she walks away, giving me a little over-the-shoulder waggle of her fingers as she does. I'm left staring after her with pain meds in one hand, a subpoena in the other and a whole hell of a lot of questions that need answering.

5. HEARTBROKEN, IN DISREPAIR

When I swing open the door to the flat I find Arden sitting on the kitchen floor chowing down on the raw rabbit. Holding the carcass with his good hand, he crunches down through flesh and bone. He glances up at me from where he's sitting, a sinew dangling from his mouth. It takes all my effort not to hurl.

"Stop!"

I watch the pulse of his throat as a mouthful travels down toward his stomach, and just the idea of that slimy texture makes me heave a little. Pursing my lips, I avert my gaze in order to prevent a gag reflex.

"You can't eat raw meat," I tell him. "Not anymore."

He seems tired when he asks, "Why not? I've done it my whole life."

Do I really have to spell it out for him? I mean, it's possible based on the evolutionary science Boadicea explained that raw food is actually safe for Arden's consumption since his physiology is different from the average human. But a part of me says not to take any chances. "Because you'll make yourself sick."

"What am I supposed to do with it?" He stares at the

carcass.

"I don't know. Boil it or bake it, I guess."

"Bah! I've lost my appetite."

I would say the same if I wasn't trying so hard to not throw up. Disheartened, he sets the rabbit down on the floor next to him. I notice that there's an entire leg missing. The next two weeks suddenly seem more daunting than everything that's gone down in the past two months. I never imagined I'd have to lecture anyone on Being Human 101. In the meantime, I toss him the package of painkillers and the pills that Roul prescribed. After swallowing them he struggles to get to his feet. When I make a move to help he lets out a snarl and digs deep to manage on his own. Without another word he heads to his room and leaves the animal carcass on the floor where he set it down. With a pair of tongs I pick it up, give it a rinse and stick it in the fridge in a casserole dish. That's when my stomach finally lets out a growl of protest. Since I'm basically in quarantine, I might have to come to terms with the fact that I just looked my supper in the eyes. Other than that, the best I can hope for is the possibility of a cereal bar in my backpack. I grab my schoolbag from the floor of Arden's bedroom, leaving him lying fully clothed on the queen-size bed.

In my own room, I sit on my bed and scavenge through my backpack. I find a package of flattened Reese's Peanut Butter Cups that my mom sent in a care package after I mentioned not being able to find any in Paris. As I devour them, my eyes fall on the manila envelope that I tossed next to me and my pulse quickens at the thought of what's inside. There's no sense in prolonging the inevitable so I tear open the slim package and pull out the contents. The subpoena is addressed to me and printed on a single sheet of letterhead that states that it's from the High Court of Magdeburg. A coat of arms is embossed at the top: a crest with a black wolf standing on its hind legs and the motto "*Non sibi sed omnibus*" below it. Besides naming the prosecutor and defendant (Heaven's Hand vs. H. Boguet), it also lists the scheduled date and time of my appearance in court. "*You are hereby commanded to report in person before the High Court of Magdeburg in Harz, Germany.*" Exactly one month from now. That's all the time I've got to figure out how to keep my inner wolf at bay.

As I read the instructions, which includes the general detail that transportation will be provided, a hollow sensation overcomes me like there's nothing left inside from which to squeeze out the fear. It sort of takes the edge off the harsh reality of the words. I don't understand what they hope to get out of me. Whatever happened in Boguet's lab when I was kidnapped from the party at La Pleine Lune occurred while I was completely out of it, recovering from Amara's bite. How much can I offer as testimony in court? Before I can seriously consider skipping out on the whole affair I read on and confirm my hunch about a penalty for doing exactly that. "*Failure to comply with this subpoena without lawful excuse is a contempt of court and may result in your arrest.*" Arden once said that we're all just pawns to the Hounds, and Roul called them oppressors. If biting incurs a death sentence, I'm not sure what the punishment for contempt would entail. All the same it's probably better if I don't find out first-hand. With all their archaic rules, I imagine werewolf prison is somewhere in the ballpark of Madame Tussauds Chamber of Horrors.

To distract myself, I pick up my things and spread out on my bed with my laptop in order to Google rabbit recipes. I'm hungry enough to convince myself that eating a bunny is a case of mind over matter. It doesn't take very long for the Internet to prove me wrong. One diagram showing cut points to butcher the carcass and I'm done. Disgusted, I shut down my computer and lie back with my eyes closed for just a second. I must be more exhausted from the day's events than I realized because sleep comes instantly.

It's dark when I open my eyes again except for a light that illuminates the hallway in a pale glow. The sound of retching wakes me. Quietly, I pad down the corridor toward the bathroom. Sure enough, I find Arden curled up around the toilet throwing up into the bowl. So much for the theory behind evolutionary science. In a way I'm glad about not having eaten much of anything today because I'm certain it would it come up now. Taking care to breathe through my mouth, I sit on the edge of the bathtub and wait for a pause.

I say, "In case you're wondering, this is called food poisoning."

He's too weak to tell me off but casts me a withering look. For the first time since we parted ways, I wish Amara were here. There's not much I can do to comfort Arden. The memory of going through a similar thing myself last year is still vivid. Sleep was my only relief. My distaste for raw anything, vegetables included, comes mostly from an experience with a bad batch of sushi. I overdid it at an all-you-can-eat buffet in K-Town and a few hours later the symptoms came on strong: stomach cramps, chills, nausea and eventually vomiting. For the longest while any time I even looked at a maki roll I'd remember tasting the undigested food on its way back up. The retching noises finally ease up.

"How did you live like this?" Arden asks hoarsely.

He's never been sick a day in his long life. Roul started an entire industry creating pharmaceuticals based on their biochemistry. I have to wonder if there's a quick-fix pill for food poisoning.

"You get used to it," is all I can say.

After a long pause it seems as though there's nothing more for him to regurgitate. Arden flushes the toilet and leans back against the tiled wall with his eyes closed, defeated by his body. All the color is drawn from his skin, which is covered in beads of dampness. The Green Day T-shirt I loaned him days ago clings to his body with perspiration. For a long while we just gaze at each other in silence. The cold reality of what he is — what I am — sets in like cement and our former selves have been buried and smothered to death beneath the thick concrete of our separate fates.

"Roul's right," he says finally, his voice raw and ragged. "You can't live without the pack."

I don't want to talk about it. Not now, at this hour, surrounded by the acrid smells of bile and sweat. So much of my life is out of my control. It can't be too much to ask that I have a choice in this matter. In a way I've been a lone wolf all my life. All the same, I have to acknowledge that navigating through the pitfalls of this newer existence can't compare with my previous life's complaints. Nothing prepares you for being the stuff of nightmares — not unless you were born into this skin. Like Arden was.

Ogling him, I ask, "What does he know that you can't tell me?"

His amber eyes come alive and I'm haunted by the former wolf in him, casting a ghostly shadow within. Maybe it's cruel of me to ask him to share his knowledge. Am I just prolonging his inevitable severance from this world? Right at this moment all I know — all I care about — is the fact that we need each other to survive. I extend my arm to help him up off the bathroom floor and there's a pause between us like when we were first introduced and he refused to shake my hand. This time, he grabs on and I hoist him up to his feet.

"Follow me," he says and leads me into the kitchen.

Curiosity gets the better of me as he opens the fridge. "What's up?"

"The first thing you need to learn as a wolf," he starts, "is how to eat."

He tosses the rabbit carcass at me. As it flies through the air I dodge its trajectory, watching as it lands with a wet and disgusting thud on the kitchen floor.

C. INCOGNITO

Incognito: *adjective & adverb*. Having one's true identity concealed.

La Défense business district is the exact opposite of everything anyone pictures when they think of Paris. It's just a sea of steel and glass skyscrapers and its centerpiece, La Grande Arche, is like a giant monument that screams, "*In your face, history*!" It's this ginormous hollowed-out glass cube that's as tall as a building and the sides actually have government offices in them.

Boguet Biotechnology has to be the tallest building in this area. Looking up as I walk up the front steps I wonder what the bird kill rate is on a building like this. It's not like they can put up hawk silhouettes on every one of these windows, if they do at all.

When I reach the top of the staircase it gets real. Why I'm here. What I'm about to do. My reflection in the glass says it all. If I'm going to sneak in and snoop around Boguet's labs with a stolen employee card, I have to look the part. My story is that I'm a friend of Boadicea's dropping in for a lunch date. My hair is tucked beneath the Burberry scarf I took from her bag, bangs just touching the rim of her oversized Jackie O sunglasses. I'm even wearing a dress beneath my fave coat. It's bright red and I bought it like an hour after I moved to the city from a vintage shop I haven't been able to find again. Pretty swanky even if I did swipe my accessories off a girl I shot dead.

Adjusting the Louis Vuitton tote strap on my shoulder, I walk through the front doors and into the sterile foyer. People in suits move around the lobby in the way that people in suits do. Like if they stopped for even a second the sky would rain down a firestorm of fail. All the women, even the ones in lab coats, wear high heels that click and echo in the open space. I'll give props to Boguet for at least being an equal opportunity badass because the place is practically the UN of mad science. I take a deep breath and try to act businessy.

The security desk is by the elevators and that's where my two feet take me. Ballerina flats are the best I could do because spy work and high heels don't mix, and it kind of makes me crazy when I see it on TV and in movies, but at least I'm wearing enough lip gloss to be a Hollywood heroine.

When the guard greets me, it hits me that I have no sweet clue what her last name is, so I hesitate. *Get it together, Maddy. How many Boadiceas could work here? One. That's how many.*

"I'm here to see—"

"Madison?" a voice calls from behind me.

Do *not* freak out. Just turn around slowly and see who it is. I do as my brain tells me and come face-to-face with

Trajan, my antivenin dealer. I mean literally face to face. What he lacks in height, he more than makes up for in muscle. His colleague Attila hangs back with full-on ennui to match his hipster look. Any time I've dealt with these guys they always appear as a set of two, no doubt for the intimidation factor, even if Trajan could pass for a walking Gap ad. I have no idea what to say.

"Hey."

I play it cool but I'm now totally conscious that I'm wearing all of Boadicea's things and my bright red coat suddenly seems like a redonkulous warning flag. So this deception isn't going very far. I take a little step to one side so that my way out is at least a bit clearer if I have to run. But I notice Trajan glancing around like *he's* the one who's nervous.

"What are you doing here?" he asks.

OMG. He has no freaking clue. Whatever he does for Boguet is clearly well below the need-to-know level, not to mention it probably takes zero observational skills. Luckily I've always been pretty much invisible to Attila. He'd rather be watching *Shark Week* or being ironic than dealing with me. I hate myself for what I'm about to do but I don't see another way out of this. With a vacuous head tilt, I put on my prettiest flirty smile.

"I thought I'd pop in to see you."

Attila lets out an exaggerated sigh, like this happens all the time. Meanwhile, Thomas Edison shudders in his grave at the light bulb dimly flickering over Trajan's head. The confused look on his face is so extreme that he almost looks like a manga character.

"That's cool, right?" I ask, laying on a sugary voice. "I mean, if not, I could totally bounce."

"No, I—" he starts, unsure at first, then clearing his throat and shifting gears back to his usual cocky self. "Yeah, hey, that's dope."

He exchanges a look with Attila. There's not a subtle bone in his body. They're mentally high-fiving each other in their stupid boy brains. I roll my eyes before taking off the sunglasses and shoving them into the tote.

"Later," Attila says as he pulls big noise-canceling headphones from his messenger bag and walks out the main doors.

If I keep smiling like this, I'm going to pull a facial muscle or something. "Wanna show me around?"

"What, like a tour?"

I nod. "Yeah, totes."

He shrugs then leads me past the security desk and down a hall of elevators, each one marked for different parts of the building. We crowd into one in the middle with some lab geeks and take it to the thirtieth floor, where he shows me everything I *don't* want to see. Getting into a lab at Boguet Biotech should be more exciting than this. The scientists in this department develop bio-plastics. Yawn.

He explains, "It's, like, plastic but made from stuff like vegetable oil. So it biodegrades faster than the stuff that's made from fuel and whatever."

Yay for the environment, but that's not why I'm here. Either he finds this department as uninteresting as I do or he sees the snoredom oozing out me, but he takes us to another floor. When we exit this time we're on the other side of a glass enclosure where scientists wearing blue rubber gloves and eye protection handle Petri dishes.

It all looks a little more serious than what was going on ten levels below us until Trajan says, "They're growing cultured meat."

I scoff a little because I picture cows in tuxedos touring the Louvre.

"It's basically grown in those test tubes. Chicken that's never been part of a chicken."

"Shmeat," I blurt out.

Gag. I'd rather eat tofu. Just the idea of in vitro meat makes me want to go vegan. He glances over at me, grinning and obviously pleased with himself for having been able to gross me out. We walk around the perimeter of glass, looking in at the employees like they're on exhibit. After a few minutes of uncomfortable silence, Trajan escorts me back to the elevator and down to the lobby again. So much for my career in corporate espionage. I should have pretended to be more interested.

"That's the grand tour, is it?" I ask.

"Nah, I'll take you up to my office. What we do there is secure. Separate from the other departments."

He seems really proud of this tidbit of information so I nod like I'm in on the big secret — and hopefully I will be soon enough. All I know is the Hounds made some kind of deal with Boguet or at least laid out some ground rules for whatever he's doing here. Some questions are better left unasked. I'm basically just a go-between. All I know is that he sells me antivenin, under the table, and I don't ask him any questions.

When we arrive on the main floor he leads me to an elevator that's separated from the long line of others. It opens as we approach and inside there are no buttons, just a biometric fingerprint scanner. He wasn't joking about not mingling with the riff-raff in the other departments. Finally, we're getting somewhere.

We stand in silence. I can feel his eyes on me so I glance over and force another smile. Eventually the doors slide open and we enter a large, modern office space that's also enclosed in glass. There are four separate workspaces, one in each corner and a main sort of conference area in the middle. We're the only ones here right now, though. A bare hallway without windows or doors rings the room. I have no idea if we're up on the penthouse or fifty floors below ground. There's another elevator diagonally across from us, probably leading to creepier labs in other parts of the building.

"What exactly do you do here?" I ask.

He brings me to his workspace, which is a tidy desk without any personal effects on it. The names of all the shifters — Boadicea, Trajan, Attila — are so bogus that I know they're not real. Still, it's weird how sterile all their desks are. I know the feeling. After I was bitten, I deleted everything too. No pictures to haunt me. It's like they have no lives. That, or they left a life behind after they chose this one. Josh told me the Hounds basically looked the other way while Boguet genetically modified shifters from a select group of terminally ill kids. Charity cases who can transform into full-fledged wolves — limited in number so they don't pose a threat to the Hounds — and since they're unable produce venom they're no risk to humans either.

Trajan gestures for me to sit in front of a giant monitor, then with one hand pressed against the back of my chair he leans over me to move diagrams around the screen with his index finger. From the corner of my eye I can see his biceps flexing beneath his polo shirt.

"My research is mostly in recombinant DNA," he tells me. "Specifically, werewolves. Born *and* bitten."

Mind = blown. This has got to be a joke. A career counselor must have accidentally swapped profiles between Trajan and some poor nerd who's now flipping burgers at a fast-food megacorporation. I blink at the screen, staring at multi-colored double helixes. With a tap of his hand on the monitor the helix breaks apart into separate little squiggles.

"This here," he starts and moves his fingers on the touchscreen to zoom in on a specific marker, "this is your evil stepsister. The thing you have to live with. It's what Boguet calls 'the curse.'"

I glance up at him. He moves his fingers to form air quotes around "the curse," which makes it sound absurd. Like he doesn't believe in that kind of thing even after having seen what we are with his own two eyes.

"We just give it an alphanumeric code: LYCN1."

The 3D strand stares back at me from the screen, color-coded in a harmless pink. Evil stepsister. As if.

"Stop me if I'm boring you."

Not knowing what else to say, I try to put the pieces together. "No, this is interesting. So you're, like, a geneticist?"

He just smiles with surprise. "Yeah."

I'm the one who's really shocked. Not in a million years would I have guessed there are actually brains beneath all that brawn. He's built like a gladiator with wide shoulders and an embarrassing abundance of muscles. Friends from my previous life would have swooned over his body, not to mention his chiseled features. But he's *so* not my type.

"I thought you were..."

"Eye candy?" he suggests with a smirk.

I give him the eye roll he's looking for. "It's just, outside of here, you're kind of the muscle. I didn't really expect you to be *this* too."

"The job's got a lot of perks," he admits. "What high school geek wouldn't want to be able to wail on haters? Being a shifter is sick."

That explains his cocky attitude: overcompensation. "How *are* you a shifter, anyway?"

"It's called atavism activation," he says, swiping the image off the screen and picking another strand. "We've got a genetic marker that's like an on/off switch. The most common theory is that an extinction event wiped out the Neanderthals, most likely humans taking over their territory. Our theory is that Neanderthals didn't die out when threatened with extinction, they evolved into werewolves. We're pretty sure Neanderthals were the ones who domesticated wolves into dogs. Like humans, they had forty-six chromosomes. Wolves have seventy-eight. A virus carried by these pet wolves infected the Neanderthals around 30,000 years ago and wiped out most but not all of their population. The virus attacks on the genetic level, breaking down the DNA of the host. In the case of the surviving population a bridge fused the strands together, merging the two sets of chromosomes and creating extra genetic material, the side effect of which lets them switch between both forms."

Sitting back, I let the information sink in. "Okay, so how does that explain me?"

He taps the screen and pulls up side-by-side images of two people.

"The virus is still alive in the werewolves and can be passed into the blood through their venom. When bitten, most humans die right away. They can't survive the genetic reconstitution. But there's this small percentage of the population, like you and me, with Neanderthal DNA. About 2.5 percent. It's left over from when the two species mingled, if you know what I mean. Unfortunately for you, because the species evolved separately, your marker is outdated. Your evil stepsister is basically werewolf 1.0."

"So, I'm a Neanderthal."

"Partly. But so am I and about 150 million other people."

With another touch of his fingers the images animate, one transforming into a wolf and the other a monster. "The virus tries to merge wolf and Neanderthal DNA like before, but all that humanity gets in the way. What you get is what you are."

I watch as the misshapen human-wolf hybrid rotates on the screen.

"Your boyfriend, though," he goes on with a shake of his head, "he's a bit of a freak of nature. A kind of mutation or something. I wasn't involved in that research. But based on his DNA, we figured out how to switch off LYCN1."

Most of those words blow right by me. "Wait. Boyfriend?"

"I thought you and fre—" he catches himself before saying something. "Aren't you and Lewis an item?"

I can't stop my face from whatever it's doing. Half-smiling and slightly embarrassed, I throw back, "Why would you think that?"

Trajan gestures to a wall of CCTV screens. Stalker cams. My heart kind of sinks. Who the hell *are* these people?

"C'mon. You're not here to see me."

My brain kind of stammers. The guy isn't the dolt I thought he was and now I'm in way over my head. When I don't answer, he pulls open a desk drawer. My heart skips a beat as I scan the room and prepare to go on the defensive. If it's a gun, crotch-punch and run. Lucky for both of us it's just a bunch of yellow highlighter colored tubes.

"You don't need to play me if you're just here for the antivenin, alright?"

I start to nod obligingly at his excuse when the elevator door pings, saving me the trouble of coming up with a real answer. Attila must be back from lunch.

"Who is this?" asks a female voice with a thick French

accent.

The woman who steps out of the elevator has a Cleopatra haircut and moves with the slither of a snake, her body swaying in a curvy peacock-blue skirt suit. I'd put her in her early forties. Confidence screams out of her pores and she looks like she's perfectly prepared to crush us with her stylish but surprisingly sensible heels if it comes to it. She's clearly management.

"Relax," Trajan says. "This is Madison."

She obviously isn't impressed. She crosses her arms, staring us down and not relaxed in any way. I've never seen brown eyes look so fiery.

"I'm with Heaven's Hand," I tell her with an authority I don't actually have.

"Do you have a warrant to search the premises?"

Trajan straightens up by my side. "Be cool, Sev."

"My name is Severine," she tells him while her eyes are locked on me. "And I will thank you to use it. Get her out, now, or I shall have security remove the both of you."

Sliding the drawer closed, Trajan silently escorts me back the way we came. Severine's gaze never leaves me even as the elevator doors slide shut. We're quiet for a very long time before I ask, "So, um, who's Queen Bee?"

He smirks. "She *is* a bitch, isn't she?"

I laugh because for a genius he's kind of clueless about other things.

"She's the money," Trajan tells me. "At least on a couple of our projects. We've been calling her Cruella."

"Do you have a lot of financiers?"

"You'd be surprised," he says then moves on lightning-fast. "Listen, I know Boguet's in trouble with all of you but Boadicea ... what did she do?"

The question makes me freeze up as I think about how much he might actually know. I try to shake my head like I have no clue.

"You're just the messenger, hey?"

My voice is small, laden with guilt, when I answer, "Yeah."

"Well, if you see her, tell her 'hey from Tray.'"

"Sure."

He thinks we're holding her in custody too. It's taking forever to get out of here! Why didn't it seem this long when we were going to his office?

"It's just a job, you know," he says.

I find his words inexplicably annoying. "So, what, you'll work for whoever's the highest bidder?"

"Money's money, isn't it?"

Trajan looks like he expects me to say something more. I don't because I have no idea what his story is. I figure whatever happens on this side of being bitten, or in his case being genetically modified, is covered by Vegas rules. He clenches his jaw. When he talks again, it's in a biting tone that tells me over-sharing goes against his better judgment.

"Look, Boguet stepped up for me — got me out of a jam when he didn't have to — and I feel like I owe it to him to stick it out."

Something about those words actually strikes a chord

with me. It's exactly how I feel about the Hounds. Sort of onside with them because they saved me, but also not because of their sketch factor. Finally, the elevator doors slide open. As I get out he grabs my arm. I turn to face him and he hands me an EpiPen. He releases his hold on me and we each take a step back.

"You know," he adds, "at least until something better comes along."

When he leans forward to send the elevator to his office again he winks at me, and while the doors close I get the sense that if I catch him alone again, he might actually let me in on the rest of Boguet's secrets.

6. COME ALIVE

The rabbit carcass stares up at me with its lidless eyes, one leg grotesquely missing. Arden left me here alone to deal with it, shutting his bedroom door behind him. Barring me while he rests was the smart thing to do since I'll have to shift to make this work. I can't even wrap my head around what's supposed to happen here, chowing down on raw meat the way Arden wants me to. The thought of it is revolting. If I were a wolf out in the wild it wouldn't matter, just like it didn't concern me when I ate that rat the first night I shifted. Well, that is until it came back up on me the next morning in disgusting undigested chunks, tail and all. My stomach rumbles audibly and I close my eyes. I'm only aware of the sound of electrical humming and the sensation of my stomach roiling from the absence of food and the presence of desire. All I can smell is pure, unprocessed meat. The memory of blood from that night overcomes my senses. And then it happens again.

I stand in the kitchen, four paws on the cold tiled floor, staring down at the remains of a kill. Saliva floods my tongue in a thick wave, gushing forth from my mouth and drooling down from my lips. I can't bear it. Crouching, I pull

90

the carcass into my maw and in a matter of minutes make short work of it. My teeth chew straight through sinews and bones, each crunch cracking open an intense flavor from the marrow. The human part of me is beyond disgusted yet the urgency of my hunger is so overpowering that I allow it to happen. When I'm done I lick my chops first, then my paws and even the floor. Chasing remnants of rabbit, I sniff around for more but there's nothing left except the vague scent of other wolves. The most concentrated odor is on the sofa. I leap onto it and the familiar smell of another male fills my nostrils. It pulls at me until I scent-roll into it, mashing my face into the cushions then pulling forward onto my chest. I toss around onto my back and repeat this ritual, occasionally nipping at a pillow until I eventually thrust it away with a headbutt. Sated and camouflaged in a musky odor, I stretch out and fall asleep on the cushions.

An intruder wakes me in the morning. Before he enters the room, my ears prick up to the sound of his footfall. He halts by the hallway as I rise on my front legs. The man stalls in his tracks as we stare each other down. Even though I'm aware that it's Arden, there's something about acknowledging his presence in this enclosed area that makes me nervous. The hairs bristle on the back of my neck. My instinct is to put as much space between us as possible. He moves slowly toward me then he crouches, not making eye contact. He speaks to me in a quiet and reassuring voice. As before, his words are stuttering and incomprehensible until finally I catch one.

"Focus."

I stare at his outstretched hand, palm turned down. Looking into his eyes would be a mistake. He may be human now, but even the shape of them will ever remind me of the wildness that he left behind. It takes all my mental effort to concentrate and think of all the things I can't do in this form: texting, using a pen, opening doors. When I feel myself slip back into human form he rises and tosses a pile of clothes at me, silent and without judgment. I get dressed as he heads to the kitchen in search of food.

"Why does this keep happening all of a sudden?" I ask, pulling on my long-sleeved T-shirt. "I was bitten over a month ago but these shifts only started with the full moon a few days ago."

He looks at me as though he just caught me in a lie. "Before then you mauled a pillow. In your sleep one night."

"What are you saying? That I turned into a wolf while I was dreaming?"

With a shrug he replies, "It happens."

At Madison's I shifted from wolf to human form while doped up on Valium. I guess it can happen in the reverse.

"I've only seen this lack of control in whelps," he adds.

A flush rises to my cheeks. I don't know why but it embarrasses me. My infantile abilities shouldn't be such a surprise. Like humans, I imagine most werewolves grow up learning the basic ins and outs of societal norms and behaviors. Me, on the other hand, I never knew what I was until I was bitten. Now my challenge is to squeeze years of knowledge into a one-month crash course. My advantage is that Arden was by all accounts a model werewolf. A "wolf to the core," in Roul's words. It explains Amara's attraction to him, beyond his looks. I wish I could offer him the same kind of expertise but I'm as poor a human specimen now as I've ever been.

"Yesterday, you said you left school early … why?"

The memory is still fresh in my mind and I have to shake myself out of it lest I lose control again. "At lunch I started thinking about what would happen if I shifted in the middle of all those innocent bystanders. Something twigged in me and I felt like I was losing it."

"Think wolf; be wolf."

"So what you're telling me is all I have to do is try not to think about it?"

"No." He pauses in taking stock of the fridge for a second. "The reverse. You must be … present. Always. Man or wolf. That's all there is."

He makes it sound so Zen. Or Jedi. Like some kind of Wolf Yoda. *There is no try.* And maybe that's all there is to it. Don't over-think the shift. Just embrace the form that I want to be in. All the same, it's not foolproof because I'm pretty sure even he had a slip-up. That fateful night when I told him his world was about to end and I was the reason for it, he lost control and turned into a wolf. If he couldn't hold it together then what hope is there for me?

"We need groceries," he says. "Write a list of things we can eat."

Arden heads to the bathroom to shower as I tear a piece of paper from a school binder and start frantically scribbling down words. When he finally reenters the kitchen I hand him my list. Back in his own stylish clothes, at least he's dressed in the role of his old self. His eyes scan the paper as I await a response. All I want is to push him out the door so he doesn't waste another second prolonging the moment when I can finally sate my appetite. Even though I devoured an entire rabbit — minus the haunch that Arden wound up regurgitating — it somehow didn't even begin to make up for the meals missed yesterday. This must be how an addict feels. I can't even remember half the things on the list anymore.

"Gatorade?"

"That's for you. I doubt you've got much of an appetite but you need to rehydrate."

With an arched eyebrow he asks, "And the chips?"

I grin but it fades quickly when he tells me, "No. You'll make yourself sick."

"Look, I'd go myself but Roul and Madison both said—"

"When did you see her?" he asks tensely.

"Yesterday, when I picked up your pain meds."

Arden tucks the paper into his pants pocket. "You shouldn't trust her."

I don't know if I want to argue the point because my feelings about her are still very mixed up. Madison Dallaire is like a fire in many ways. Although I find warmth in her company and she's shed some light on this new world order, I've also been bitterly burned by her.

"You'd be dead right now if she hadn't given me the

antivenin," I remind him.

He doesn't respond and it's clear that my words haven't done much to further my argument. His eyes scan me. In the stillness of the moment I'm aware of how jittery I am. I didn't realize it until now but this pent-up energy must account for why I took up running after I was bitten. Standing in place makes it more obvious. I'm suddenly intensely aware of the animal within. It wants all four paws on the ground, to feel grass and earth on the pads of its paws, to take in the sounds and scents of wilderness and wide-open spaces. I understand why Arden was always so irritable. Apartment living is like being caged.

"You're your own worst enemy right now," he observes.

"How's that?"

As if reading my thoughts, he asks, "When's the last time you ran? You need the distraction."

I shake my head as though the answer might rattle out. "I don't know. It's been a few days now. We both know I can't go out there."

"There are other ways to exercise your body in order to calm your mind," he says. "You need control before you can take the next step."

After he pulls his leather jacket down from a hook at the entryway he slings the left side over his cast then slips his other arm into the sleeve. I follow him to the door, shutting it behind him without twisting the deadbolt. The worst thing that can happen to me at this point is dying from starvation. Alone in the flat, ordinarily I'm a master at the art of filling time. There's only one thing on my mind now, and nothing — not even my favorite online RPG — can distract me from it. His tough-love approach means I have to think of a way to expend energy without leaving the flat. My first thought goes to Phys Ed class. I'd rather play the Wii version. There was a time when I would have given anything to be in my current position, contained within the privacy of my own room without any commitments to the outside world. Just me, my laptop and a bag of chips. At one point, my physical activity consisted of getting up for refills of Coke, and now I'm doing push-ups in the living room. The monotony of the exercise combined with the physical exertion is definitely unwelcome but I have to suck it up in order to regain some control of my life. By the time I get through the first set of fifty, I begin to feel that peaceful ease moving in. For a change I switch to sit-ups. Through the sweat and grunts I gain clarity. My body aches from the effort but maybe that's the point. The sensation reminds me of my human form. I hold on to it. I cling to it, relishing all the parts of me I took for granted. Fingernails, opposable thumbs, even the way my tongue curls to form words.

When Arden returns, he catches me standing in front of the mirror at the entryway making a face at myself — a wide, gaping yawn and surprised-looking eyes. I regain my composure as he sets a bag of groceries on the kitchen table.

"Good," he finally remarks and I assume he's referring to the fact that I stayed human and didn't rampage through the flat destroying all his valuables. When he slips out of his jacket, I notice writing on his cast.

"What's that?"

On closer inspection it's a phone number in fuchsia lipstick. With a grimace he ignores my question and struggles to single-handedly open a Lemon-Lime Gatorade.

"Are you *kidding* me?" I take the bottle to remove the plastic safety features then hand it back to him. "You got a girl's number while you were out shopping for groceries?"

He takes a swig of the fluorescent green fluid, wincing at the false promise of citrus. "I had trouble because of this," he tells me with distaste as he gestures toward the cast. "A woman helped. Then ... she defaced my plaster."

"Is that what the kids are calling it these days?" I joke.

No surprise, but Arden doesn't laugh.

"It's called picking up. This..." I tilt my head to read the lettering, i's dotted with x's. "Emilie ... wants you to call her."

"Why?"

Rather than being flattered, he sounds put off. Maybe I *do* have more to offer him in terms of human behavior than I originally gave him credit for. "If I were to guess, it's because she wants to get in your pants. You know, to..."

"I'm injured and weak," he notes, perplexed by the concept. "An unworthy mate. It's foolish."

"Welcome to being human," I say sarcastically.

7. FURR

The rest of the week passes pretty uneventfully. We have most of our meals together, and our former silences are replaced by life lessons. Arden instructs me on how to make it in the wild and the many dangers of getting caught. Our conversations don't include typical talking points found in wilderness survival training. His instructions are about the dos and mostly don'ts of living alongside humans, urban wolf etiquette and detecting the territory of other packs. Between all these lessons, he frequently has me switch to my other form. I wouldn't dare risk it in the absence of the EpiPen that Madison gave me. Although the shifting comes easier with practice, the wolf in me is still hard to control. I'm not wholly me in that form. It takes all of my concentration to hang on to my human thoughts. My self-awareness is easily lost at the slightest distraction. Transforming in the apartment comes with a safety net. There are fewer things here to divert my attention, being in a confined space. Out in the real world I won't have that luxury. If I'm to gain real control, we'll have to eventually take this training beyond the apartment threshold. But the timeframe for doing so shortens with each passing day. I haven't had any contact with the Hounds — besides my most recent encounter with Madison — and Roul has left me alone under the guardianship of Arden. Somehow I have a feeling that they're waiting for me to slip up.

Meanwhile I give Arden tips on how to survive in the captivity not just of this apartment but of his own body too. My pointers seem so trivial in light of everything that he's shown me, especially since he's been living among humans, albeit grudgingly. It doesn't help that Arden is no less irritable a man than he was a werewolf. At least he's learned the basics of human survival, including how to cook meat to a proper temperature and how to safely prepare raw food in order to prevent a repeat performance of his food poisoning experience. Still, I can see that he's not wholly himself. Sometimes I catch him just staring off, amber eyes filled with lost moments. I wonder how long it will take him to recover, on the inside I mean. At least he appears to be starting to accept his lot in life. That's no small comfort to me. I've twice pulled him from the brink of death, against his will, but now that he's among the living I don't think he has it in him to off himself.

Whether he has the same heightened wolf senses as before remains to be seen. I hope not. Every day that passes the scent of Amara diminishes around the flat. One day, I accidentally catch him taking in a deep breath of her pillow. He buries his face in it, trying to inhale whatever he can. Even then he must know that lingering smell will disappear. He must be hyper-aware of her absence, albeit more viscerally. He had a tendency not to be around the apartment without her. Regardless, he was usually in his preferred form, posing as her dog. All physical signs of her have gone. Things that I hadn't really noticed or paid much attention to highlight the fact that she's missing: her messenger bag, jackets and shoes, the sketchpad with tattoo artwork. It's like I can see the pale silhouette of her belongings scattered around the entire flat.

Today, precisely two weeks after Arden started the drug that Roul gave him to speed up his recovery, a thin man in a suit comes by to remove the cast. He's as efficient in his practice as he is with his speech and doesn't say more than five words. The doctor — or at least that's what I assume he is — pulls a chair from the kitchen table, places it flush against a wall and motions for Arden to sit. From a medical bag he produces a handheld electrical saw that we stare at with apprehension. Although Arden's face is a blank page, I can read his nervousness through the tension of his muscles as he sits upright with his spine pressed against the back of the chair. The high-pitched whirring of the blade, like a dentist's drill, cuts through me as easily as it does the plaster. The doctor peels back the outer shell that has shrouded Arden's arm like an insect cocoon. He places the plaster in a waste bag set on the nearby table. The whole process is over in a matter of minutes. As Arden gawks at his pale arm — two shades lighter than the rest of him — the man packs up and wordlessly readies to leave. On his way out, I ask about payment but he merely shakes his head and says, "It's been paid for." Without a word more — what's the point? — I merely shut the door behind him.

Arden hasn't moved. He continues to stare at his arm. It's the first time either of us has seen his tattoo in two weeks. A brown wolf stands beneath a tree, looking off toward some distant point that's missing now because the matching tattoo spans Amara's back. When paired together the images paint a picture of what their life was supposed to be, each wolf longing to be with the other. The art is forever etched on his skin as a further reminder of what once was and what will never be again. A thin scar runs across the wolf's neckline where his bone tore through flesh. It's bogus, this concept that werewolves mate for life, when walking away is apparently an option. Forever isn't supposed to have an expiration date.

"Arden?"

He doesn't look at me. I wait for him to say something, unsure of my own words. Rising, he grabs the back of the chair and sets it back at the table. There's an efficiency to his movements that comes out when he has purpose. He takes the bagged plaster, discards it in the garbage bin beneath the kitchen sink then moves past me.

"Get dressed," he says. "We're going out."

"Wh—" I can't get the single-syllable word out.

Standing barefoot in the kitchen, still wearing my pajamas, I stare after him as he makes his way down the hall toward the bathroom. He shuts the door and the sound of the shower running travels down the hallway. I haven't been outside in two weeks. I knew from the start that the day would come when I'd have to step out into the real world but the idea scares me a little now. With all the extra time I've had cooped up in the flat, my thoughts have been preoccupied with the impending court date and what that might entail. Time has felt stretched out and all at once not long enough. What if I lost myself entirely to the bloodlust I felt before?

Before I even realize any amount of time has passed, Arden clears his throat. He stands shirtless in the living area, toweling off from his shower. Although he looks like his old self again — unencumbered by the awkwardness of the cast — I know he's still not the same. While he dries his hair, I notice he wears a black vambrace, an armguard I've never seen before over his forearm where the cast used to be. The leather is worn with age and it's tied tightly with a thin rope of suede that crisscrosses his inner arm. It's from another era altogether. I don't know much about his past but there was a time when life was more primal, hundreds of years ago. The leather brace is a relic of that time, an object meant to protect a warrior from dangers in combat. Maybe it means he's still fighting. Or maybe he just doesn't want to be reminded of what's underneath it.

Catching my gaze he tosses the towel aside and pulls on a black sweater. "I told you to get dressed."

There's no sense arguing so I comply robotically, every step heavy-footed. It's as though I'm walking on death row, only I'm the executioner. I throw on the first things that catch my eyes: my favorite pair of jeans and a Giants sweatshirt that's seen better days. Arden waits for me at the front door in his black leather jacket. In his hand he gently works his fingers against a rope of some sort, testing out movement now that he's free of the cast. I shoulder into my own fall coat, checking my pockets to ensure the EpiPen is still there.

"Here." He hands me the rope.

It's actually a braided leather cord. The ends are tied in a fisherman's knot to form a loop that makes it look suspiciously like—

"What the hell is this? A dog collar?"

"It'll help you."

"I don't need help turning into a wolf. It's staying human that's more of the concern."

"That's not what it's for." He takes the leather collar from me and pulls it over my head. "If you can touch it with your fingers, you're not a wolf."

To test it out I grip the braid and stroke the rippled texture. He makes a valid point. In my other form this wouldn't be possible. I remember the ring he used to wear at the end of a gold chain and wonder if it served the same purpose for him at some point. Amara took possession of the necklace the night he supposedly died. When Arden unlocks the deadbolt and swings open the door my heart skips a beat. All the anxiety that I've been pushing down about this moment comes back urgently. Despite having moments of hermit-like cloistering where I've stayed at home for days at a time while lost in gaming, I never once thought of myself as a shut-in. At this moment the idea of it is very appealing. Stay here forever. Get food delivered. Never leave.

"Let's go," he says.

I take a deep, calming breath to chase away my unease.

Taking a few steps forward I edge closer to the exit then cross over the threshold, and the world doesn't end. A brief sensation of relief washes over me. We head down the narrow staircase and out into the world together. At first there's that rare moment of calm in a big city where, by some miracle of timing, not a lot is going on at street level. It's in that pause when I'm deluded into thinking I can pull this off. Then a motorcycle flies by in the lead of lines of traffic, bringing with it a cacophony and the suffocating scent of diesel. I want to turn back right away — and physically I do — but Arden grabs a handful of my jacket at the back of my neck and forces me in the other direction.

"Talk to me," he says, keeping a firm grip on me.

"I ... don't have much to say," I answer distractedly.

"Words are a tool for you right now. Use them."

The only thing on my mind at this moment is precisely what I blurt out. "What happens if this goes wrong, Arden?"

"It won't," he says through his teeth.

"If it does, though—"

He thrusts me ahead, gesturing with his now free hand. "Have I taught you nothing? There is no *if* in this. *If's* get people killed. *If's* change the world. It's not like it used to be. If this goes wrong, there's no undoing what people see."

A shift in broad daylight would be all over the world in seconds. On Twitter, Facebook and — more terrifyingly — YouTube. For a second I wonder about his motivation for bringing me out here. And, if he made it out alive, where would that put him? On the most-wanted list of the

Hounds and maybe other packs. My brief doubt about him
is quashed quickly. He could have easily unleashed me days
ago or simply not tried as hard to help me manage my inner
wolf. I have to trust that he knows what he's doing and have
faith in myself to stay human when it counts most.

We walk together and because casual banter has never
been part of our relationship, I quietly hum a tune to myself.
Eventually, it becomes clear that our destination is Gare de
Lyon. The street opens up to the train station with its clock
tower that every time I see it reminds me of Big Ben. Besides
an airport, this location is probably the busiest, noisiest hub
of action he could bring me to and I now know that this is
a test. Before I even reach the Hounds I'll have to travel in
a confined space for a long period of time and this is the
closest way of preparing me for that. I stop in my tracks.

"Keep moving, Connor."

"I can't. I just — I need a second."

He pauses. "There's your second. Now let's go."

Arden walks on without me. I follow in a panic. I should
have expected a sink-or-swim approach from him. The
closer we get to the station, the more hectic our surroundings become. A combination of sounds blend in a chaotic
symphony: plastic wheels of luggage rattling against the
sidewalk pavers, trains rumbling in and out of the station,
and the low murmur of conversations. An array of smells
marry between sweet roasting chestnuts sold by street ven-
dors, the noxious poisons carried in cigarette smoke and a
rich aroma of coffee. People shoulder by me and I'm jostled
around as we line up to buy tickets. Arden's watchful eyes

are on me. There's a lot riding on my ability to focus right now so I go to my human thoughts: espresso, ice cream, goosebumps, brain freeze. When Arden hands me my ticket I quickly scan the details and see that he's taking us on a forty-minute train trip to Fontainebleau.

"What's there?" I ask as we make our way to the platform.

"A forest."

"And we're going there *why*?"

"You need to control the wolf. Out in the wild. Where it matters."

"What if I take off?" I press as we board the waiting train.

Over his shoulder he tells me, "I brought a leash."

I whisper back urgently, "And if I bite you again?"

He doesn't respond as he takes a window seat in an empty area of the car.

"What then?" I sit across from him. "I brought the antivenin just in case but there's no way you could keep control of me while injecting yourself. Not when your arm just came out of a cast."

I reconsider the armguard Arden put on earlier and realize I might have over-thought it. Maybe he's wearing it to protect himself from me. Instead of answering, he stares out at the platform. All the noise and odor of that world still cling to me. I forget about it quickly as an errant backpack hits me in the side of the head. A number of tourists walk by, loaded down with hiking gear. They navigate the narrow aisle, bottlenecking when more passengers approach from the other direction.

Finally, when they've passed out of earshot Arden comes out with it. "I brought a muzzle too."

When I look over at him he still averts his gaze.

All I can say is, "Awesome."

Any further discussion on the matter is curtailed by a college-age couple who plant themselves next to us. I slump back in my seat in preparation for the long silence ahead and accidentally knock my leg against the girl sitting beside me. When our eyes meet her hand goes to push back a curly lock of unruly hair behind her right ear. I give her a little grin of apology and she smiles brightly back. The guy she's with is blasting his iPod, bopping his head and gesturing emphatically to the tunes. Catching our exchange, he says something to her in Italian as the train pulls out of the station. I turn my attention away as they lean across their seats toward each other. He hands her an earbud and together they listen to one track after another. More annoyingly, they start dancing in their seats, hands up high in the air and heads shaking while their bodies sway from the waist up. They're far too irritating to ignore, swaying to a private beat. In a way their presence is a mixed blessing. The pair's complete disregard for their surroundings makes it impossible for me to think anything but human thoughts.

Forty minutes later, our train pulls into Fontainebleau-Avon station. Arden stands without a word and pushes through the narrow gap between the couple, knocking out the girl's earbud. This time when I half-smile at her in apology it's met with less enthusiasm than before. Disembarking from the train I notice the backpacking tourists taking our same route out of the station. When they pause briefly to consult a map I try to urge Arden ahead. I want to put as much distance as possible between us and them. Common sense and movies both dictate that hikers and werewolves don't mix. Arden leads me off the beaten path and soon we're ankle-deep in oak leaves and underbrush. He's in his element out here. While I stumble to gain my footing on the uneven forest floor Arden takes in his surroundings without so much as a misstep. I have to wonder if I'll be this clumsy as a wolf. We make our way into a denser area filled in by a copse of evergreens. Our presence disturbs some creature in a nearby bush and the swoosh of foliage catches the attention of my inner predator. Stopping in my tracks, I fondle the leather braid at my neck and take a furtive glance over at Arden. He reaches absently for his own throat but doesn't find what he's looking for. His fingers linger at the dip of his collarbone. He takes a seat on a fallen tree, propping up a leg and stretching out as if on a sofa or park bench. The awkward pause between us gives me the opportunity to look around. This isn't Gare de Lyon but there are subtler noises and scents to capture my attention, all just as frequent as at the train station yet speaking more directly to the wolf in me. Creatures stir all around us, a mixture of fur and feathers. Movement brings up the odors of earthy decay from decomposed leaves, in stark contrast to the freshness of evergreens. The wind carries all of it to me like a gift.

When Arden finally speaks, he brings up a topic I've

been avoiding. "They'll want to talk to you, the Hounds. You're bitten. Part human. They'll offer you an ultimatum: join the pack or join them."

"What if I don't want either?"

He leans forward, casually resting a forearm against his knee. "I've thought about it. You have another option."

Although I'm skeptical, with time closing in on me and no other way out of the upcoming court date, what else can I do but hear him out? "I'm all ears."

With a sweeping gesture, he says, "It's this."

A breeze hushes through the length of the forest, sending goosebumps up my body.

"You mean living as a wolf."

He nods. "There's a place near the Alps. The hunting is good. The water pure. Untouched. The Hounds would never find you. Not as a wolf. Humans leave fingerprints in so many ways. Out in the wild ... your tracks wash away. You disappear. You wouldn't exist."

Tilting my head skyward, I mull over his words. The trees stretch upward, a mix of pine needles and bare-armed beeches embracing the cloudless blue sky. I grew up in a city filled with people. Without Arden as my guide, I wouldn't know how to get out of this forest and back to the train station.

"Do you want that?" he asks. "To not exist?"

I would truly be a lone wolf without another soul to confide in. It would mean living among creatures that aren't my own species, existing in the spaces between worlds. I'd spend all the rest of my long years alone. Neither human nor werewolf. Like Arden. Then I realize that's what he's telling me. For someone who barely strings his sentences together, he makes a clear point. Even though his life was taken from him, he's still alive.

"I—" Something catches in my throat.

He smiles thinly. "I didn't think so."

Turning his back toward me, he repositions in order to leap off the log on the side. A slew of thoughts race through my brain as he slowly walks away. I'm not the one who sentenced him to this life. I didn't take away his choices. Boguet did that. But it's a lie. At best a half-truth. As much as I don't want to acknowledge it, I have to accept my part in Arden's fate. Good intentions or not, I had something to do with handing him this life.

"Arden, wait."

He pauses without looking back.

"I'm not going to apologize for saving you."

"Twice," he reminds me.

"Yeah, twice now." I fight to get the rest of my words out. "But I hear you. Loud and clear. I won't do it again."

With a nod, he murmurs, "Good."

I push down the swell of emotion flooding my eyes. Ours has been an uneasy relationship since the beginning. But he's had my back all this time and I thought I was doing right by Arden. Instead I might as well have been the one to deliver the cure myself. He whistles and gestures over his shoulder. When I get to his side he takes a chain leash from out of his pocket.

"It's time."

"You're getting too much enjoyment out of this," I say in an attempt to lighten the mood.

He doesn't deny it and I catch a hint of smile, which puts me oddly at ease. I slip out of my jacket. My hands grab at the back of my neckline and I pull out of my shirts in one fluid motion before completely undressing. Heat rises off my bare skin. It's colder than I thought. Shuddering, I allow him to attach the leash to the braid around my neck. Closing my eyes, I bring my full attention to all the things I've been subliminally aware of that have been calling out to the wolf in me. The last fully human thought I have is—

Rabbit!

I take off after it. The entire woods are alive. As the chain drags through leaves behind me it churns up dirt and the pungent aroma of the forest floor. The swooshing sound disturbs the wildlife around me but my focus is on the hare darting into a hedge. I'm so attuned to the hunt that I'm only half-aware of being chased myself. The sound of human feet thrashing through the dead foliage is an unnatural one, but my focus is on my prey. So much so that I don't have time to prepare for the tackle as the full brunt of a human's body slams me against the dirt. I topple beneath the weight of my attacker and my brain switches into fight mode. With a snarl I twist around to bite but as I do my senses are overcome by a scent so familiar and unexpected — and so distinctly from my human life — that human thoughts take over my mind. I shift back, my teeth lingering against her neckline as I exhale the scent of vanilla.

D. PRETENSE

Pretense: *noun.* An attempt to make something that is not
the case appear true.

Connor pulls away from me suddenly, trying to compose
himself as he lies back breathless against the upturned
leaves. His hair is all bed-headed as usual but his eyes have
a kind of wildness to them, like the wolf is still rattling
around in there. He has a hold of me by the arms and my
hair cascades around his face like a waterfall on fire. I should
be really mad at him for losing control out here in the real
world but instead I'm trying hard not to think about the
fact that he's naked and panting beneath me. His mouth was
just on my neck and I can still feel the trace of his lips there
like a ghostly kiss. Arden jogs over casually like he knew
all along that I was out here. He tosses a heap of clothes
over to us and I roll back onto my elbows by Connor's side
so he can get dressed. Connor's totally blushing when he
removes a chain leash and pulls on his jeans. I try my best
not to look. Meanwhile, Arden just glares over at me.

"You're either suicidal or straight-up crazy," I tell him.

He doesn't come back with a response, not even a facial

tic to give me the satisfaction of knowing I got to him. Arden's one of those people who knows there's power in silence. And it pisses me off.

"That or you were dropped on your head as a kid — or pup — or whatevs."

"What are you doing here?" Connor asks. He's fully clothed now, including the expression that he wears like an old hat: worried and confused all at the same time.

"I'm keeping your handler in check, for starters."

They exchange a loaded look. Good. They *should* be taking this in. Things are screwed up enough without adding human casualties into the mix. I can see Connor working out some kind of answer while Arden just stands there. Ugh! I want to flick Arden between those amber eyes just to get some kind of a reaction out of him.

"You know he bit me just now," I tell Arden.

Connor glances between us, like he's trapped and looking for a way out. "I did not!"

"Explain the hickey you just gave me then," I say, turning my head to stare right at him.

He looks at his shoes. Maybe he's not the one I'm mad at but he could stand to learn a lesson from all of this.

"It's not like I broke skin," he mutters.

"And you stopped because *why* exactly?"

Chestnut-brown eyes meet mine for like a second but he doesn't speak up. I don't know why I bother. Would it kill a guy to express a single feeling in words? Seriously.

"*It would crush me if ever I hurt you,*" said no guy, ever.

Really, what would it matter if he *had* bitten me? It's

not like I can become more wolfy. Maybe I'm the one who's crazy/suicidal/dropped-on-her-head, but it didn't even spark in my brain that he could actually hurt me. I mean it's not like I ever, in my craziest nightmares, imagined Josh turning into a werewolf and biting me the night that he did. I may have issues but I know that love isn't a fistful of rage.

"What you're doing here," I start on a different tack, "it isn't allowed. You're basically supposed to be under quarantine until you've got everything under control."

Arden finally speaks up. "This is where we belong."

"You say '*we*' like it still applies to you."

Hello! *That* got his attention. Everything about his body language shifts. Even though I'm lying prone on the ground, getting up would mean breaking eye contact so I stay put. I won't let him win this round so easily. He's a boring old human now who gets to live out his existence without all these stupid rules. After a few more seconds, Connor positions himself directly between our staring contest.

"Why isn't Josh with you?"

I get up slowly, dusting off the sleeves of my hoodie and nylon vest. Even when I'm decidedly *not* thinking about Josh he manages to invade my life. It would be super awesome if I could just have one conversation with Connor in which my very ex-boyfriend didn't come up as a topic.

"Do I look like I need a chaperone?"

"I thought you worked together or whatever."

"Did I not make myself clear?" I ask, annoyed. "What you're doing here is not allowed."

He raises his hands in frustration. "I don't know what

that means, Madison. Are you going to arrest us? Issue a citation? What?"

There's a tone in his voice that comes from someone who hasn't broken very many rules in his life. At least none that really matter.

"The Hounds don't know she's here," Arden notes smugly.

In a calming voice, I say, "I'm not here officially, okay?"

"What are you doing here then?"

Seriously, he's so dense sometimes.

"Just pack up the circus tent and go home, already."

Arden lets out an irritated noise — does he make any other? — then picks up the chain leash and heads back the way they came. Hot *and* bothered. I guess he's someone's type too. He and Amara (a.k.a. Mr. and Mrs. Congeniality) were suited to each other in their own way. It's a shame it had to end.

Connor follows without saying a word. As he walks by I put a hand on his arm. He's definitely been working out. I reach up on my tippy toes to pull a leaf from his hair and he pauses to look down at me. When his eyes travel away from my face, I feel his fingers on my neckline where he almost chomped through. Pulling away, he holds up his index finger to show a pinprick of blood at the tip. He looks devastated, like he's playing out in his head what might have happened.

"Next time just practice making hickeys on your arm like everyone else."

He shakes his head with a laugh. In the distance, Arden

whistles for attention. I roll my eyes for effect as we slip out of each other's reach and Connor walks away. Aquila put a lot of faith in Arden to do all this training and I'm not sure why. When the Hounds find out, I'm sure they'll put the kibosh on their little arrangement. If they knew about all these near misses, they'd lock Connor up.

But I know something about Connor Lewis now. Something that he doesn't even know about himself. I met with Trajan again. Our last conversation stirred up a hornet's nest of questions that needed answering. Turns out he has a theory about Connor's DNA. One that could tip the scales of power. Trajan wasn't joking about working for the highest bidder. And it wasn't even that hard to find someone with deeper pockets than Boguet. It was right under our noses, actually.

8. WAITING FOR THE END

Despite Madison's warning, the two weeks leading up to my fateful court appointment are filled with similar training in similar scenarios on the outskirts of the city until we're comfortable enough to venture out around the city as pet and owner. I get a new appreciation for everything Arden went through those first few weeks when he was posing as Amara's dog. It's humbling to say the least. Human contact is unavoidable in the busy streets of Paris. Sometimes I can smell fear rising up off the pedestrians amidst all the urban scents. Other times, I'm thankful for the muzzle as sticky human hands thrust themselves upon me unbidden and I react with instinctive savagery. The more I shift, though, the more control I gain.

Arden also takes it upon himself to teach me the fine art of throwing a punch: boxing. Never in a million years would I have imagined myself actually sparring with an opponent outside a console game. He's incredibly lithe and eager to educate me. At first I find it frustrating, not being able to land even a glancing blow. Worse is getting clocked on more than one occasion. He insisted that bare-knuckle is the only way to learn, and I have a sense that my initial ineptitude is pure entertainment for him. It isn't until my fist finally connects with his moneymaker that I understand the appeal. Not that I feel good about myself when it happens. In fact, I'm mortified at the sight of blood running from his nose, and frankly my hand hurts like hell after. But a rush of endorphins floods all my senses. I understand now the purpose of that fight club room at La Pleine Lune. In the absence of being able to transform regularly, throwing a few punches around is a way of unleashing the pent-up animal within. None of this training can distract me from the impending court date with the Hounds. Last night I received a text from Madison: *CU @ 10 AM*. Since this is my first court appearance I have no idea what the procedure is for transporting witnesses, but it sounds like I'll be in her custody until we get to Germany. When Arden and I return to the flat after a morning jog the picture comes more into focus. Madison stands at the landing outside the apartment door with Josh crowding in behind her, my underused bike propped against the far wall behind them. It's the first time I've seen Josh since the fight with Boguet. He seems different. All the familiarity of friendship has been replaced with a businesslike coldness.

"Ready to go?" he asks.

Arden squeezes by to unlock the door and I can see that they're both trying to suppress smiles at the sight of a leash around my neck. As soon as the door opens I take off to my room. When I shift back to my human form a hot flush of embarrassment rises to my face but I try to put it out of mind. From the entrance, I hear their heated voices overlapping for a few seconds.

Arden snaps, "You're not welcome inside."

Brash and overtly hostile now that their laws don't apply to him anymore, I can only guess that he's ready to take out centuries of pent-up hatred on them.

"We're just here as your escort," Josh tells him calmly. Ever the voice of reason.

"You can wait out there," Arden says and slams the door.

Escort? Now that he's human I never imagined that Arden would be called in to testify also. I grab my passport and schoolbag, packed with a change of clothes and the few things I'll need, and seek him out in his room to get an explanation. He slings an overnight pack onto his shoulder.

"What's going on?" Without a word he pulls a familiar manila envelope out from a dresser drawer. A subpoena.

"I thought they had a 'No Humans Allowed' sort of policy."

"Like I said, we're all just pawns to them."

In an effort to get answers — real answers — I race to the front door and swing it open expecting to see one of Madison's many expressions of distaste, but the landing is empty. They must have decided to wait for us downstairs. I don't know why he kept this information from me, or even why I care so much, but something about this gives me a bad feeling. Like I may be coming home without him. Even though my promise to live or let die is still fresh in my mind, there's a part of me that's oddly protective. We've been through too much to have our fates determined by the Hounds. He prepared me for the choices that they'll likely offer, but will they present him with options too? Is there even a chance that they'd allow him to live the rest of his years free of their rules? Thing is, the issue of who bit me has yet to be resolved and I know he'd never let Amara admit to it. At the best of times he would have fallen on a sword for her. Now that he's got a human expiration date I have no doubt of it. I charge down the steps as Arden locks up. Outside, Madison and Josh looked bored already, which doesn't bode well for the long journey ahead.

"What the hell is up with Arden coming along for the ride?"

"Easy, Rover," she teases, referring to my status as pet dog.

With a sigh of frustration, I ask, "Are there any other surprises I should know about?"

"He's just evidence," Josh interjects. "Proof of what Boguet can do."

Right. Evidence of mad science. In what other reality would this even make any sense?

Madison's eyebrows knit.

"We're not the ones who made this a surprise," she says, casting a glance up the stairs.

Arden emerges from the narrow stairwell as if on cue and Josh leads us toward a vehicle parked at the corner. Not just a vehicle: a white Rolls-Royce Phantom limo, its windows blacked out. My jaw drops a little as Madison shepherds us forward and Josh opens the back passenger door. It's a modern interpretation of the classic car, still showcasing a silver grille and marque ornament of a winged woman on the hood. Not a car you see every day. I slow in my approach then stop to fully appreciate the metallic beauty, my hesitation about the trial temporarily on hold.

"He told us you were ready for this," Madison says, appearing by my side. "I can give you a Valium or something if you're not."

She misreads my hesitation, but it brings my concerns back to the forefront.

"What exactly are we walking into?"

"Um ... a limo?"

"I mean this trial," I turn to face her.

"I've only been to one of these before, Connor."

"And?"

She shakes her head. "Not going there. What's up with you?"

"I don't trust any of this."

"Nobody's asking you to."

It does nothing to alleviate my anxiety. That's her brand of honesty. Sometimes hurtful, but always to the point. Her eyes dart toward the vehicle, telling me to keep moving. Josh looks back at us patiently. I walk toward him and Arden, committing myself to the journey. Talking about it further is pointless. It's not like there are any words that will make this easier. I'm not sure what it will take to make things right. Arden appears to take all of this in stride, sliding across the black leather seats to the furthest side without so much as a glance at the car. I move in to take the seat across from him while Madison edges behind me impatiently. There's plenty of space to stretch my legs out across the flat floor, on which soft woolly rugs have been laid out. There's a soft scent and touch to the leather upholstery, and the piano black wood veneer of the interior adds an extra layer of elegance. After shutting us in Josh taps on the opaque black Plexiglas that shields the driver from us. I'm seated facing the back of the limo so when it pulls into traffic, a slight wave of motion sickness hits me to add to the nauseous unease I have about what lies ahead. In a few hours time I'll be in Germany at the High Court of the Hounds of God. I'll have to wait until then to judge their intentions for myself.

The first part of the trip is a quiet one. Madison is never this silent, which makes me wonder what she's hiding. Arden ignores us altogether. His body language makes it clear that he wants nothing to do with us: angled toward the window, not making eye contact, wearing the noise-canceling headphones from the in-vehicle entertainment system to further tune us out. I thought we would have at least stood in solidarity somehow. He does everything in his power to avoid conversation or any kind of contact. I wonder if he's even listening to anything — I have a hard time imagining what kind of music he'd listen to — or if he's just using the headphones as a visual cue that he's occupied. I let him have this alone time. Without his help, I wouldn't have been prepared for this journey, confined in a car for what I estimate will be around a ten-hour drive.

After we get on the A1 and pass the massive complex of buildings that is Charles de Gaulle Airport, we leave behind the congestion of the busy streets of Paris, leaving me nothing to look at out the windows but highway signs and stretches of farmland. Now that we're in such close quarters I sense an odd tension between Josh and Madison, more so than usual. They probably had yet another falling out. He looks different somehow too, with a fresh haircut in addition to a dress shirt and slacks that have replaced his sporty attire. There's a serious air about him and it makes me want to turn back time to that point when we were just a bunch of teenagers hanging out together, or at least I thought we were. Josh pulls a *Sports Illustrated* from his duffel bag and commences reading in silence. Madison grabs a book from her rucksack. It's a dog-eared copy of *Scott Pilgrim's Final Hour*. If only I could handle my problems like a video-game style battle against a boss. But there are no power-ups in real life. No FTW moment when I can declare total pwnage. I don't even know who the bad guys are.

Some time in the afternoon, the driver pulls into a rest stop for lunch on the outskirts of the city of Liège in Belgium. He parks the limo in front of a cluster of small bars and restaurants that surround a large, bright red Total gas station. Josh and Arden step out of the limo, but Madison puts a hand on my arm to hold me back. When I glance over at her, she shakes her head. I'm not allowed out of here. A twinge of anxiety shakes me as I momentarily think about what would happen if I somehow lose control when I finally step out of the limo. The idea of sitting around in awkward silence for an hour doesn't appeal to me in any way, though, and I mutter as much.

"Deal with it," she says, then asks, "What do you want to eat?"

I shrug in non-compliance. Madison presses an intercom button and tells the driver to get us some waffles, a café crème for me and her usual blend of hot chocolate and coffee, which comes with a grunt of disapproval from beyond the divider. We hear the driver exit the vehicle with a slam of the front door. I slouch back in my seat and we sit in silence until I can't stand it anymore.

"Waffles for lunch?" I ask to break the ice.

She shrugs. "Who doesn't like waffles?"

It's a valid point.

"Aren't you going to try to sell me on how great the Hounds are?"

"Why would I do that?" She sounds like I just asked her to kill a kitten.

I let out a sigh. "I don't know, aren't they going to try and recruit me or something?"

"If you're looking for a sales pitch you should talk to Josh."

"Don't you have *anything* good to say about them? You know, to make me feel better about this werewolf version of *Law & Order*?"

"What do you want me to say?" she snaps. "That I'm omigod-over-the-full-moon-crazy-in-love with being a Hound? Like I said, if you ask Josh—"

"I'm not, though, am I? I'm asking you."

She bites her glossy lip.

"Well?"

When she speaks, her words are tinged with a hint of bitterness. "You don't get it, Connor. The bitten can't live with humans, and unlike you we don't get invitations to join wolf packs. That doesn't leave us with a lot of options."

"If it's any consolation, the pack isn't all that."

"Don't be stupid."

"How is that being stupid?" I sit upright in irritation. "I'm not like them. I wasn't born a pack werewolf. I don't understand the way they think or act. I was born human just like you. Besides which, you have choices. Like you said, life's what you make it."

She leans toward me. "There are so many things you have zero clue about. The Hounds put rules in place to keep us safe — to keep all of *this*," she says with a wave of her right hand indicating the city around us, "safe. The wolf packs don't care. They'd just disappear into the forests and abandon us if they could. Maybe it would be easier if we could just peg whole groups as heroes or villains but the world doesn't work like that. Everything is just a shade of gray. Sometimes all you can do is side with the lesser evil."

"You're not exactly making them out to be shining beacons of light."

"They're not, but they bring order to all of this chaos," she says as she sits back in her seat. "You wanted the truth. That's my version of it."

There's a tap on the window next to Madison. Josh stands with the chauffeur, who I can see now is dressed in a very formal double-breasted uniform, and each of them holds an order of food. Madison rolls down the window and passes along my coffee and waffle, which is piled up with some kind of whipped cream. I cram a mouthful of the delicious cooked batter into my face as I look around for Arden. I spot him sitting alone at a table by a café window across the way looking unsurprisingly bored.

"Having fun babysitting Mr. Congeniality?" Madison teases Josh, who leans into the window as she sips on her hot beverage.

"How'd you live with him for so long, bro?" Josh asks under his breath, sounding more like his old self.

I shrug. "He kind of grows on you."

By a coincidence, Arden glances over at us. His disdain for the Hounds of God seems pretty evenly distributed. In his mind they've been cast as the dark overlords, restraining the packs from living free. His view can't be completely unfounded but I take Madison's point about black and white. When we're done eating Josh walks across to his temporary ward and signals to the waitress in order to pay. The woman leans flirtatiously into Arden's personal space, saying something with a smile. There's something about the way he responds in his body language that brings to mind an animal caught in a snare. Nowhere to go. No action to take that won't just tighten the wire. It's the same way he reacted the other week when I asked about Emilie of the fuchsia lipstick graffiti on his cast. That another woman is flirting with him is no big surprise. It's his ineptitude at turning on his own charms that throws me for a loop. The poor waitress has no clue what's she's getting into. She brushes his arm in a casual, kittenish sort of way and I think he's going to lose it and react inappropriately. Instead he kind of freezes, still unsure of how to respond. Josh must have cleared his throat or something because she casts him a glance before pulling away, blushing. Arden takes his sweet time, sipping the last of his water then slowly producing the money to pay for his own meal, all the while glaring at Josh. It doesn't faze Josh, who demonstrates the patience of a saint, and eventually they return to the limo so we can continue on our journey.

"Want one?" Madison asks, thrusting a handful of brightly colored Double Bubble Twist Gum packages toward me as the car pulls back onto the highway.

I take one. Madison chews two pieces and commences blowing bubbles, swiveling in her seat to pop them near my ear. She does this about a half dozen times, trying to get a reaction out of me until I finally it works.

"Don't make me pop your bubble."

She snaps the pink balloon and sucks it back with a mischievous grin.

Arden watches the exchange and when his eyes meet mine he says, "*L'on est bien faible quand on est amoureux.*"

One is weak when one is in love.

Beyond embarrassed, I sink further into my seat. My entire face must be an exact match of Madison's cherry-red hair at this point. From across the aisle Josh peers over at us. Madison snaps her gum loudly at him too before picking up her book and seemingly losing herself in Scott Pilgrim's plight. I wonder if she's also fazed by the comment, but then I remember she's Madison.

There's something about the motion of planes, trains and automobiles that invariably puts me to sleep. With nothing to look at again but countryside and farmland, I fall in and out of sleep with the quiet humming of the vehicle. Each time I wake we've lost more sunlight. The farmland slowly turns into forest and the countryside into low hills. I only wake up fully when the chauffeur makes an announcement telling us we'll be entering Quedlinburg in approximately twenty minutes. I think back over the previous month as I glance over at Arden. As we draw closer to our final destination I have a sense that time may be running out for both of us.

9. ILLUMINATION

The closer we get to our destination, the more I start to notice an unsettling pattern in the town names on highway signs: Wolfsburg, Wolfenbüttel, Wolfen. Obviously wolves have had a strong presence here throughout history. At some point humans must have known on some level about the dangers that lurked in the woods. We reach Quedlinburg long after dusk, passing through the gates of an ancient town wall. It's a medieval town of cobblestone streets and half-timbered buildings with red-tiled roofs like something out of a fairy tale. I have a sense of stepping back in time and half expect a knight on horseback to come charging toward us. Even the outdoor lighting fixtures look like old metal lamps, albeit electrically powered. Our limo, as beautiful as it is, is out of place here — a metal monstrosity. I'm mesmerized by the buildings as we wind through the streets, all decorated for Christmas with lights, wreathes and candles in every window. In the distance, towering above the village like a guardian, is a fortified stone castle sitting on a craggy rock lit up by floodlights. It's the nucleus of the entire village and appears to be where the driver is taking us.

We make our way up the hill toward it and stop by the

sloping cobblestone entrance. I'm the first one out of the car, but that doesn't seem to be an issue anymore. The coolness of the air hits my lungs like a swift punch and my breath escapes in a frigid mist. Below us the village glows faintly, a market square lit up by strings of light hung between houses and vendor stalls. In the square I see a Christmas tree standing tall by the spire of a church. As simple as the decorations are in comparison to my memories of Rockefeller Center, I'm struck with a homesickness that the holidays bring to mind. We walk together in silence through an arched passageway then stop in front of a Renaissance castle of worn stone walls that have seen better days and topped with a red roof like all the other buildings here. The courtyard is dominated by a cathedral with two matching square steeples that, if they weren't covered in the sooty wear of time, would remind me of the Tower of London. My parents had a souvenir book they brought back from a trip from before I was born and I've always been fascinated by the many famous historical figures who were once imprisoned there. I guess if Boguet is here, one of these buildings would have to double as a jail of sorts, and who would guess a church? Following Madison's lead, I leave the courtyard and walk in through the curved stone front entrance of the large castle. Arden is the last inside, hesitating for a moment outside the wide door before entering.

We're greeted by two passing nuns, dressed entirely in white, who shake our hands and say, "Peace be with you."

Arden walks past them without so much as acknowledging their presence. Clearly, there's no limit to his poor manners. On the inside, the building is as simple as the exterior with very little furnishing or artwork on the bare stone walls and floors. A wrought iron candlelit chandelier hangs overhead, casting long shadows around us.

"What is this place, exactly?" I ask.

"Quedlinburg Abbey," Josh tells me. "It was built about a thousand years ago. Some kind of religious college was set up here for noblewomen, and the town was ruled by them for about 800 years until Napoleon invaded in the 1800s. Shortly after the Hounds of God took over."

"Enough with the yawn-fest," Madison intervenes. "Breber is expecting you, Connor."

"Who?"

"Our fearless leader," she says, her voice rich with sarcasm.

Her eyes flash past me toward a room by the stairs, door ajar so that a flicker of light from within frames the entry in a pulsing glow. Josh casts her a concerned look. Irreverence toward their leader is probably a no-no. Not that Madison would care. Stepping toward me, she grabs the strap of my backpack from my shoulder and says, "I'll bring this up to your room."

I hold on to the strip of fabric for a moment, trying to play it cool despite my unease. The last thing I want is to be left alone with their leader. She tugs quickly, claiming possession of my backpack, and casts me a reassuring smile, but the moment is interrupted.

"*Hola*, Madmen," a guy's voice taunts in a Spanish accent.

Madison squints and braces herself before turning to glare at a couple of guys about our age standing behind her. The taller of the two is sable-haired with inky eyes and a leer that permeates his coppery face. The other is a brown-eyed brunet who has lackey written all over him. They're both dressed as if for private school, except the one with the attitude wears his tie loose around his popped collar. There's something about him that I instantly dislike.

"Madmen?" I ask Madison quietly.

Before she can answer, the guy grins and replies, "Do you not know? Madison, she drives men mad. Is that not right, Josh?"

He raises a fist at Josh, who doesn't oblige with the requisite bump, so he punches Josh in the shoulder instead. Josh grins in spite of himself and taps his friend back. I'm suddenly aware again of how much I don't fit in. It's no different than my old life. I'm on the outskirts of what's normal even here among this clique of the bitten. The shorter guy walks over to me, clearly amused by the antics of the others, and I feel the anxiety of trying to blend in build in my throat. No matter, because the dark-haired friend, obviously the alpha male, moves to block his path.

"Take care, Javier," the alpha says. "The pup may bite."

Then he glances over at Madison, that playfully cruel expression never leaving his face. "Madison, you are looking exceptionally tasty."

"Daniel," Madison acknowledges as she crosses her arms. "Still a complete douchebag, I see."

He clutches at his heart, falsely hurt. "You wound me

with your words."

Madison rolls her eyes.

"Who is your new *compañero*?" he asks. "I didn't know you liked dogs."

Arden leans against a wall, watching everything unfold. I want this humiliating initiation to just be over with already. I know how it works. Some cool kids get off on making newbies uncomfortable and dishing out some kind of pain before going back to regular programming. If I play things right, it won't come to anything more than that. Regardless, my fingers rub against the leather braid around my neck in an effort to stay calm.

"This is Connor," Madison says, nudging me toward my exit. "See Connor leave."

"Why you gotta be like that, Maddy?" he presses, putting on an American accent before turning his full attention to me. "*Un momento*, Connor. What brings you here to Area 51?"

I have no idea what response will make him go away.

"Leave him alone," Madison tells him. "He's a pack wolf, not some froshdog."

He lets out a scathing hiss. "What?"

Daniel's fists clench and the tension between all of us escalates exponentially. Instantly I mimic his gesture, taking on a defensive stance. Arden pushes off the wall and stands directly between us, laying a palm flat against Daniel's chest.

"Go play somewhere else," Arden says.

Daniel's smug look turns malicious as he squares off his

shoulders. "Do not touch me, dog!"

Arden pushes him back with more force than is called for, the way he did to me at Club Cin-Cin so many months ago, and Daniel stumbles back a few feet but doesn't fall over. Knowing this situation can now only go one direction, I prepare for the blows to come and am glad for my bare-knuckle boxing lessons. When Daniel steps forward, Josh agilely jumps in and holds him back. Javier lingers in the background, ready to pounce even if his anxiety betrays him. There's a fire in Daniel's dark eyes and I sense he's out for blood. Josh pushes against him and whispers something in his ear. I can't hear what he says, but his words have the effect of redirecting Daniel's attention, and as he looks between Arden and me the fire in his eyes is replaced by something else.

"Does your big brother always fight your battles for you?"

I don't bother responding since it's clear that the threat is over and he just wants to get the last word in. We all watch as Daniel turns away and marches outside to cool off. Javier lets out a little sigh of relief and follows on his heels. It's only then that I realize just how fast my pulse is racing and how close I was to losing control again.

"Ignore him," Josh says to me by way of apology. "He's just bit of a hothead."

"He's a complete douchebag," Madison argues. "And everyone knows it."

He shakes his head. "C'mon. We'll see you in the morning, Connor."

I watch as they all head up the staircase single file. At the rear of the pack, Arden throws me a look that I can't decipher. It has the effect of making me even more anxious about what lies ahead. With a deep breath, I walk toward the room with the flickering candlelight. Now that I'm alone my senses pinpoint all the creepy little things that allow my imagination to run wild. All I hear are my own footsteps as I make my way to meet the leader of the Hounds of God. Pausing at the doorway, I catch a musty scent like whatever waits for me on the other side is ancient, but I push past the creaking door and come to stand in a cluttered office. There are candles everywhere — on wooden shelves that line the walls, crammed with books and papers, on table-tops, chairs and all available surfaces. It's seriously a fire hazard. Below a simple square window that's recessed into the stone wall is a large wooden desk inlaid with elaborate panels, including a coat of arms with the crest of a wolf standing on its hind legs. Behind the desk sits a man reading a large and timeworn tome. I feel his eyes on me as I make my way to a bookcase and touch the spines of some of the books. Everything on the shelf is practical — maps and encyclopedias, medical texts and legal cases. Maybe when you're a mythological creature you don't really have a need for imagination and fiction. When our eyes meet he stands, close to seven feet of him stretched out like a giant. There's something austere about him. His long wispy blond hair is worn loose at his shoulders and his eyes are the color of a glassy lake. He's dressed in a long-sleeved white wool tunic that falls below the knee with a plain leather belt knotted at the waist and matching pants tucked into his boots. I expect him to channel David Carradine from *Kung Fu* and call me 'grasshopper' as he bows in greeting.

"Welcome to Quedlinburg, Mr. Lewis," he says in a clipped German accent that sounds at the same time cordial and intimidating. "I am Breber of Heaven's Hand."

Roul told me once that the Hounds go by different names. I turn to face him. There's no point in prolonging the inevitable.

"What is it you wanted to see me about?"

"There are necessary details that must be discussed ... lycanthrophic bureaucracy, if you will," he says almost apologetically. "Frankly, I do not know what to do with you, Connor Lewis. They tell me you are a hybrid. Not born a wolf, yet you may take their form. Part of neither of our worlds."

"That seems to be the general consensus."

"And that you are a relation of the renowned Rodolfus de Aquila."

"So he tells me," I add nervously, unsure if my blood relation to him is good or bad.

"Not to worry," Breber assures me, probably reading me like one of his many open books. "We were founded on principles of doing no harm. As you know by now, were-wolves come into the world in two ways: the true-born and the bitten. Since the former have proven incapable of doing so, Heaven's Hand governs both in order to safeguard our secret lives. Above all else we must ensure precautions are taken for the protection of all life."

"Precautions like the antivenin?"

He nods appreciatively. "Like so, yes."

Before I can consider the consequences of challenging the authority of the Hounds' leader, I ask, "Don't you think that's a little hypocritical? I mean, aren't you using the antivenin, the very technology that you're about to put a man on trial for?"

He considers my words calmly and without any indication that he's put off by my question. "Ah, yes. How do you say? You must make lemon juice from the lemons?"

"When life hands you lemons, make lemonade."

He laughs abruptly. "You Americans have such wonderful turns of phrase. Yes, there is no undoing what has already been done by Boguet. But his work may yet prove useful to us in the future."

Boadicea said the antivenin was the result of money from a significant investor. If the Hounds protect humans from the knowledge that werewolves even exist then it stands to reason that they're the only ones who would be interested enough in this research to back it financially.

"Didn't you fund the research?"

"Unfortunately, this is a matter before the courts and, as such, one that may not be discussed at this particular moment. All truth will out itself in due course. In the meantime I must complete the troublesome affair of ensuring that you understand the rules of this new world of ours. Under normal circumstances we would have had this parley sooner, but yours is an unusual case. There is but one tenet — one golden rule — that applies unwaveringly to all bitten and true-born: transforming of humans is strictly prohibited. The penalty is rather permanent."

"You mean death."

Wagging a finger at me, he smiles. "You are very percep-tive."

"There must be exceptions."

"I am afraid not. We must be steadfast."

"What about in Madison's case?"

He lets out a long sigh and shakes his head dramatically. "Such a tragic example. Joshua Emerson was a minor when his transgression occurred and therefore could not be held wholly accountable for his actions. As with human laws we treat underaged offenders with some leniency."

"So there *are* exceptions," I insist.

"No, I am afraid his father paid the ultimate price for his crime."

In plain English: they executed his dad. No wonder Madison didn't want to talk about it. All the same, how could Josh be a poster boy for the organization that murdered one of his own family members? Breber examines me as I process what he's just told me then moves lithely in my direction, stopping to gesture at a candle that's at my eye level.

"You see, life is precious. It is a light much like this candle. The one who has a hand in putting out such a light—" he grabs the flame between a thumb and forefin-ger, then shows me the blackened tips, "—will be forever marked. It is neither an easy task nor one that we take lightly, but eventually the one who bit you must repay your life with theirs."

I back away. Although I expected that this topic would come up sooner or later, I didn't imagine it would be one of the first orders of business. I take a slow step backward. I haven't figured out how to handle this yet so I need to get away before he asks me outright who bit me. Breber stops me with a wave of his hand.

"But this is not a question for this evening."

Again, he has read me like a book.

"I have no doubt that your pack leader will want a word with you on this matter before we discuss it in further detail. Ah, and speak of the devil."

He gestures toward the door where, to my relief, Roul stands assessing the situation.

"Better the devil you know," he says in return.

My heightened animal senses immediately pick up on the tension between these two. There's a forced civility between them right now, but for all intents and purposes they're two pack leaders, one in the other's territory. Looking at them together, they seem diametrically opposed; where Breber represents the past and tradition, Roul — although possibly much older — is the modern werewolf who embraces progress and change. Roul comes to stand by my side and the conversation is put to an end.

"Yes, a discussion for another time," Breber concedes. "However, there is one last matter. Before the trial resumes Henri Boguet has requested a visit from you, Connor Lewis."

Mention of the name in this context makes me nervous

and I can hear myself swallow. "Why?"

"Why does anyone wish to do anything?" he ponders aloud. "It is a question of philosophy. Perhaps the man has a guilty conscience. Or perhaps he wishes to impart to you some words of wisdom. I see no reason to deny his request. Given, of course, that your pack leader accompanies you."

Before I can say a word, Roul says, "Of course."

With a shared glance, we leave together quickly and quietly. He leads me out of the office and into the empty courtyard. I feel at once relieved and annoyed. In no way did I agree to pack representation. I've been comfortably riding out this whole lone wolf lifestyle and am not about to give it up without a fight. At least until I have enough information to make an educated decision.

"You're not my pack leader."

"I'm well aware of that," he replies, turning on his heels. "You don't seem to understand that these bitten werewolves have their rules, ones they take quite seriously."

"Do they have a rule about lying to their leader?"

"I didn't lie. I merely misrepresented the truth."

"Whatever you want to call it, is it going to come back to bite me?"

He takes a deep breath before slowly exhaling a long plume of mist. "I can't even begin to tell you how many laws they create to govern us all. They crave the structure of human society even though, or perhaps because, they've been forced to live outside of it. For my part, I keep the pack safe. Lone wolves are considered a menace by more than just the Hounds. One gone wild is a detriment to us all."

Raising my hands in surrender, I want to say, "I'm not about to go on a crazy rampage," but that's exactly what I'm afraid of doing. Instead, I tell him, "That's not my intention."

"You don't need to convince me. Believe me, Connor, when I tell you that I don't offer a place in my pack lightly. But let's be clear: if not mine then find another."

He sounds more like a dad than my own father. And it annoys me.

"You do *not* get to call the shots in my life."

With a calming hand on my shoulder, he peers into my face with his piercing gray eyes. "I think you misheard me. I've given you options."

"And what about the Hounds?"

"What of them?"

"Aren't *they* an option?"

He chooses his words carefully. "A very questionable one."

"Says the big, bad wolf."

Withdrawing his hand, he lets out a little scoff. "Do you know what the locals here call January? *Wolf-monath.* The month of the wolf. That's not *our* doing. Despite what Breber may think we're not the ones who are the stuff of fairy tales. We learn self-control from an early age. It's paramount to our survival that we not expose ourselves to humans. That level of discipline comes much harder later in life, as I'm sure you can appreciate."

The names of so many of the neighboring towns come to mind. All those precautionary childhood stories like

Aesop's Fables and *Grimm's Fairy Tales* that cast the wolf as a menacing, predatory antagonist go back a long time. But who were they in real life? Henri Boguet made a career of taking down the pack, but was that just a grudge? Was he chasing the wrong creatures? After all, bitten humans seem to be the mentally unstable ones so far, clinging to distinctly human motivations like revenge. Even with all the history between Roul and Arden, I've never seen them exhibit any hatred for one another. Roul said it best: humans have never been particularly mindful of the fact that predators don't kill other predators.

"Where does that leave me, Roul?" I ask. "Look at me. I'm just a pathetic human with freak werewolf DNA."

Pulling off his tie and folding it neatly into a suit pocket, he says, "You're my kin," effectively ending the conversation. "I'll take you to see Boguet in the morning."

"Where are you going?"

With a furtive glance up at the looming abbey, he tells me, "There is nothing on this Earth that I would barter in exchange for being forced to sleep even one night at Quedlinburg Abbey."

That does not bode well for me. I walk with him down the path toward the archway for a while until, just outside the perimeter, I catch sight of a black wolf in the distance. I recognize her at once as Amara. As we step closer I can just see, dangling from her neck, the gold chain that once belonged to Arden.

"What's *she* doing here?" I ask, anger and concern rising at the possible meaning of her presence here.

He pauses from unbuttoning his shirt. "You're surprisingly distressed."

"Arden was subpoenaed too."

"I'm well aware."

"You know, before you interrupted our little chat Breber had one burning question: who bit me."

We both look to Amara, stalking the length of the passageway. She should be participating in this conversation, at the very least. Instead she's taken a form that makes it impossible for me to communicate with in any meaningful way.

"Yes, so I heard," he responds.

"What am I supposed to do? You know that Arden would lie to protect her. And that lie comes at a pretty steep price."

Removing a pair of cufflinks and placing them in the breast pocket of his suit, he says, "I can't compel you to do anything."

A sigh of frustration escapes me. "If you want to be my pack leader, you need to do better than that."

"What would you have me tell you? Whether you proffer the truth and sacrifice Amara or back Arden's lie and allow him to fall on the sword, someone's life will end. There is no way around it. What you need to ask yourself is: whose execution are you more willing to play a part in?"

I run my hands through my hair. "Do you understand how messed up this all is?"

"Of course, I do. It weighs on me unremittingly. Everything a pack does comes back to its leader. I am ultimately responsible for all of their actions. And yet each of them is held accountable for their own deeds. Not all mistakes are made equal, Connor, and not all punishments fit the crime. This is the world you live in now."

He turns to leave then hesitates before speaking again.

"If you recall, Amara wasn't the one who brought you and your friends to La Pleine Lune the night you were bitten."

He seems to want to say more but instead makes his way toward the gate.

"She should know I made a promise to Arden," I tell him, loud enough that I hope she hears me. "I swore I wouldn't save him again."

Roul nods. "Rightly so. No man's life should be a debt to another."

He walks down the path and meets Amara on the other side of the archway. I watch them disappear into the darkness together before turning back. I don't get far before I see Daniel leaning by the entrance of the abbey. Although I halt in my steps I can't withhold the sigh of irritation that escapes from my lungs.

"Where do you think you are going?" he asks, straightening up from the wall.

"To sleep," I mutter.

"I'm sorry," he says with a malicious grin, "but there are no pets allowed inside."

When he steps in front of me I catch a glimpse of a large, oddly shaped scar across his neck that I assume is a memento from being bitten. For whatever reason, clearer than all the days since it happened, my mind flashes back to my first day in kindergarten. Now that I know the things that I know, I've wondered lately about that kid and what might have happened to him.

"What are you looking at?" Daniel asks.

I shake my head, hoping to jar the memory, but it just rattles around.

"I said, what are you looking at, *perro?*"

He pushes me and I let him. As we stand in the middle of this ancient courtyard all I can think of is that blur of a childhood memory, bathed in blood. He grabs a fistful of my T-shirt and my eyes travel back up to his neckline. Did I do that to him? Do I deserve the world of hurt that he wants to unleash on me?

I can barely get my words out. "How'd you get that scar?"

"How do you think? One of you mongrels did this to me last year."

I swallow hard. Last year. He's not the same kid from kindergarten. He's just some jackass on a power rush. Even still my heart pounds with adrenalin. All the fear and tension of the last couple of hours gives way to aggravation.

I look him directly in the eye. "If you think about it, and I seriously doubt you have, bitten humans are actually the mongrels."

He thrusts his hands against my chest and I stagger backward. When he comes at me, I can see that with every motion he's losing control and transforming into the monster that lurks within. His skin gives way to fur and his clothes tear at the seams as his mutating body stretches them out. Fingers become claws and his nose and mouth morph to take the shape of something like a muzzle. There's no time for me to undress so I slip out of my jacket as he lunges. I'm thankful for all of Arden's training that allows me with a single thought to dodge out of his path as a wolf. My clothes hinder my movement slightly before they fall away mid-leap, but not before I feel a sharp bite of pain as his claws rake against the fur along my haunch. Spinning around with a snarl, I crouch into an attack position and snap at his hand, which he pulls away before I can make contact. He lunges at me again but I roll to his left and take advantage of his unstable footing, leaping up from behind and pushing him to the ground. His jaw hits the cobble-stones beneath the brunt our bodies. I snarl into his ear, bearing down my full weight across his back with the heft of my paws in order to keep him in place. He tries to turn and break my hold, so I lightly clamp my teeth around the back of his neck as a warning. He goes still and I begin to sense the fear enveloping him.

"Enough!" a man's voice booms.

Breber marches hurriedly toward us. Daniel takes advantage of the distraction and grabs a hold of the scruff of my neck with his claws then effortlessly flings me off of him. I crash against the cobblestones, landing several feet away. With the air knocked out of me, I collapse gasping to the cold stones. Daniel's nostrils flare, breath coming out in a mist. He's either too dumb to know the fight is over or too overcome with fury to care, but he closes in for another attack. Breber heads him off effortlessly. He's a giant of a man, even facing the wrath of the upright beast in front of him. Fearlessly, the older man pushes the young werewolf away with his human hands as if Daniel were no more than a child.

"He doesn't belong here," Daniel rasps. "He belongs outside with the dogs."

He paces, apparently trying to find a way around Breber in order to get to me. The cold air is filling my lungs again and I get to my feet to shake off the blow. I switch back into my human form and begin picking up my clothes, looking Daniel in the eye to show him that I don't consider him a threat. He growls ferociously but Breber doesn't budge in the slightest. Instead the man simply points to the cathedral across the courtyard. The leader of the Hounds holds his arms out like a cross and shepherds Daniel away from me with every step forward. Finally accepting defeat, Daniel gives up the fight and turns away obediently. Only once I see him safely behind the door of the cathedral do I begin to breath normally and get dressed. Breber doesn't look back. I don't know if it's the chill of the air on my bare skin or the idea of sleeping as an unwanted guest among the Hounds, but I shiver involuntarily before turning back toward Quedlinburg Abbey.

E. SAUDADE

Saudade: *noun.* An intimate feeling and mood caused by the longing for something absent that is being missed.*

This place still creeps me out. I head upstairs in silence together with Josh and Arden, deeper into the fortification and closer to all the zealots that walk these halls. Downstairs Breber is still lecturing Connor on the finer points of Heaven's Hand. That's what he prefers to call us. Like it's more civilized or something. The Hounds of God is an old name but at least it's more on the up and up.

I've only ever heard their side of history. The way Josh tells it, they were forced to form a secret society. The Hounds seriously got with the program a few hundred years ago. First they organized just to survive and then eventually to lay down the law. They wrap it all up in religion because everything back then was but I've seen for myself how Darwinian things can get, even if they'd never admit to it.

Arden knows that other version of history first-hand, no doubt. He hangs back now, brooding like some character out of a Brontë novel. Josh leads the way, as comfortable here as he is on any football field. Mr. Team Captain. He's supposed to be the hero of the story. The one who comes to the rescue. I'm all for girl power but I really wish someone had saved me from him.

The abbey is ginormous and my memory isn't clear from the first (and only) time I was here. This is the last place on Earth I ever wanted to come back to. Especially with Josh. After the accident, he brought me here to get better. Apparently it's standard practice but all those months being trapped within these walls, I couldn't even look at him. Somehow I hoped the truth of what happened would collapse between us like a mineshaft and forever bury us apart. For such a long time I wished he would disappear. But even when he was out of sight, a ghost of him haunted me.

When we get to a landing, the staircase opens up to a wide hall with lines of doors on either side. The only sources of light are torches in wall sconces. It triggers a memory and, as the guys continue walking, I know without looking that the doors on their wrought iron hinges have locks on the outside. Most bitten werewolves would have seen the inside of one of these rooms before.

One of the heavy doors slams shut and I snap out of it. Arden is gone and Josh stands alone now beneath a flickering fire. My room is up another level with the girls. Living arrangements are never co-ed among the Hounds. Too much werewolf mojo to be trusted. The idea of walking up those steps alone, though...

"Madison?"

His voice carries in the long corridor. I pull myself together and walk over to him. There's no way I can let on that this place is getting to me already. We stand at the threshold of his windowless room. There are no windows in any of the dorm rooms. The walls are bare brick and the door is thick oak. Dark and dungeon-like but practical. I tried tearing through one of these doors once, and if they weren't all sealed off, I probably would have thrown myself out a window.

There are too many memories lurking here. I really can't deal with this right now.

"'Night." My voice comes out unnaturally husky.

"Wait," he says before I can move. "Can we talk?"

I don't have to think before answering, "No."

He goes quiet, reorganizing thoughts for a different plan of attack. Cutting him off at the pass is my only option.

"Seriously, Josh, we've been traveling all day. Aren't you tired?"

Leaning his head against the wall, he looks me up and down. I try to meet his gaze but the memories in this place plague me and tear away my grip on everything. Even his eyes remind me of what happened. They don't change when we shift. They were the same that night when he bit me as they are now. Blue like a clear sky. I was once supposed to find safety in those eyes.

"Yeah," he finally concedes. "I'm tired."

He closes his eyes just a millisecond too late to hide the buildup of tears. It's been a long time since I've been moved by his tears, though, and I almost say the words I've said a thousand times before: *"Don't say you're sorry."*

But he doesn't give me reason to. He just turns quickly

on his heels, steps into his room and shuts the door quietly behind him.

And then there was one.

This is usually the scene in a movie when the dumb protagonist heads deeper into the darkness where, obviously, the psycho killer is waiting. I'm alone in the hall, still holding onto Connor's backpack, and scared to death of every flickering shadow. So this is what it takes to freak out a werewolf. For two seconds my resolve almost breaks down and I think about barging in on Josh. He's the reason I got dragged, kicking and screaming, into this world in the first place. But I don't want to give him the satisfaction of my needing him. And I sure as hell don't want to see him crying now. Or ever again.

I think about the wolf pack roaming the forest outside of town. I wish I had their freedom now to curl up beneath the stars instead of being trapped here inside Castlevania. This is silly. I just need to keep busy so I don't lose my mind. The room Connor's been assigned is a few doors down the corridor, so I head there to drop off his backpack. An old voice in my head makes me pause at the threshold.

The room itself is almost empty. Exactly the same as all the others. A lone candle shines a small halo of light for a single bed with plain white linens topped with a coarse wool blanket. I remember the reek of bleach on those sheets. I would pull them over my head at night and try to pretend I was back at home, but the stink of bleach would never let me lose myself in the illusion.

The first full moon here was the worst. All I remember

is the pain. My scars weren't fully healed yet so my stitches tore open. Then came the screams. I was surrounded by shrill, maddening shrieks. They all sounded the same. It took a while for me to realize all those screams were mine. As I step into the room, I can almost hear them again.

The whole time I was on the edge of death, all I wanted was to give up. To die. To end it all. Being bitten made me regret being alive. Coming back here wasn't a good idea. Josh and I are still a long way from having a normal relationship. I doubt anything will make it right again. Being here brings all our issues to the surface. And I'm not ready to look at them yet. All of this is exhausting. I'm so freaking tired. Of everything. I collapse onto the bed like a rag doll and close my eyes. Darkness sweeps my mind.

"Madison?"

Sleep is like an anchor, dragging my consciousness. I sense someone by the bedside and my eyes flicker open to Connor Lewis. Only he isn't staring at my face. My sweater shimmied up in my sleep and cool air shivers across the exposed skin on my side. I totally know what he sees. It's something I try to avoid looking at altogether.

His sad brown eyes linger right along my ribcage and down to my belly where I've been marked as bitten. Long and jagged and horrible, ugly scars. I pull the fabric back over my side, mortified. Nobody has seen my scars before and I wanted to keep it that way. I'm just glad he keeps whatever commentary is running through his head to himself.

I watch Connor move around, unsure of himself and looking for a place to sit. He picks up his backpack from the floor where I dropped it and sets it down by the foot of the bed. I sit up and dangle my feet from the edge of the mattress, socks mismatched because I gave up trying to pair up things that only wind up getting separated anyway.

"So? Now that you've been schooled on the Hounds, are you a Brelieber?"

He grins before answering. "Not exactly."

Still standing awkwardly by the bed, it's like he's waiting for me to get up.

"The locks on the outside of the doors..." he starts but can't quite finish the sentence. "This feels like a prison cell."

"Yeah," is all I have to say. He has that look of putting two and two together. "What time is it?"

He shrugs. "My guess? Past midnight. What are you doing here, anyway?"

The truth is too pathetic, so I say, "I *loathe* everything about this place."

His hand goes to the footboard of the bed, but he doesn't sit at the end. I pick at tiny pills of wool on the surface of the blanket.

"There are a lot of memories here," I finally admit. "Bad ones. I thought maybe we could just ... talk."

Turning, he slumps against the foot of the bed. "Isn't it kind of late for that? I'm exhausted, Madison. It's kind of been a rough night."

"Look, I can't sleep alone in this place."

With a frustrated gesture toward me he says, "You were doing pretty well before I got here."

My head leans back against the brick wall as I gaze up at the ceiling. "That's different. I knew you'd be coming back."

The candle flickers, making our shadows pounce across the walls. It's dangerously close to going out. When it does the room will be barely lit by the torches out in the hallway. That's if someone doesn't come by and lock us in. He must have the same thought because he goes to the door and leans out past the threshold.

I fold my arms around my legs, hugging them against my chest. When he glances back, I'm sure all he can see of my face is my eyes peering back over my knees.

"If you don't want to talk, can we just sleep together?" I offer.

His eyes widen and I keep my smile hidden behind my bent legs. Even though it was all clear a second ago he scans the corridor again for fear of an eavesdropper. In a hushed voice, he whispers, "We're in a monastery, Maddy."

"So? It's not like we haven't shared a bed before."

"Not like this."

"Yeah, I kind of expect you to keep your pants on this time," I tease.

He casts a glance toward the floor. It's kind of adorable how easily embarrassed he gets. The first time he shifted I gave him a Valium and brought him back to my room at the boarding house. He was too doped up to know what he was doing. One minute he was a wolf sprawled out on a pink throw rug, the next he was a naked boy in bed with me.

"Nobody checks the rooms," I tell him. "It's just ... the

last time I was here ... it wasn't good. I really don't want to sleep alone."

Connor runs his hand through his hair the way he does when he's nervous. I grin and say, "I promise I won't try anything."

Struggling against his better judgment he says, "Alright."

Without a millisecond's hesitation I crawl under the sheets as he leans over to blow the candle out.

"Don't," I tell him.

He shrugs and kicks off his sneakers before lying down beside me. "You know, *we're* the things that go bump in the night now."

"Seriously, keep your pants on, lover boy."

"I..." he starts and fumbles for words so awkwardly that I have to laugh and let him off the hook.

As we face each other on the narrow bed it's obvious that he can't decide where to put his hands. Folded across his chest: awkward. Along his sides: uncomfortable. It's going to be a restless night unless he figures it out.

"We're better listeners in the dark now."

"So, what is it that you *don't* want to hear?"

Absently, I tap the knuckles of his now folded hands with my fingertips as if testing out the keys on a piano. "If these walls could speak ... I think they'd scream."

Gooseflesh rises on his arms and it makes me shudder. Not knowing what else to do, I giggle and pull the blanket up over my nose. He pulls the sheet down below my chin. His expression is a mix of worry and confusion. I put on my poker face and hope he thinks I'm just messing with him instead of trying to cover up my own little worries.

"Not funny," he says.

"Not joking."

I tilt my head and a lock of hair falls into my face. Without a pause, his hand pushes it back behind my ear and lingers there. My mouth twitches at a smile. But he has a serious look on his face again, one that tells me he's mulling something over.

Before I can change the conversation, his fingers comb through my hair and he asks, "Why do you hide behind all this camouflage, Madison?"

My instinct is to go on the defensive but I make the effort to fight it. He props himself up on an elbow. Partly lit from the glow of the candle he has an expressive, shadowed face surrounded by darkness. He reminds me of a Caravaggio painting. Right now I know this could be our last chance before we never see each other again to steal one little kiss.

"I'm not hiding," I tell him in as even a voice as I can. "I'm moving on. Nothing good ever comes of looking back. There's a version of me that died in a forest last spring. I've had to leave her behind."

When Connor smiles it's full of tragedy like the hero in one of those old paintings. "She said she was a ghost, too."

Who is he talking about?

"Boadicea." He fills in the blank.

"Banshee is more like it," I mutter, annoyed that he'd

bring up her name right now.

"You're right," he muses. "Did you know that Banshees are messengers of death?"

"How do you know all this stuff?"

"I'm a fount of useless knowledge."

He grins but my Spidey sense tells me he was into Boadicea. Most guys would have been disarmed by her guile, which she used like a secret weapon, and I doubt Connor was any exception. Knowing now what Connor did back then — that Boguet's genetically modified shifters were all hand-picked kids on the verge of death and owed their lives to him — it only shows the kind of power she must have held over him. I don't know how he could have trusted her even for a second when she was so far in debt to the man behind the mad science.

"You know, I thought I was saving your life when I pulled that trigger," I explain.

"But you didn't."

Sitting up slowly so we're eye to eye, I want to tell him about the gun I found in Boadicea's bag and that I haven't stopped thinking about that night. My most horrible mistake ever. The sound of that gunshot still travels with me. I'm not Supergirl. I can't outrun it. All I can hope for is a little bit of understanding. I did it for him. I did it because I couldn't lose him. Even before the words spill out of his mouth I know he's going to say the thing that we've both been avoiding.

"You ended hers, though."

His tone has so much accusation that I can't stop the

pain and remorse from taking control. I scramble over his body, pushing him out of the way as the hot sting of tears swells in my eyes. Grabbing my boots and rucksack, I march out of the room, flinging the door shut behind me. Even though the memory of this place has scarred me for life, the last thing I ever thought could happen here was being hurt again.

* **Saudade:** alternatively, a vague and constant desire for something that does not and probably cannot exist.

10. TIE UP MY HANDS

A gust of air from the slamming door slaps me in the face and blows out the candle, leaving me alone in the dark. Part of me wants to follow after her, instantly regretful for having said those words. But another part holds me back, unsure of what consequences lie in wait for me. I'm sure now that Madison had my back in the cemetery. She made the worst kind of mistake, the permanency of which will follow her for the rest of her life. If things had been different — if they'd gone down the way she expected and Boadicea had pulled a gun instead of a USB flash drive — I'd be thankful. I'd owe her my life. It didn't happen that way, and I wound up instead with Boadicea's blood literally on my hands.

Without any source of heat, I'm suddenly aware that the room is icy cold. Cold enough that it makes me consider sleeping in wolf form — a thought that hasn't crossed my mind before, but the fur would be pretty nice right about now. Fully clothed, I yank the sheets around me. They reek of bleach and the wool is itchy. Everything about this day is just too much to process: the Hounds and their laws, the pack and its surprising lack of power, the likelihood that

I'll have to eventually choose between Arden and Amara's life. My fight with Daniel has made it painfully obvious that I'll never fit in here. Granted, fitting in has never been my M.O. The lone wolf lifestyle has been my lot in life. Up until recently, anyway. Then I met Madison.

I shut my eyes in the dark, willing her out of my mind. With a sea of thoughts flooding my mind, sleep doesn't come easy. Madison left the scent of her perfume on my pillow. My thoughts and senses are filled with her. It was my fault that the gun was there at all, left out in the open because I'd been afraid that one of Boguet's thugs was about to ambush me and turn me into some kind of lab rat. I would never have fired it and said as much to Roul when he gave me the weapon. He told me that I would if it meant saving someone I cared deeply about. Madison pulled the trigger to protect me. Part of me wishes I knew what room she was in so I could go to her. Instead, I give in to the wolf and shift. With the door shut, I have no way out. No way to do any more harm.

If I dream, I don't remember any of it. The sound of church bells wakes me. It's a muffled toll due to the thick stone walls but the sound is unusual enough to my wolf ears that I bolt upright. The room remains pitch dark. I have no sense of the time. I can only imagine it's some kind of ungodly hour. Shifting back to human form, I fumble around for my backpack at the foot of the bed and pull out my iPhone. It's 8:01 a.m. My internal clock never wakes me up this early. Tapping the flashlight app I set the phone down on the bed and quickly put on a change of clothes. I notice that there clearly used to be a window in the room but it was sealed up. The inner stone is a different color and my guess is it was done long ago. When I turn around with the light in my hand, my heart leaps into my throat at the sight of heavy claw marks that cut deep scars into the thick wooden door.

I pull open the thankfully unlocked door and step outside. The hallway is bereft of life. I expected there to be more of a commotion. At the very least I imagined monks and nuns in white robes running around frantically preparing for some kind of mass or daily rite, but I guess this whole area is reserved for 'guests.' I pad around the corridor, cautiously peering down its length. Josh emerges from his own room just a few doors down.

"What's going on?" I ask.

"*Prime,*" he says calmly, pronouncing the word so that it sounds Latin. For my benefit he adds, "Morning prayer."

Now that I know there's no fire, I rub my eyes and consider going back to sleep. Then I notice how Josh is dressed: a shirt with a button-down collar and flat-fronted khakis instead of his usual sporty attire. He looks like he's going to church, and it's not even Sunday. Yawning, I figure that catching a bit more shut-eye while everyone else prays isn't a half-bad idea after all.

Before I can head back to my room he asks, "Have you seen Madison?"

It brings me back to reality in a hurry. I shake my head. She must be really mad if she couldn't even confide in him about what happened last night. The night I broke into her boarding house after discovering werewolves were real, Josh got all the details before I could even explain my side of the story.

"Look, if you see her—" he starts but then lets out a defeated sigh. "Never mind."

Barely awake, I waver in the middle of the hallway as he starts to walk toward the staircase. I'm still there when he pauses to look back at me.

"You hungry?"

I nod. I'm always hungry.

"Come on, I'll show you the mess hall."

The casual way he makes the invitation brings to mind the first day of school when we met. His friendliness seems strained now. We haven't really spoken since I found out I was a werewolf, and I have a feeling that to him I really was just an assignment.

"Don't you have somewhere to be?" I ask without meaning to be rude.

He shrugs. "Prayer's optional."

I follow his lead down the stairs to the ground level mess hall, where we're the only souls in the place. It's a large room filled with long tables and wooden benches. Ancient tapestries hang on the walls, embroidered with hunting and battle scenes, knights in white tunics and — unsurprisingly — wolves. Massive wrought-iron chandeliers hang high above our heads on metal chains, filled with unlit candles. There's a buffet table by the large windows and we head straight toward it. An orange glow from sunrise breaks through the thick and hazy glass. It's December and we're inching toward the shortest day of the year. Most people are thinking about Christmas and the holidays. It's the furthest thing from my mind. I pile a plate with cured meats, cheeses and breads and scoop up some jam and honey just for good measure. Josh and I take seats across from each other at the nearest table and for a few minutes we just eat without any words. Without Madison around as a conversation buffer, I'm not sure what we could possibly talk about at this point.

"You honestly buy into all of this?" I ask.

"What do you mean?"

"This whole self-governed secret society of werewolves wrapped up in religion. It's like—"

I'm about to say *Vampire: The Masquerade* but I doubt he'll get the RPG reference.

Before I can think of a better analogy he tells me, "It's not a cult."

"I wasn't going to call it a cult," I tell him honestly.

"Don't you believe in some kind of afterlife?"

I shrug and he looks me up and down. He starts to say something else but stops for a long pause.

"My granddad used to say you shouldn't talk about politics and religion in polite company," he finally says. "You can't change anybody's mind on either, but it's the surest way to start a fight."

It's hard to steer clear of those topics when the Hounds represent both. I cram more food into my mouth as an excuse not to talk.

"As for buying into all of this," he continues, "the rules

are for our own good. And like I said, you don't have to pray to belong here."

"If you say so."

He grimaces, setting down his fork. "Bro, it's not like I don't question it sometimes."

"Do you?" I ask. "Breber told me what happened. After you bit Madison."

He squints as he tries to figure out my meaning.

"With your dad," I whisper despite the fact that we're alone.

"No, you don't understand, Connor," he replies quietly, looking straight at me. "That was on me."

I knew from the start that Madison had her unique brand of issues, but in spite of our differences, Josh always seemed like the one who was together. Aside from pining over his ex-girlfriend, I wouldn't have guessed he was carrying such a heavy cross. Religion was not a part of my upbringing so all of this is foreign to me. I'm aware of people having what's called a crisis of faith where they question their beliefs. I just don't get it. Religious quandary aside, if I'd suffered through what Josh did at the hands of the Hounds, the last thing I'd want to do is go back to them. He picks up his utensil again but only moves the food around his plate.

"There are consequences for everything we do," he says.

He shoves food into his mouth. I do the same. We chew in silence, avoiding eye contact. I don't need to hear the details of what happened to Josh to know that it was horrible, but his relationship with the Hounds still confounds me. How can he forgive them?

"He was a werewolf too, my dad," he tells me after a while as he stares at his plate. "A few years after we were bitten, my dad walked away from all of this and took me with him. He was tired of the rules. Said they were out of touch with reality. I was thirteen at the time. By then we thought we were in control of the shifts and all we wanted was some kind of freedom. Full moons aside, we were ... *normal*, you know? The Hounds blamed my dad for taking me away but I never wanted to come back to any of this."

His voice becomes emotional and he pauses to finish his last bite of food before continuing.

"I met Madison freshman year. Living on the military base gave my dad and I all the structure we needed. We really thought we could get away with it. Having a life where we didn't have to answer to anyone but ourselves. Pride is a deadly sin. And we had to pay for it. My feelings for Madison threw me for a loop and one night I lost control. I lost everything. My dad, Madison..."

"I'm sorry about your dad," I say. "But why did you break up with Madison?"

He swallows hard enough that I can hear it straight across the wide table. "That's ... part of my penance."

Finally, the piece that was always missing from the puzzle. Even before he punched me at the mash-up party I knew his feelings for Madison ran deep and that he definitely wasn't over her. Now that I know my hunch was right it doesn't make it any better. In fact, it makes things more awkward than ever.

He changes tack. "Look, Madison said you were weighing all of your options. That you were thinking about striking out on your own."

He looks to me for a response but I keep my mouth shut, a little annoyed that they still talk about me behind my back.

"Connor, if you walk away from these rules, you have to know it works both ways. You won't be protected by them either. You should know the good and the bad. Life outside the Hounds makes you an outlaw. And there are worse things out there than us."

If it was anyone else, I might think it was a threat. But his voice is that same collected calm that he usually exudes. When I don't respond he simply stands up, taking his empty plate with him.

Before he turns to walk away, I ask, "Do you know where the wolf pack is? I'm supposed to meet Roul."

"Try the gardens behind the cathedral. The pack wolves don't come in here if they can help it."

He turns toward the door and his entire body freezes in place, the fork falling from his plate and bouncing with a sharp ring. I follow his gaze. Madison stands by the door haloed by the light that streams into the room. Her long cherry-red dyed hair and blunt bangs have been shorn into a choppy pixie cut. The short style shows off all of her features: the high cheekbones, the almond shape of her eyes, the pouty lips. The bright red of her hair has been replaced by her natural brown color, which brings out the honey tone of her skin and the gold in her hazel eyes. I imagine somewhere there's a photo of her from before she was bitten in which she looks exactly as she does now. Last night when I asked her why she was hiding behind the dye, the makeup, the constantly changing eyebrow rings, I never imagined she'd take my words to heart and change any of it. It's like she basically buried whoever that person was.

Madison hesitates at the sight of Josh. Then, like the ghost she's supposed to be, she backs out of the room and leaves without so much as a word. When I look to Josh again, his blue eyes shimmer and he rushes after her. He was right. There are consequences for every little thing that we do.

11. SUPREMACY

Talking to Madison is out of the question, at least for now, so I head outside hoping to find Roul. I follow a path past the cathedral that opens up to an expansive garden with a clear view of the clutter of red rooftops of the town below. In the summer months the garden is probably quite beautiful and lush but in December it's achingly bare. Squared patches of grass are yellowed like straw from the cold. Footpaths lead off in a few different directions through the grounds and I take one along the edge of the garden to admire the view. Terraced houses crowd around the hillside. In the distance I catch glimpses of the town's old fortifications, including an imposing stone wall and watchtowers. Beyond these the mountains far in the distance send a chill through me as I consider what Roul said about the history of wolves in the region. Rather, werewolves. Creatures that came down from the mountains or lurked among the trees and preyed on the unsuspecting. Pack wolves, as Breber claims, or the bitten, according to Roul. I imagine the angry villagers in all those old horror movies running into the forests with pitchforks and torches to hunt them down for revenge. And maybe this lawlessness is why the

Hounds banded together in the first place. It all started in the interest of self-preservation, to protect their kind. But somewhere along the way it turned into something bigger. Or maybe Josh was right when he said there's something worse out there.

My eye catches movement to my right and I turn to see Roul has been sitting on a stone bench at the far end of the garden all this time. I walk toward him. He's dressed casually — by his standards, anyway — in a gray cardigan over a navy blue dress shirt and beige slacks. Given that he slept out in a forest without so much as a sink he still looks clean-shaven and well put together, without a hair out of place. He taps away at a cellphone, sending an email or text. I guess he does still have a multi-billion-dollar pharmaceutical company to run. As I step toward him, he glances up at me like he's been waiting for me this whole time.

"How did you sleep?" he asks.

"Not great. You?"

Standing up, he pockets the phone. "I'd wager better than you, but I'll admit I've become rather fond of some creature comforts that the woods don't provide."

I can't hide my surprise. "Like what?"

After a moment of pursing his lips he lists off a few of his favorites. "Indoor heating. Thousand-count Egyptian cotton sheets. Eiderdown pillows. Pillows are vastly underrated."

Judging from the wistfulness in his voice, he isn't joking.

"All the same," Roul continues more soberly, "it's a fair trade to sleep without those comforts than be confined in a cell."

The only logical response is a grimace. "Yeah, I see that now."

"Are you ready to meet with Boguet?"

I remain firmly planted on the path, unable to summon the courage to move forward. "What do you think he wants from me?"

"You would know better than I."

"I've barely spoken with him."

"Well, your blood alone is worth a small fortune in research. Perhaps he's looking to barter for more of it."

His answer is not comforting in the least.

"How is this helping?" I ask.

"Better to know the truth, isn't it? You've been dissatisfied with my reticence up until now."

True enough. All the same, my dealings with Boguet have been cryptic to say the least. Maybe now that he's unraveled the mystery behind my DNA, he'll be more forthright. I'm nervous still and I can't hide it. Roul comes over and puts an arm around my shoulders.

"He's behind bars," he reassures me. "How much harm can he do?"

With a hearty pat on my back he leads the way. Taking a deep breath, I follow him down the path and toward the cathedral with its two looming towers. My eyes travel upward and catch the carved frieze that runs across the width of the building just along the edge of the roof. Decorated alongside other animals are what appear to be wolf- and serpent-headed monsters. When we reach the metal door,

Roul pulls the handle, a wide ring decorated with a medieval leaping wolf. To the casual observer these are all just interesting bits of architecture. To me, the combination of it all screams werewolf HQ so much that it's hard to believe they've remained undiscovered for this long. Who'd ever believe it though?

In stark contrast to the weather-worn stone exterior, the interior looks almost bleached. The main part of the cathedral is a long and open expanse that leads toward an altar where wide staircases on either side lead up to the choir. Romanesque archways line aisles on either side all the way to the back. High above us, windows with similar arches allow natural light to flood in below. There are more engravings running below these openings, and although they match the ones on the outside in style, there are no wolves, snakes or creatures of any kind represented here inside the church. Roul ducks past a column and I stay close on his heels, walking toward a closed iron-grilled door. A white-robed monk waits for us on the other side, holding a torch even though the area is well lit. Jangling a set of ancient keys on a large metal ring, he lets us in then locks the door behind us. We enter a small room with a vaulted ceiling. At the far end is a sunken alcove with a stained-glass window featuring some kind of bird. I get the distinct feeling that we're in an above-ground crypt. The monk kneels by what appears to be a sarcophagus, as though he's about to pray. Then he shoulders into the stone coffin, pushing to reveal a secret passageway below where a narrow set of stone steps spirals down into darkness. I guessed right when we first arrived. This place doubles as a prison and there's probably a hidden dungeon below us. I edge closer, trying to catch any glimpse of light, but Roul extends his arm and bars me from getting ahead of myself. With his free hand, he gestures to the staircase.

"After you ... brother."

The monk descends the steps and I trail behind Roul. We don't get very far before we stop at a wide landing where the monk places his torch into a metal rung in the wall. He takes the few steps back necessary to reach the underside of the coffin that doubles as a doorway and tugs at the lip with both hands. The sound of stone grinding against stone accompanies the loss of natural light as we're shut in underground. Task complete, the monk continues to lead us, leaving the torch behind and slipping his hands into the wide sleeves of his robe. The air is much cooler here than it was outside. Our descent of the circular staircase is lit by other well-placed wall torches set at even intervals along the wall to cast just enough light to allow us to find our our way. I take care to watch my feet on the narrow steps to make sure I don't misstep on a broken stone or slip on some moisture, but it has the effect of giving me a mild case of vertigo as we descend. Not wanting to fall behind, I keep my eyes on the outer wall and just hope my feet will land on each stone. Fortunately, we don't circle for much longer and we finally reach the dimly lit dungeon. Although the architecture of the room is similar to the one directly above us, the thick stone is crumbling here and metal beams have been inserted across columns to bear the load of the ceiling. Jail cells line both sides, housed within the columned arches. More torches hang on metal rungs, lighting our path to the very end of the passageway, where I can easily make out the form of Boguet behind thick metal bars. He's dressed in a canvas cassock like a monk. No orange jumpsuits for werewolf criminals. Seated on a short wooden stool in the passageway directly outside his cell is a severely businesslike dark-haired woman with a Cleopatra haircut. Roul reaches suddenly for something concealed at the back of his waist, presumably some sort of weapon, but doesn't pull it out just yet.

"What's the meaning of this?" he asks.

The monk, perplexed, replies, "Silent observers are to bear witness to this trial and its proceedings."

Although the woman exudes a calculated certitude, she doesn't look like much of a physical threat and I'm confused by Roul's extreme reaction. Dressed in a suit with matching pumps, she sits perfectly still in profile. Unless we're at risk of a corporate merger, I don't see the danger. Roul's hand doesn't leave his weapon as we continue following the monk, and my anxiety builds with every step. We stop close enough for me to see that the woman is wearing a white armband with a handprint embroidered in gold thread on the sleeve of her jacket, and I wonder what it means. With a solemn bow the monk takes his leave. Roul stands in front of one of the torches so that he's backlit, the wolf tattoo on his face lit up and staring back at me menacingly. The flickering light makes it appear as though he's snarling. His attention never wavers from the woman, who merely continues to stare ahead blankly. As I approach the cell, Boguet also lopes forward toward the bars that separate us in a way that makes me think of *Silence of the Lambs*. I stop moving to ensure I'm out of arm's reach.

"What did you want to see me about?"

Boguet looks pale in the dim light. His face is thinner than the last time I saw him, gaunter. They must have been keeping him holed up here underground since his capture about a month ago. Human physiology wasn't built for subterranean living. This is all to say, without sunlight or activity he really doesn't look in great health and I have to feel a little empathy for the old werewolf.

"Ever to the point," he says in a voice that's stretched. "Life's short."

"I believe you'll find that no longer to be the case."

It's impossible for me to withhold a sigh. "Do *you* have a point? Because I think you'll find I'm tired of waiting around for people to tell me things I can figure out on my own."

He nods, slowly. "Fair enough. I want you to heed my words: these Hounds are not your allies."

Boguet doesn't seem to care about the presence of so many unwanted listeners. I suppose being on death row does that to a person. I'm assuming that's what the outcome of all this will be. That a guilty sentence means an end to his life. Despite the theatrics of a trial, it seems unlikely that he'll be found innocent.

"And you are? An ally?"

"Such formal cooperations may be entered into for a mutual benefit, would you not agree?"

Roul was right. Boguet still needs me for his research.

"What exactly do you bring to the table?"

His smile broadens, flourishing his palms open toward me. "Salvation."

"From what?"

"We must all stand before the judgment seat of our Lord," he begins to recite, "that each one may receive what is due him for the things done while in the body, whether good or bad."

Although what he's saying is clearly some sort of religious passage, I have a feeling it's more than just biblical scripture. Like there's supposed to be a message for me directly. But I'm not getting it. "What are you saying?"

"There will be a reckoning in the days to come."

He must be losing it. "Yeah, you're on trial for crimes against werewolves."

"All misdeeds will be accounted for, not just mine."

"Are you talking about the scenario where you wipe all of us out? I hate to break it to you but you're on the wrong side of these bars to be able to make that happen."

An expression of annoyance briefly crosses his face. "My intention has never been to vanquish them. I merely intend to free them of the beast. Come what may but this battle isn't over. Far from it. Four hundred years is a long time to endure this curse. Longer than any human in known history has ever done. My legacy on this Earth will be that I did not survive in vain. Regardless of the outcome of this trial, more heads will roll than mine."

"Do you really think all of these werewolves are going

to let you walk away?" I shake my head in disbelief.

For a long, uncomfortable moment he observes me with those icy blue eyes of his. Then he smiles in his grandfatherly way as though everything is right and safe in the world, which make the words that come out of his mouth all the more shocking.

"My dear boy, in due time you will live or die by my command."

Shaken, I back away further, comforted only by the fact that Roul has witnessed his mad ramblings. "You've lost it, haven't you," I say more as statement than a question. "You have no power anymore."

He extends his right arm past the bars of his cell and I flinch as his hand gnarls then one of his bony fingers points directly at me. "I know now who you are."

Roul stirs from his place behind me and Boguet switches his gaze toward him.

"And you, Rodolfus de Aquila, your secrets cannot hide from science."

"It's time to go," Roul says.

Even before turning around the wolf in me senses the danger and I can feel it bristling beneath my skin. Roul's focus shifts rapidly now between Boguet and the woman. There's a fragment of movement from one of them, I can't tell which, but it's enough to make Roul draw his gun. With his arm outstretched, he points the weapon squarely at the businesswoman and motions calmly for me to move toward the exit. I don't hesitate and back straight down the passageway toward the stairs, careful not to put myself in the crosshairs as Roul covers my exit and backs out of the dungeon himself. We circle back up the stairs as quickly as we can move even though I hear no signs of a pursuit. Other than Boguet's threatening words I saw no gesture of aggression. Still, I feel the urge to run with Roul fast on my heels. I do my best not to trip up but wind up doing so just as we reach the wide landing.

The monk stands patiently waiting for us and although he must have heard our hurried approach is startled not just by my abrupt appearance at his feet but by the gun in my pack leader's hand. I realize as Roul helps me up with one hand, while still aiming the gun and keeping watch down the steps, that I trust him unequivocally. Something snaps into place, and for the first time ever I have a pretty good idea of where I fit in. That despite what went down with Arden, I belong among the pack werewolves. Boguet is a righteous egomaniac bent on forcing his moral convictions on our world and if I choose a life of isolation I could very well end up just like him. The Hounds may be guided by a sense of greater good but they've applied their rule to such zealous extremes that I can't in good conscience side with them either.

The monk interrupts my epiphany by stammering incoherently at us.

"Get us out," Roul demands. "Now."

Stumbling over his robes, the monk races up the few steps to the coffin and trembles with the effort of pulling open our escape route. My heart thrums in my throat. I envision the woman shifting into a horrible half-beast creature in an expensive suit clawing her way up the steps. In an effort to calm myself, I rub at the leather braid around my neck. I've never seen Roul in combative mode. If anything, he's the reason my brain got all ramped up with adrenaline the way it did. No, I'm fairly certain that the threat down there was Boguet and his words. His message was received, loud and clear, and it's obvious now that the words were never meant for me in the first place. No sooner has the sarcophagus been moved aside than we push our way past the monk and up to the aboveground crypt. Roul waits for the dungeon to be sealed off once more before stashing his gun. I follow him through a back exit to the gardens. Relief begins to calm my nerves but it isn't until we're completely outside again that we both breath a sigh of relief. In the openness of the garden I pace back and forth, rubbing my hand through the hair on the back of my head.

"What the hell was that? And how does he know we're related?"

Although his eyes dart over to me when I speak, Roul is very still as he stares off into the distance. "It doesn't matter."

"What do you mean, it doesn't matter? It was a big enough deal for you to go all Stathem-esque down there."

"Just let it go, Connor," he says. "There are bigger factors in play here. Things you won't understand."

For all the calm he displayed below ground, his brow is now beaded with sweat. Somehow Boguet's words got to him. I'm not sure which ones but I've never seen him this way before. Boguet struck a chord. I'm beginning to suspect there's more I don't know about Roul's motivation for reconnecting with me, his long-lost kin. But he's already shut down that line of questioning so it'll have to wait. I start down a different path.

"Who was that woman?"

My question has the effect of returning his attention to the present. He faces me when he speaks this time, regaining that cool confidence I've grown accustomed to from the pack leader of the werewolves of Paris.

"She leads the Luparii."

The last word means nothing to me so I hazard a guess. "Another rebel werewolf faction?"

Shaking his head, he turns to press his hands against a stone ledge seemingly to take in the view. "The armband she was wearing is the mark of an untouchable."

"Meaning?"

"It's a form of social exclusion usually meant to segregate a minority from the mainstream. A human concept. Untouchables are ostracized in order to protect societies from contagion, whether it be disease, beliefs or otherwise. The practice has been around for centuries, and it still is in some places."

I shake my head in disgust.

"Save your moral indignation, alright?" he says soothingly before continuing further. "When the Hounds took power, untouchability became a basic tenet of their rule. Only in our case it's humans who are, quite literally, untouchable and we're the ones who pay the price for making contact."

"Wait, she was human?"

"Yes."

"And she's dangerous?"

"I never underestimate what humans are capable of."

I sigh and he leans forward on his elbows, slumping his head. "Yes, the Luparii are dangerous foes. They're an intergovernmental European task force for limiting and maintaining control of our populations."

"Wait, what?" My head is spinning from all the information he just delivered in that last sentence. "So humans know about us. And the government has created a program specifically to wipe us out?"

"Not all humans are privy to this information. And their goal isn't to eliminate us, but to keep us in check. Much like wolf culls that take place in some countries, including yours, the Luparii believe that limiting our numbers is vital for human conservation and as a form of *pest* control."

"Werewolf hunters," I mutter.

Where was my training for that? I walk over to his side and mimic his stance as though it might bring me some of his calm resolve. It doesn't. I feel completely powerless. The Hounds have us backed into a corner due to their sheer numbers. I have no idea what this government-appointed division of werewolf hunters is capable of doing or what their role could possibly be, but it's no doubt more bad news. Something crosses my mind: Boguet's so-called 'cure.' Before Boadicea died she said that scientists were conducting field tests, whatever that means. It can't be good.

"What are the Luparii doing here?" I ask.

"Although the Hounds have no jurisdiction over humans,

the reverse is not necessarily true. It's unusual but not unheard of for the Luparii to appear as observers in a high-profile case such as Boguet's. They don't distinguish between the born and the bitten. We are all an equal threat in their eyes. It may be that they're here to ensure the trial is handled with a blind eye turned to personal beliefs. But I suspect they have other interests. There has always been an uneasy alliance between the Hounds and the Luparii."

I let out another heavy sigh. "Is it just me or does it feel like we're surrounded by our enemies?"

I understand now why the born and the bitten were-wolves are all so opposed to lone wolves. Josh was referring to the Luparii when he said there are worse things out there. Lone wolves are outlaws, unprotected and probably the first to be picked off when it comes time to thin the pack. There's safety in numbers. That's what Roul's been trying to tell me all along.

"We?" he asks.

"I don't want anything to do with these Hounds or Boguet," I say flatly. "And I can't sleep in that cell again. The pack is where I belong."

With a reassuring hand on my shoulder he says, "You have my word. I will not leave you here."

Staring out at the town below us, I picture all the people in their quaint little half-timbered medieval houses just starting their days. They're completely unaware of what goes on up here. All the injustices done in the name of justice.

"Have I mentioned lately that being a werewolf sucks?"

"I can help with that," he says, gently chuckling. His eyes give me the once-over. "Let's start with your clothes. Did you not bring something more suitable to wear?"

I stare down at my faded jeans and 1UP mushroom T-shirt. Both have seen better days. The shirt has a rip at the back of the neckline from where I tore out the label because it kept sticking out. Truth is, I didn't think much beyond the subpoena. I'm not exactly here of my own free will, and I sure as hell didn't figure there'd be a dress code.

"I'm not the one on trial." I shrug.

He grimaces, clearly unimpressed by my response. "Every time we come here, we're on trial. One way or another. Remember that. Go get your things and I'll book a hotel in town."

I head back to the abbey as he pulls his phone from his pocket. I feel much better now that I've placed my loyalties firmly with Roul's pack. Whatever Boguet has planned, he can't possibly be able to anticipate what we're capable of. Especially when I'm not even sure myself.

12. LITTLE TALKS

I'm no sooner up the stairs than I see Arden in the hallway for the dormitory. Apparently he's had his fill of the Hounds too. I find him facing off with a monk who speaks frantically in German. Even if the plea was in perfect French, Arden isn't in the mood to listen. It's almost comical watching the white-robed monk as he spreads his limbs out as a physical barrier like some kid trying to get a prized object back in a schoolyard game of keep-away. Arden merely shoulders by, knowing full well that he can't be touched. In my room, I quickly stuff the clothes I was wearing yesterday into my backpack and rush out the door to follow him down the stairs.

"What are you doing?"

"Leaving," is his one-word, unhelpful answer. He'd never let me get away with a response like that to one of his questions.

"Where are you going to spend the night?"

"The mountains."

I shiver at the thought of it. "Do you have a death wish? It's freezing out there. You're human. You'll die of hypothermia."

183

That's when he decides to ignore me too.

"Did you hear me? Or do you want a repeat of your hospital visit?"

At the base of the stairs, he turns on me so suddenly that I almost crash into him. Although I tower above him from where I stand one step up, Arden will always have an air about him that makes him more of a physical threat. Like he's just on the edge of being murderously dangerous.

"We have an agreement," is all that he has to say.

Right. The one where I'm supposed to just let him die if he wants to. In response, I stammer. There must be a way to reason with him. No rational person wants to end his life. It's the final refuge for those without hope.

"I didn't think that applied to suicide," I argue.

That word makes him hesitate slightly. "I've lived in the woods longer than I have between stone walls," he says grudgingly.

I take a second to examine him more closely. He's dressed like a character from *The Bourne Trilogy* about to high-tail it through some snow-covered hinterland on a mission to blow stuff up. Still all in black, he's wearing a wool sweater and heavy pants with a Polartec jacket over top. It's almost as if he'd planned for this eventuality. I should have expected as much.

"Take care out there," I say.

When I put a hand out as a good-bye gesture, he merely stares at it like that first time we were introduced. I withdraw it quickly, feeling foolish. Without further ado, Arden heads out the front door. When he pulls it open I catch a glimpse of Roul, who glances up from his phone, expecting to see me. His expression changes minutely in surprise as Arden pauses at the threshold. They have such a strange and strained relationship, even more so now that Arden is no longer part of the pack. Far be it from me to judge or even understand the complexity of it. When Roul took over the pack after Arden's father died at the hands of Boguet, he introduced radical new ways for them to survive. Arden, the traditionalist, never approved. Differences aside, their loyalty to the pack is precisely the same: unwavering in every way. After a moment of hesitation Arden continues on, the door shutting behind him and obstructing my view of the outside world. I take the final steps down the staircase and consider looking for Madison or Josh to let them know I'm leaving, but I don't know where to start. Besides, a quick escape is probably for the best so I continue toward the door. Breber interrupts my departure from his hallowed halls. He moves to stand by the exit, smiling. In an attempt to appear nonchalant, I nod cordially.

"Are you to leave us as well?" he asks as I reach for the door.

"Yeah." I hope that will be enough to end the conversation.

I open the door a crack but before I can get even a foot past the threshold, Breber reaches out to bar my exit. My eyes flit between him and the door.

"That's allowed, isn't it?"

"Of course," he assures me. "This is hardly a prison."

I beg to differ but keep that to myself. Still, he doesn't

move. He seems on the verge of saying something when the metal handle slips from my grip as the door is opened from the other side.

"Is everything alright?" Roul asks, assessing the situation.

Breber doesn't hesitate or lose his composure. "I was merely bidding Connor Lewis *adieu.*"

He moves his arm back to his side without another word and I squeeze past him and out into the courtyard with Roul.

"Did you talk to Arden?" I ask as we make our retreat.

He shakes his head.

"These archaic rules about ostracizing your own — it's messed up."

"I don't make the rules but I have to abide by them," Roul says. "We all do."

"I'm getting pretty sick of hearing that line. You don't seem to get how steep a learning curve this all is — me being a werewolf, Arden not."

"The moment Arden was cured by Boguet, he became an untouchable. We're not permitted to associate with him. Literally speaking we're supposed to avoid all physical contact. It would stand to reason that the punishment for defying this law — certainly in this case — ought to be overlooked entirely."

"What's the punishment?"

"In older days it used to be that the offender would lose the hand that made contact. Of course, that was back when we could avoid humans altogether. Over the years our worlds eventually overlapped and we've been left with little choice but to coexist."

It would be difficult for a wolf to hunt in the absence of an appendage. Back in the day it would probably have meant starvation. A death sentence would be more humane. The Hounds govern with harsh laws.

He adds, "I haven't tested whether the punishment still stands today."

Ahead of us I see the silhouette of Arden, standing at the end of the archway looking at something further down along the passageway. As we approach, Amara comes into view also and I realize why he stopped in his tracks. She stands in her human form looking back toward him and I'm awestruck in the same way I was when we first met. Her unique beauty has always left me a little tongue-tied and I almost forgot the involuntary effect she has on me. They stand an appropriate distance from each other across the short passageway, just taking each other in. Amara catches sight of us approaching, but she isn't abashed the way I would expect. She watches me in the same predatory way that she did when we first met. Sensing our presence, Arden starts to walk away and as he moves past her she says something that I can't hear. He stops and turns toward her but I can't see his expression. With one hand, she pulls something from beneath her sweater — the necklace with the sundial ring — and dangles it from her hand for him to retrieve. Instead of reaching for it, he shakes his head. He backs a few steps away to gaze upon her one last time then without a word continues down the path. Amara stands stock-still for what seems like an eternity as we approach. The law disallows them to make a choice for themselves, to look past their differences and live the life they've always known. She tucks the necklace out of sight again and makes a move to leave.

"Amara!"

She stalls before glancing back at Roul, who simply shakes his head once. All this wordless communication makes me realize how much I've missed of their conversations. It's why Arden uses words so sparingly. Why does he need any of them when he can say so much with a gesture? I make a mental note to pay more attention to their body language and mine as well. As we walk toward her, Roul holds her in his stare.

"Not in their backyard," he warns her.

For the first time since I met Amara, she looks lost. Our eyes lock, and seeing the sorrow hers hold, all the pent-up anger I've been feeling on behalf of Arden begins to thaw. None of this is fair. She breaks our gaze so she can face our pack leader.

"If not theirs, then where else?" she asks.

"You know this cannot be."

He turns away, ending the discussion, but I interject. "Why not?"

"Don't rattle the cage, Connor," Roul warns over the shoulder. "Someone's liable to get hurt."

"Seems to me someone's liable to get hurt either way," I argue. "Or dead."

"Yes," Amara agrees. "The Hounds will want blood and

it should be mine, not Arden's."

Spinning around to face us again, Roul lets out a low growl. Although he barely moves, the slight shift in his posture tells me his patience has worn thin and he's not about to be challenged on this point. He motions at her to emphasize the severity of his words.

"Not under my watch."

"It is my crime," she continues softly.

"And it's a fool's errand to try to pay for it." He comes forward to lift her chin and look her fully in the face. "You know damn well that Arden will never allow it."

"That is why he cannot know."

Whatever control Roul had over Amara has slipped away somehow. She stands defiant now and it's clear that her loyalty to Arden outweighs her allegiance to the pack. There is no bargaining chip greater than that, no words or gestures Roul can apply to sway her and he knows it. His hand retreats to his side. Soul mates come once in a lifetime and the only way it's supposed to end is with death itself. A long silence follows. None of us knows what to say next. Suddenly she envelops me in her arms and I'm so surprised by the embrace that I can't return it. When she pulls away, she puts her hands on either side of my face then kisses my cheeks. Even though I know this is her final goodbye I can't think of a single word to say. She smiles sadly before turning away and I watch her slowly disappear down the path back into town.

"Where's she going?" I finally ask Roul.

"She's relieved you of the burden of having to choose

between them," he tells me. "She intends to forfeit her life. What does it matter now if she breaks one of their rules?"

I realize that she's heading in the same direction Arden did. She's going to say another final goodbye. Roul lets out a long sigh then leads me down a different path. We walk down the narrow cobblestone streets of Quedlinburg in silence. Enclosed balconies jut out over the street and an old woman props herself on pillows at a window of one of them to watch the foot traffic below her. Many of the half-timbered houses are decorated with geometric shapes carved into the wood and as we stop at an intersection my eyes are drawn to one house in particular, decorated with a row of hexagrams.

"Welcome to Hell," Roul says.

I glance over at him to see that he's gently smiling, which is a relief. It's clear he doesn't want to talk about the fate of his pack member. Truth be told, neither do I. Even if I tried to intervene, her fate is out of our hands now.

"This building formerly belonged to an alchemist," he notes. "The residents considered that practice the devil's work and called this place *Hölle* or Hell."

The corner of the building has a little blue sign with white lettering that marks the street as such. Roul quietly adds, "They don't know the half of it."

The place that Roul booked is on the same street in one of the old half-timbered houses. He enters a pass code to unlock the wide wooden doors then shows me inside. The interior of the house is kind of a blend of modern and traditional with exposed wood beams, whitewashed hardwood floors and a mix of historical and contemporary decor. It's a private home that we have to ourselves and it's clear that he spared no expense even with what I would assume are limited options in this small medieval village. He spends money the way the extremely wealthy do, like it's air. I guess it's called disposable income for a reason. The shared living area on the main floor is open-concept and includes a small kitchen that overlooks a private courtyard with an old tower in one corner. Roul ushers me upstairs to one of the private bedrooms. They take up an entire floor and mine is up top. I would have settled for a room with just one window and a door that locks from the inside. He waits by the threshold as I enter the room, which has a wall of exposed stone and is grandly decorated with a large armoire, Oriental rug, a writing desk and other expensive-looking furnishings. Even the ceiling is embellished with elaborately carved wood. On the king-size canopy bed sit a large paper shopping bag and a garment bag, each with the German name of a local shop.

"I think you'll find everything you need here," Roul says.

"What's this?" I ask, gesturing toward the bags. "And when did you have time to go on a shopping spree?"

"I placed the order by phone. It'll have to do since I had to guess your sizes. If need be, you can have them tailored later."

I arch an eyebrow.

"Why do you care so much about how we look in the eyes of the Hounds?"

"Appearances matter. It's the kind of world we live in."

"Says the guy with the facial tattoo."

"I earned this mark," he informs me sternly. "Tattoos have been a part of our culture since well before my time. They represent important milestones in our lives. Some are decorations for bravery, others are pledges of devotion. Every last one of them is a story, whether a rite of passage or a mark of status and rank."

"Sorry," I say. "I didn't mean to be ... this is all just a bit overwhelming."

"Get some rest. You have an interview with the prosecutor in the afternoon," he says before shutting the double doors behind him.

Kicking off my sneakers I leap onto the bed, landing face first and burrowing my face into the sheets. Roul was right. Pillows are underrated. Maybe this rental just happens to have the softest pillows in the world or maybe a night in a cold, dark cell with its monastic decor took more of a toll on me than I realized. In any case, I fall asleep almost instantly.

When I wake up some time later, I feel well rested and prepared for the rest of the day. I head into the adjoining bathroom hoping to rinse off the stratum of grime that's settled on my skin. There I'm faced with a spa-style shower stall with a complicated a panel of dials that must have been specifically imported from two hundred years in the future. I fiddle with the control panel until a blast of cold hits me in the ribs from a hidden spray in the wall. It'll have to do. I try to be as quick as I can. Toweling off, I unzip the garment bag to reveal a black suit and tie with a white dress shirt, clearly meant for tomorrow's court date. The other bag contains slightly more casual clothes neatly folded and wrapped in tissue paper. There's a striped green button-down shirt with beige trousers and leather belt. He even threw in socks and underwear. At the bottom of the bag is an uncomfortable-looking pair of dress shoes. Despite my reservations about dressing to impress the Hounds, I suck it up and swap my regular clothes for an outfit that's entirely too preppy for me. It reminds me too much of private school except that I can't even wear my sneakers. All the same, the smart thing to do is trust Roul on this. I'm intimately acquainted with what it's like to be judged on appearances, and I get a sense that the Hounds might hold a grudge. First and foremost, the bitten are human. Their curse wouldn't exist if werewolves didn't. It's hard to find forgiveness in your heart when your brain is storing that kind of information. If Roul thinks that keeping up appearances will in some way make them less critical of us, then preppy it is.

Emerging from my suite, I notice low, murmuring voices coming from downstairs and guess the prosecutor has arrived. I must have overslept and I'm late for my meeting which I hate, but I'm not really here of my own accord so it doesn't bother me that the attorney might be waiting. Heading downstairs, I notice the voices seem to be coming from Roul's room. His door is ajar and I approach quietly, unsure of what to expect.

A man's voice says to him in French, "It's your estate. You could leave it all to a pet dog for all I care."

If I'm to fill in the blanks, Roul is talking to his estate lawyer about a last will and testament. Is Boguet's threat more serious than I thought? Why else would he take this moment, the day before a big trial, to make changes to his will? Maybe I should be more worried than I am. Awkwardly, I stand by the door and wonder if I should knock.

"Far be it for me to judge, but..." the man starts.

"Just write it in."

"My friend, if it were me I would want to know."

"Thierry, it would kill him. You don't know Arden as I do."

Arden? I step back, aware suddenly that I've intruded on the wrong conversation. The synapses in my brain misfire. The words don't make sense to me and yet they do. And that both saddens and maddens me.

The man in the room jokes, "Being human is not without its charms, no?"

I slowly back away, hoping to remain undetected, and not watching where I'm going in my retreat, I knock into a display table. The sound of a vase rumbling makes me turn in alarm and I make an attempt to catch it before it shatters on the hardwood floor. It fumbles between my hands for what seems like minutes before finally slipping from my grip and breaking into several pieces. I don't know what to do. Panicked, I bend to pick up the shards of porcelain and wonder how much it'll cost to replace while at the same time trying to process what I've just heard. The door opens and I sense his presence there at the threshold, staring down at me. My hands stop moving as I peer up at him.

"The problem with living alone for so long is that it affords a privacy that's easily overlooked," he says in English. "How much did you hear?"

The even tone of his voice and his level stare make me feel like a kid who just accidentally destroyed a family heirloom. Standing, I place the shards of vase on the display table like an exhibit of deconstructed art. I stare at my hands, ashamed and unsure why. Whatever this secret is, it runs deeper than any trust I could possibly have earned up to this point. He stands back and gestures for me to enter the room. Inside, a man sits at a desk with paperwork spread out in front of him. On the surface he has the appearance of being part of the established boys' club: middle-aged, well-dressed, thinning hairline and a deeply lined face. But I know he doesn't belong here.

"My lawyer," Roul starts by way of introduction, "Thierry Mercier. This is my kin, Connor Lewis."

The man ogles me then shakes his head. Addressing Roul, he continues to speak in French. "He's the spitting image of your son. How could they not know?"

Roul grimaces. "Connor is here from New York on a French language scholarship."

With a meek look of apology, for whatever reason his lawyer switches to English. "Look at me, always putting my foot in my mouth. You should have killed me when you had a chance, my friend."

"Is there anything further we need to discuss?" Roul asks.

Thierry smiles despite himself and rises, patting down

his pockets until he finds what he's searching for, a gold pen. He holds it out to his client.

"Sign here."

With an efficient flourish, Roul adds his signature to the document then watches as his lawyer packs up. Thierry pats him on the shoulder like an old friend.

"*Santé*," he says. *To your health.*

On his way out he takes one last look at me, shakes his head again and leaves. No sooner has he shown himself out than I begin my line of interrogation.

"He was human," I observe.

"Yes."

"Your lawyer is human and he knows we exist."

"If perception were measured in stating the obvious, you'd be quite masterful at it."

"How about a little help here filling in the blanks?"

"I saved his life. You'll find that's a surefire method for securing someone's loyalty. In Thierry's case it was a disease of the heart."

I wonder how many other fatal diseases he's cured through drugs developed from werewolf biochemistry. Of course, Fenrir Pharmaceuticals doesn't work purely for the greater good of mankind, and it isn't exactly a charitable organization. A shortlist of wealthy clientele is enough to keep his business profitable, and, more importantly, anonymous. Tracing back medicines to our DNA isn't exactly in the best interest of the pack. But I guess the desperate don't ask many questions.

"You should never have been privy to that conversation."

"I'm sorry," I start half-heartedly, "but it seems to me there have been a lot of things that I never should have been a part of. For the record, I thought you were talking about me. What I'm confused about is what Arden has to do with your will. You told me his father died four hundred years ago."

Roul slips his hands into his pockets again. It seems to be a nervous tic of his. A tell. A clever one at that because it gives him an air of nonchalance when in reality he's deep in thought, considering the words he has to say next in order to slip out of the snare before it tightens. The words that I heard suddenly become an event horizon as I piece together their meaning, pulling me into a black hole that I can't escape. He *was* talking about me in a way.

"Thierry said I look like your son," I speak as a realization dawns on me. "Arden's your son, isn't he? And that means he's related to me too."

His voice is low, almost a whisper, when he tells me, "He can't know."

There's only one good response I can come up with on the fly. "Why?"

"I made an oath that he'd never know. When I gave him up, I relinquished our blood ties. Besides which, the pack — everything we are, everything we stand for — is all that he's ever known."

"He's not a wolf anymore," I remind him flatly. "And he's as good as dead to the pack."

I think back to Arden lying prone on the hospital bed in

the hours after the wolf in him was forcibly removed, and consider our stark reversal of fortunes. Me thrust into the realm of wolves, him into a human life. Turns out we were both hybrids from both worlds all along, only he doesn't know the whole picture and if Roul has anything to say about it, he never will.

"The least you can do is—"

"Destroy him?" Roul cuts me off. "Is that what you would have me do?"

"Hyperbole much?" I channel Madison's snark for a second but it doesn't pay off.

"Arden has fought tooth and claw against our integration into human society," he says. "Having the wolf removed is one thing, but knowing he was half-human all along? How would that not destroy everything he has left to hold on to?"

"I thought there were rules in place about being with humans. How did you get away with it? With his mother? Your soul mate."

"It happened long before the Hounds came to power," he says. "It was a time when we were at war with humans. She wasn't my mate."

I don't know why but my heart sinks. "Arden told me werewolves mate for life."

"I was orphaned as an infant," he tells me, speaking slowly to draw out the memory. "A human army slaughtered my pack and the general took me as a prize, a pet for his young daughter. I grew up among humans. It wasn't until I was about your age when I broke free and returned to pack life. Loneliness impoverishes a child. Even though I knew how perilous it was to reveal my secret, I was desperate for true companionship when I shifted for the first time for the girl. It was like a game at the start, hide-and-seek in my own skin. As young as we were, we both knew the risks of being found out. Not only had I seen first-hand the decimation of my pack, but the general would regale his daughter with tales of conquest when he returned from war. We both understood how fear of the unknown wrought death and carnage in the adult world.

"In my private human moments with the girl I learned their language. We grew up together, entirely too fast, as playmates and fast friends. A kiss would change everything. It was foolish to think it would last. I had no place among humans. In any case, when the general discovered the pregnancy she was sent away to live with relatives until the birth. Imagine living almost your entire life knowing only the adoration of a single person, then having that taken away. It was an impossible situation. I went mad with rage, broke free, sought her out."

He leans back against the desktop, taking a moment as I absorb all the little details. What happened all those centuries ago between Roul and this girl resulted eventually in me and the cure. Was it all just the outcome of a one-night stand?

"Wolves typically have multiple whelps in a litter," he continues. "While such a thing is an anomaly in humans, twins are not so uncommon. One of the babies was taken by a family member to be raised as their own son, but as was the custom in the day with unwanted infants, the other was left at the edge of the city to die. One child lived and died as a human to carry on my bloodline in you, the other left to perish from the elements. I may have been young and foolish but I couldn't allow that. Yet I knew nothing about being a father. I hardly knew what it was to be a wolf. It's no small miracle that he survived that month with me as his caregiver. I found the first pack that would accept us and I made a bargain with their leader to share everything I knew about their human enemies. To ensure my loyalty to them, they demanded I give up my son and relinquish all ties to him so he could be raised by the pack. It was all a gamble but after the alpha female nursed him, he shifted for the first time and I knew I'd done right by him. All Arden has of me is the name that I gave him."

I'm struck by the irony. "A month ago you left him to die out in the woods as a human."

"It was no easy decision."

"Would you have done the same to me?"

He glares at me. "What does he know about leading a human life? Now that the Hounds govern us, everything has become infinitely more complicated. First and foremost: I made an oath. When our pack leader died, he took this secret with him to his grave. I will not dishonor him. I will not renege on my promise."

I run my hands through my hair. "When you brought me here under false pretenses of a scholarship — this isn't supposed to be my life either."

"You have centuries ahead of you to come to terms with

your lot in life. Arden will grow old and die in the blink of an eye. How would you have him spend those last moments? I would not burden him with the truth, knowing it will only amount to chaining him to his past."

The doorbell rings and puts an abrupt end to the conversation before I can ask him anything further about what I overheard with his estate lawyer. Roul pushes off from the desk and walks toward the door to head downstairs.

"That would be the prosecutor," he says as he moves past me. "Please fix your hair."

I do as I'm told then put on a neutral expression and slip my hands into my pockets, prepared to play their game the way Roul taught me.

F. TESTIFY

Testify: *verb.* To make a statement based on personal knowledge or belief; bear witness.

Josh showed me the secret passageway to try and cheer me up the last time we were here. It was after my wounds had healed over and ideas of self-harm were fuzzy in my head, mostly because I was doped on anti-anxiety meds that left me confused and disoriented. There are stretches of days that I don't remember at all, but it's probably better that way.

The entrance isn't hard to find again, in the library where I spent most of my time whenever I was allowed out of my room. It's nothing fancy. No revolving bookcase that gets activated by pulling on a special book or statue like on *Scooby-Doo*. Just a cutaway in the brick that opens and closes like a regular door if you know that's what you're looking for. It's hidden away in the back recesses of the library where nobody goes.

That first time we didn't explore very far. I held his hand in the dark as he led us by flashlight away from prying eyes. We sat in this very alcove, tucked away together. A little hidey-hole in the middle of the giant castle. We were like tiny mice that had found a place that felt just our size. I remember laughing at something he said and it echoed down the long unlit corridor, carried away like my laughter had wings. That feels like a long time ago.

Now I sit in the same spot, alone with a pink glow stick as my only source of light. I pull the file folder from my rucksack and just stare at the red 'classified' stamp on the manila surface. Trajan leaked the damning information for a price, the way he said he would. I've been wracking my brain trying to decide how much I'm going to say to the prosecutor. Just enough information to make things right but I'm stuck on figuring out how much that is.

Time is running out. The trial is well underway and the prosecution will wrap up tomorrow after questioning Connor and the true-born. I need to decide fast what to say. Boguet can't walk away, I know that much. But he's not the only one who's been up to no good.

Voices travel down the corridor. Quickly, I stash the glow stick into my rucksack with the file folder on top. I don't know why I thought this place was safe. Maybe I can still get out of here before they see me. I peer out of the alcove and see the figures lit in torchlight walking toward me: Breber and Severine with someone trailing behind them.

I squeeze as far back into the alcove as possible.

"...dangers in hybridization," Breber finishes a thought.

"Henri Boguet saw a useful purpose for his DNA," Severine argues. "One that benefits us all."

Everything I know about the Luparii I learned from Josh. They're the werewolf hunters, the heroes in some books. Not in ours though.

He scoffs. "We do not entirely approve of these scientific methods. If you are not careful, you will soon have an uprising on your hands. The wolf does not make the beast. Boguet does not seem to understand this undertaking of his puts us in danger of all-out war with the true-born."

"What would you suggest?" Severine asks.

"Far be it for me to advise you. I am but a humble servant at your disposal."

Their footsteps halt as Breber stops to bring a point home.

"Perhaps," he starts slowly, "you might allow Heaven's Hand to consider ... enacting a form of martial law."

The way that he suggests it sounds as though he just asked if she wanted cream in her coffee.

Silence.

"Purely as a precaution," he continues, "in order to prevent unnecessary bloodshed."

"You wish to assert total control," she says flatly. "I could see some advantage in that. But it's an extreme measure. It would require an extreme circumstance to justify it."

"So it must be," he says and there's a smug tone in his voice. "Daniel here has seen first-hand the unpredictable behavior of this hybrid, Connor Lewis."

That grabs my full attention.

"Is this true?" Severine asks, presumably of Daniel, who must be the one trailing behind them.

"Yes," Daniel says, sounding meek for once in his life.

My heart pumps anxiety throughout my entire body. He's obviously lying. How badly do I want to strangle him right now!

Breber takes up the story. "Last night, the poor child was attacked by Connor Lewis. It was utterly unprovoked. I found them in the courtyard just in time. The hybrid had Daniel pinned to the ground, his teeth fixed around his neck. Had I been even a few moments later, only God above knows what might have happened."

"Unfortunate, but hardly enough to enact a state of emergency," Severine argues.

"Of course not," he agrees. "However, if the hybrid exhibited such a level of disdain for our hard-won judiciary system by, say, unleashing the wolf in court tomorrow ... to create such danger in the presence of humans would be injurious. Daniel worries that his presence may cause such an upset."

"If such a thing were to occur, yes, we would support your bid for martial law," she agrees with a thoughtful pause. "Are you prepared to wield such power, Breber?"

"As I have said, I am but a humble servant."

Light floods into the passageway as they push open another door and I stay very still to avoid being seen. Then with a thud I'm left alone in the dark.

My decision about the trial just got easier.

13. OLD DEVILS

The prosecutor is an older man who's average-looking in every way: short gray hair, average height and build, and a face that could easily be lost in a crowd. He introduces himself, somewhat fittingly, as Mister Smith as he unlocks a briefcase and sets up at a coffee table. Even here, I get a sense that the Hounds have home field advantage. It's their game, their rules. Even though this trial isn't about us I have a sense that somehow we're the ones with everything to lose. Smith is all business and gets right down to brass tacks while Roul observes silently from an armchair by a large stained-glass window that filters colored light onto his tan skin. I take a seat by the table while the prosecutor opens a file and places a digital recorder between us. Mister Smith explains, in his posh British accent, what I should expect in court tomorrow. He tells me that the trial has been ongoing for the past week and the prosecutor's office will rest its case within the next day before the defense team begins their testimony. Justice moves swiftly in these courts. I'm among the last of the witnesses and evidence for the prosecution.

Smith records our conversation as part of my witness

statement. His questions are pretty basic and I'm not really sure what the point of any of them are or why they need to be recorded. He asks about how and when I met Boguet, what happened when I was brought to the biotechnology firm, and that fateful night at Père Lachaise Cemetery. All the while, Roul takes my testimony in stride, shifting in his seat only once when I get to the part about Arden. It's the first time anyone outside the pack has heard my version of what all went down since I moved to Paris. I get no read on the prosecutor at all. As far as I observe he has no tells and offers no reactions to indicate whether or not I'm giving the right answers. After about an hour, I can only assume Mister Smith is satisfied because he stops the recorder, packs up his briefcase and leaves us in peace. Roul shows the man out as I remain seated, mentally reviewing my responses and wondering if I did all right by the pack. After the door shuts, there's a long silence. Roul doesn't move, just keeps his hand on the doorknob, facing away from me. An inordinate amount of time passes in which I become increasingly anxious that I've said something to concern him.

His voice is low when he speaks, eventually. "I failed Arden in the worst possible way."

My version of what unfolded the night that Boguet got his revenge has brought up a kind of guilt in him that I only now understand. The two have always been at odds with each other but I had always attributed Roul's self-reproach to a failure in his pack leadership role. Only now that I understand their true relationship do I know how deep it runs. It was a failure of a father to his son.

"How could you have known about the cure?" is all I can offer. "If you really knew how humans operate, you'd know Boguet was driven by revenge. It's not that complicated."

He shakes his head, facing me finally. "Mistakes like this come at a great price. Four hundred years. That's how long I've protected this pack. One doesn't lead this long without understanding the enemy. There's nothing uncomplicated about revenge."

"That's a pretty decent track record, Roul. Nobody's going to argue that."

"That means very little. Werewolf packs operate on much simpler terms than human societies. This failure will be seen as a great weakness."

He told me once that pack leadership is earned through sheer physical prowess. Anyone with ambition and a bit of muscle could challenge him. It'd be a brave or incredibly fearless soul who tried. Underneath the designer labels and custom tailored suits is the body of a fierce warrior. He's physically more robust than even the fittest human and covered in battle scars, which is a strong indication to me that he's seen more than his fair share of challenges. In his youth, Arden tried to best him once and failed. I wouldn't doubt that Roul has been unchallenged since then. From across the room he approaches me. Hands in pockets, he has that casual air about him that puts me at ease. I sit back in the chair.

Then he asks, "Did Arden teach you how to fight?"

I perk up. "Let's just be clear here. If you think I have the ambition to take you on, you're mistaken."

"It was a yes or no question."

I swallow nervously. "Yeah."

"This is going to get worse before it gets better."

When I suddenly rise to my feet, he stops in his tracks, surprised.

"Do you still trust me?"

"Until you give me a reason not to," I reply cautiously.

"What Boguet has planned, it affects us all: born and bitten alike," he explains. "The life of the pack has always been governed by fight or flight. And in this particular scenario, I'm looking for fighters."

I'm on edge at the thought of it. Until recently I've barely been in a fight my entire life. Rubbing the back of my head, I tell him sheepishly, "My two weeks of bare-knuckle boxing lessons aren't exactly a match for the Armageddon that Boguet claims he's about to unleash."

He smiles faintly. "I'll watch your back. Of that you can be assured."

Taking a step back he turns toward the staircase.

"He doesn't hold it against you," I blurt.

Without a word he glances quizzically back at me.

"Arden. Not that he said. I just ... I know he doesn't."

He merely nods. "I'm going out for a run. You should join me."

By the way he says it, I know it isn't a request. We head to our respective suites to change yet again. I'm eager to burn off some of this nervous energy after days of being cooped up in cars and cells, but also just to get back into more comfortable clothes. The wolf inside of me craves the run now.

Exiting the rented house, we immediately head away from the festively decorated cobblestone streets of Quedlinburg toward the outer edge of town. The temperature is hovering around freezing but the physical exertion makes me almost impervious to the cold. Roul leads us through the barren countryside where the fields were plowed in the fall and frost is the only crop visible for miles around. Despite his physical advantage, as we head up into the Harz Mountains I somehow manage to keep pace with him. Being out here clears my mind and the silence between us is comfortable. After about an hour, we crest the top of a hill and take a break by a gnarled and wind-blown tree. My heart races and my breath pours out of me in white clouds as I pause to take in the scenery below. Wide swaths of farmland spotted with the occasional house cut through thick evergreen forests. An unusual rock formation juts out like a natural barrier of sorts. It looks almost man-made, like the crumbling wall of an ancient fortification. Whatever it is, an eerie sensation crawls over my skin at the sight of it. Roul follows my gaze.

"*Teufelsmauer*," he says in a perfect German accent. "The Devil's Wall."

My mouth quivers at a grin. "You're making this up."

"Most certainly not. A number of *Grimms' Fairy Tales* reference this place. The wall is supposedly the remnants of the Devil's lost wager against God."

I shake my head in disbelief. Our place in Hell, the Devil's Wall. Either the cold is starting to affect me or this place is starting to give me the creeps because I shudder noticeably. As if to emphasize the theatrics of the moment, snow begins to fall. Tiny flakes float down upon us while dark clouds gather above.

"Can Arden really survive these mountains in this weather?"

"If he wants to, yes."

So it's crossed his mind too — the idea that Arden might decide to leave this world on his own terms. Then it dawns on me that he's not actually alone anymore.

"What happens if the Hounds find out about him and Amara?"

"As a human, he's no longer their concern," he starts. "And she won't be for much longer. Besides, I've said my piece to Amara and hold no sway over Arden now. What they choose to do is their own free will."

"Don't they hold you responsible at all?" I ask. "For the actions of your pack?"

"They could," he says dismissively. "The legal term for it is plausible deniability. And you're what's called my alibi."

He must see the confused look on my face because he explains further. "We live in an economy of power. Governments and their leaders rise and fall in due course. You have to pick your battles, and, while lying in wait, subvert the authority of those you oppose so they never become too powerful."

I'm not sure I understand and my mind goes back to Arden and Amara. The two of them have flirted with danger before — taking me in when they were unsure of who I really was, for starters. This act takes their daring to a new level. Not just because it's right under the noses of the Hounds. A bite, even an accidental one like the one that happened to me at La Pleine Lune, could kill him. I say as much to Roul. In response, he merely unzips a pocket of his Gore-Tex jacket and tosses a bright yellow object at me. I don't have to see the label — Boguet Biotechnology — before the color leaves my face.

"Where'd you get this from?"

"I think you know the answer."

Earlier this morning when Boguet spoke about allies, I didn't imagine the pack's included Madison Dallaire. Staring at the cylinder I don't know how I feel about her being mixed up in our affairs. Sometimes I wonder if I even know her at all. Still, I feel a pang of regret for having left the abbey without talking to her again.

"For the record," I start, "I don't think she cares about your well-being or that of the pack."

"She cares well enough about yours."

I glance over at him. "What do you know about that?"

"There were two graves at Vincennes Park that night."

Nodding, I swallow down the memory. Almost choke on it. "She thought she was saving my life."

"In this economy of power, we must often barter in blood."

Roul is banking that Madison's loyalty to me will outweigh any deception on her part. I have to trust that he's a better judge of character than I've ever been. It's his job, after all. Handing back the EpiPen an old thought comes to me.

"I know we're not supposed to talk about this but it's been eating away at me since I found out what I am."

Roul merely waits for me to continue.

"First off, do we have some kind of — I don't know — werewolf-leader confidentiality agreement?"

He laughs softly. "Sure."

After a moment of hesitation, I recite the words that have been floating around my mind for years. "On my first day of kindergarten, I bit a kid. Hard."

"You're wondering if you *cursed* him."

I nod.

"It happens to the best of us, particularly during childhood."

"Did you ever do it?"

"Yes."

"And?"

"Nature has its fail-safes. We age much like canines — accelerated during childhood and adolescence — on par with humans until we reach adulthood, when it slows drastically. With the increase in hormones, our venom is activated. Since your mother is human, you never received the necessary enzymes to develop as one of us. In the absence of those enzymes, all evidence suggests you would have lived and died a human had you not been bitten."

I close my eyes and take in the words, thankful for the small miracles in nature. It's bad enough to be chased my entire life by this memory. If I'd cursed that kid, I don't think I'd ever be able to live down that terrible knowledge. The world from up here looks like a yawning expanse of endless possibilities and my life is microscopic in comparison. Everything that led to this point took centuries to unfold. All the little cells that had to divide, alter and marry together before that one little mutation came about. Namely me.

"That's some kind of messed up irony, isn't it? I wouldn't even be living and breathing, let alone out here if it weren't for you. And if I didn't exist, neither would the cure."

A sad smile crosses his face as he rests a hand against the weathered tree. Do werewolves even understand regret the same way humans do? Arden is really the only one of them who's shown me any kind of genuine emotion, albeit packaged with both incivility and hostility. And now that I know he's part human I wonder if that's where it comes from. Roul grew up among humans. Does he mimic human expressions to appear more relatable? Amara certainly never did. A brisk wind picks up and blows the snow around us and I shiver at the thought of the long return run in these conditions. Turning back is always the worst. It always means there's an end in sight when sometimes I'd like nothing better than to just keep going.

"Are you ready to turn back?" Roul asks.

I shake my head. "The Hounds, how long have they been in power?"

"I first heard reports of them some time around the 1690s but it wasn't until the early 1800s when they organized formally."

"Why then?"

"The story goes — and this is typical of werewolf lore as told by humans — it was a particularly harsh January when the hungry wolves came down from these mountains and into the villages below us."

He pauses for effect as the wind picks up and carries the snow in a swirling motion around us.

"One night in the nearby town of Magdeburg, an infant was stolen straight out of its crib. After that, night upon night children went missing while the villagers slept — or tried to. Eventually the magistrate was called upon to investigate, but even he was unable to solve the disappearances. That is, until a witness appeared late one night, frantic. She led the magistrate to a field where the culprit — a bitten werewolf — was feasting on its prey. He took the creature by surprise and slayed it on sight with barely a struggle. On dying, the bitten revert to their human form. In this case, the magistrate only then discovered that the beast was, in fact, his wife."

"That's … messed up."

He nods, moving back toward the path in order to make our long and quiet run back to Quedlinburg.

"Wait, what does this story have to do with the Hounds?"

"The magistrate was Breber."

14. HANG YOU FROM THE HEAVENS

Needless to say, I sleep terribly. It's bad enough to be on the most-wanted list of a four-hundred-year-old bitten human whose primary occupation is mad scientist. Having my fate in the hands of Breber, a man who's bent on justice at whatever cost, adds yet another unwelcome element into the mix. My imagination doesn't have to stretch very far to torment me with nightmares. At 8:30 in the morning I'm fully alert and staring at the ceiling when the bell tower chime of my phone's alarm goes off. I can hear a clatter of dishware coming from below — probably meaning that Roul ordered in breakfast or is making it himself. The mere thought of food makes me hungry these days so, like a team player, I hop out of bed, shower and put on my new suit — even though I think it makes me look ridiculous. I feel like an imposter.

I find Roul fully dressed in a three-piece suit, reading a newspaper in the sitting room. In front of him is a sizable spread of simple breakfast foods: boiled eggs, milk, cheese, slices of cured meat and a selection of fresh fruits. And, of course, coffee. I pour myself a cup and wrap a block of Gouda in meat then cram it into my mouth without sitting. He glances over at me beyond his newspaper. There's something freakishly normal about all of this, though way out of my league. I can't even begin to imagine how much this house rental cost for the night. Roul goes back to reading *Die Zeit*, a national paper written in German. I wonder how many languages he's fluent in and what other things I might or might not be surprised to find out about him. With his skill set and all the knowledge he's acquired over the course of several centuries, he could easily be a spy if he was ever overthrown and out of work.

"Eat quickly," he says from behind the paper. "We're expected back at the abbey within the hour."

Grinning, I pretty much clear all the plates in a matter of minutes. Sometimes Roul has such a paternal way about him that I think it's a pity he never knew his offspring. Then again, he has a whole pack to look after now. In some ways, they must be like grown kids who just never leave the nest, or den as the case may be. His role as patriarch is to ensure their well-being and is foremost on his mind at all times. I can't even begin to imagine how exhausting that must be. Before we leave he hands me a gun and holster that he insists on fitting under my suit jacket. He won't even hear my protests. The idea of wearing a gun into a courthouse is absurd but it doesn't faze him. I guess werewolves have other means of security. In the end, I wear the piece. If the Hounds take it from me, I have to believe Roul knows what he's doing in arming me in the first place. As we leave Hell and head to the trial, the holster rubs at my ribs as a constant reminder of its presence. A group of kids play on the hillside ahead of us with raucous abandon. When they see us walking up the slope toward them they stop, one by one, eyes wide and staring. I can only guess they're frightened of Roul and his fierce tattoo. Their staring makes me feel uncomfortable, almost naked, as we continue our progress toward them. I clumsily try to calm them by saying one of the few phrases I know in German, "*Guten tag.*"

It only makes them huddle closer together.

"They won't come near us."

I glance over at Roul by my side.

"Do they know?" I ask, looking back at the children. "What we are, that is."

He shakes his head. "It will have been a long time since a human was bitten around here but they see enough to know they ought to stay away."

"What do you mean?"

"The newly bitten are brought here to be rehabilitated by the Hounds."

I think about the locks on the outside of the dormitory doors, about Madison's resistance to sleeping alone in that cell. The claw marks on the back of the wooden door, the sparse furniture, the sealed-off window — it all makes sense now. There's nothing in those rooms that can be used for self-harm. Not quite imprisoned per se, but according to Boguet the bitten are not of their right mind at the start. It takes time to adjust. Madison said she loathes this place. Josh must have been here at some point with his father too but he doesn't have the same misgivings.

Roul barks, startling me and sending the kids screaming

down the slope. Before we walk through the arch that leads into the courtyard he appraises me. My hair is ever-unruly but I did my best to at least make it look somewhat stylish by emulating Arden, though I'll never admit it. He reaches up, I think to fix my tie, but clasps the leather braid around my neck instead. The expression on his face is hard to read.

I start to explain. "It's for—"

"Yes, I know," he tells me. "Your tie will have to do for today."

Obligingly, I tuck the braid beneath my shirt collar and follow Roul across the courtyard toward the abbey. We're met outside the entrance by two very large pack werewolves, a man and woman who look like they were born to fight. They're dressed like they're part of a security detail the way I've seen in movies, covering some dignitary. It dawns on me that Roul would be that dignitary. The duo moves into action when they spot us, on high alert as we enter and move through the abbey. The halls are busier than they have been. It's not just with white-robed monks and nuns. Today, there is also a mix of civilians and uniformed guards, bitten humans and most obviously the Luparii. There are at least a half dozen of them, marked with the white armband of the untouchable. I catch sight of Arden in the crowd, forced also to wear the gold-embroidered band to mark him as no longer one of us. He's too far away to speak to but I can see that he's unshaven, unkempt and dressed in the same clothes he was wearing yesterday, which is all completely uncharacteristic of him. I get a sense that he's done it out of spite for the Hounds. The trial is taking place in a wing of the abbey that was converted into courtrooms. As expected there are no metal detectors like I assume there would be at a regular courthouse, and nobody seems concerned when Roul makes it obvious he's carrying heat by flashing open his jacket to take out a pen from an inner pocket. He hands it to me and I clue in, making a show of my own weapon as I pocket the pen. He wants them to know we're armed. Like Madison said, we're the most dangerous weapons here — the loaded guns waiting to go off unexpectedly.

"Well, if it isn't freak show," a voice says and I don't have to turn around to know it's Boguet's henchman Trajan.

I smooth my tie anxiously as I turn to face him but his expression doesn't hold the maliciousness I've grown accustomed to seeing from him. He's dressed for trial, no doubt here to testify on Boguet's behalf as one of his employees. Before I can even think of something to say as a comeback, Roul urges me on into the courtroom. He might not remember Trajan from our last encounter. Roul was too busy holding me back from trying to tear Trajan and Attila into pieces. Months have passed since then and at that time I was still unaware of the wolf that lurked within me. I guess a street fight with two thugs might not register as a big deal to a pack leader who has seen countless numbers of battles, but Trajan's presence here makes me nervous.

Roul takes a seat on one of the long wooden pew-style benches at the very back of the court near the exit and I claim my place beside him. The bodyguards hover nearby, scanning the room and assessing the dozen or so threats. Amara walks toward us, as breathtaking as ever. Her long black hair is done in a loose side braid. Shimmying past Roul she takes the seat next to me and accidentally brushes up against me in the process. Even knowing what I know the contact makes my entire body inadvertently tense up, but I try to ignore it. I wish we were given the time to talk things through. She's as good as dead and I'm intricately tied to her end. We're the only born werewolves here and everyone knows it. What's more is that the Hounds make an effort to emphasize it. The bitten leave the space around us vacant like we're a nuclear warhead that has the potential to irradiate all life within a certain radius. The Luparii are treated no differently. The woman with the Cleopatra haircut from Boguet's cell leads the group into the courtroom. They're given a wide berth as they take their place in the front row, directly behind the prosecution team. Boguet is seated in what looks like a wooden penalty box before the judge's bench. He's dressed in a tweed suit with elbow patches, deceptively looking ever like a harmless old grandfather. All the attorneys wear simple black robes and flank Boguet: prosecution on the right and defense on the left.

As the clock approaches the top of the hour, the rest of the crowd begin to take their seats. I'm not sure if they each have a role to play in the trial or are just spectators hoping to catch a glimpse of history in the making. Arden strolls into the room with the last of the stragglers. He stops right at the edge of our bench and angles his head toward our line of seats. His amber eyes take us in one by one. First Roul, then me, and finally Amara, who he holds in his gaze for just a fragment too long. Whatever bond ties these two together, I get a sense that it won't be broken even after one of them has departed from this Earth.

With nowhere else to go, Arden sits directly in front of me in the dead zone that no one else is willing to occupy. His hair is a mess and the tag of his sweater sticks up at the nape of his neck. I scan the room for other faces that I know. There's no sign of Madison yet, which strikes me as odd, but I do see Josh and the monk from the hostel in Paris. Brother Christopher, the one with the scarred face. It strikes my mind that, with exception to the Luparii, every single person in the room must be disfigured in some way. Even Josh, next to him, with his college-brochure good looks has vicious scars running somewhere across his flesh. Daniel sits on his other side and wears his collar up to hide the evidence of what happened to him. My nerves tingle at the sight of him. It's probable that most of the people here were bitten by one of their own. Maybe even someone they knew or loved. I look down at the small scar on my hand and then over to Amara, who put it there. Without thinking about it I tug at the smooth sleeve of my expensive dress shirt in order to hide the scar from sight. I've never heard of the Brioni label on the tag on the inside of my suit, but if we're going to be judged at least we're doing it in style, even if I feel like a fraud.

The whole time I scan the room there's really only one person that I'm searching for and she's still nowhere to be seen. I'm a little anxious about talking to her again, but that can wait a little while longer. My eyes return to the back of Arden's head. Seeing the tag sticking out of the collar of his sweater makes my own neck itch in solidarity. I can't handle it anymore and reach out to tuck it in, not thinking. Roul and Amara, instantly and in unison, grab my forearm and hand respectively. I freeze. Untouchable. That's how easy it is to lose an appendage around here. I feel their eyes on me and penitently withdraw without meeting either of their gazes. No more acting without thinking first. A bailiff enters through a door at the back of the room by the judge's bench. He's dressed in a white military-style uniform with black slacks and has a gun in a hip holster like the rest of the guards.

"All rise," he commands and everyone complies. "Oyez! Oyez! Oyez! All persons having business before the Honorable Judge Breber in the High Court of Magdeburg are to draw near and give their attention, for the Court is now sitting. God save Heaven's Hand and this Honorable Court."

For whatever reason I didn't expect this court to be so formal. Breber enters through a separate door on the same side of the room. His long judge's robe is black velvet and he wears a white silk cravat to distinguish himself from the attorneys.

Leaning over to Roul, I discreetly ask, "How is it fair that the leader of the Hounds is overseeing all of this?"

Staring straight ahead he whispers, "As I said before: judge, jury and executioner."

"You may be seated," Breber says.

The trial is not like anything on TV, where the lawyers make snappy remarks and finally trick the criminal into breaking down into a confession on the stand. It's exponentially *much* more boring than that. We sit through hours of questioning and exhibiting of evidence, all in English. Roul takes particular interest when the prosecutor calls an expert witness to explain the science behind my DNA and the cure that Boguet developed as a result. I expect to just sit through it all, having heard the explanation from Boadicea once before already but the scientist that's called up is Trajan. I sit up straight, confused. Did he flip sides? Or is he up there against his will? I listen as he explains how Neanderthals evolved into modern werewolf by surviving a viral outbreak that was passed on through domesticated wolves. He goes on to say Neanderthal interbreeding with early humans resulted in a tiny fragment of the Eurasian population carrying traces of Neanderthal DNA, and that without these markers exposure to the werewolf venom through a bite rapidly destroys the human on a genetic level. All stuff I've heard before. I'm more surprised by how eloquently he explains it. I thought he was just a hired thug.

"In born werewolves the marker acts like a railroad switch between each form: wolf or not wolf," he says. I notice he's very careful never to use the word human when talking about the pack werewolves. "Wolf's Bane was created by Boguet Biotechnology to permanently turn off the switch. When introduced to the subject, the marker is deactivated — the wolf decommissioned — thereby allowing a human to return back to before she or he was bitten. As a result, with the Neanderthal DNA essentially removed, a werewolf bite would be fatal in the absence of an antivenin."

Just like in Arden's case. Even though he's a hybrid like

me, the cure switched off the wolf in him permanently. Talk of returning to a wholly human form causes a rush of chatter throughout the courtroom. Despite my reservations about trusting the Hounds and their heavy-handedness, they have worked hard to give survivors a purpose and integrate them into their new reality. These are all real people who once had different lives and some who don't want this new one. The cure will be openly welcomed by many of them. I can see it in the faces around the room. They haven't seen the effect on the life of someone born into this reality. If they only consider their own personal benefit from the cure, it could lead to Wolf's Bane, as Boguet is calling it, being used for the wrong ends and wiping out an entire species.

Breber bangs his gavel. "Order."

He has to do so a few more times before the noise of the spectators subsides. It was naive of me to think this trial could only go one way. In this court of the bitten, Boguet could easily come out of this as the shining white knight of the story for them. What does that make us? The slain beasts, the hunted and cut down animals as depicted in the tapestries downstairs. I can see now why Roul chose to sit near the exit. Mister Smith calls my name and my heart skips a beat. It's my turn to take the stand. All eyes look to me as I rise. I feel like a freak of nature — which, according to science and Trajan, I am. Somehow my feet numbly carry me forward until I'm sitting in the witness box facing the crowd, Breber to my right and Boguet in front of me. I still don't understand the point of my testimony. The prosecutor has me go through all the questions that I answered for him yesterday at the house rental. He establishes my genetic relationship to Rodolfus de Aquila, that I was taken to Boguet Biotechnology against my will and finally that my DNA was used to formulate the cure.

"At this time, Your Honor, I would move to introduce the Hounds of God's exhibit number 23 into evidence. A test which proves conclusively that Wolf's Bane was derived from the DNA of Mister Lewis."

Breber looks to Boguet's lawyer, a dour-looking young man. "Any objections, counselor?"

"No, Your Honor."

"Exhibit 23 is hereby moved into evidence."

I don't have time to think before we're on to more questions about the events that led to Boguet's capture. I tell my version of what happened at the cemetery that night, omitting the part about Madison and Boadicea, and jumping straight to the ambush when Arden was bitten by Boguet. My testimony ends there because it's all that I can remember. The memory of finding Arden in Vincennes Park near the wolf exhibit is one that still resonates quite clearly. I skip the part about him asking me to kill him, hoping it might garner him sympathy. The defense declines to question me. And that's it. As I step down from the stand, all faces in the room gawking at me. I feel like I'm on display. People whisper as I pass. Even as I take my seat back next to Roul, some eyes linger on me.

I try my level best to ignore them. It's Arden's turn to testify. Our fates aren't dissimilar, although reversed. His werewolf marker was deactivated, the wolf no longer accessible. Unlike mine, Arden's answers are, not surprisingly, curt and to the point. The questions start off pretty innocuously: name, relation to the pack, etc. Eventually he's led to the point where he has to discuss what happened to him at Vincennes Park.

"I woke," he says gruffly, "buried alive by the Hounds."

He casts a glance toward the seats occupied by Josh and Brother Christopher.

"What did you do next, Mister LaTène?"

He grimaces. "I dug my way out."

"Which form were you in at the time?"

His amber eyes flash over to the prosecutor, then over to us. "This one. The only one I can ever be."

"Please explain to the court what you mean."

"Boguet bit me." He glares at Boguet and almost spits his next words. "He *cured* me."

There's another commotion throughout courtroom. Breber bangs his gavel again, louder this time. "Order."

A hush falls upon the crowd as cross-examination begins. Our lives are exposed here but it might as well be a movie to the spectators. I'll bet some of them wish there was a concession stand out in the hall. All I want is to leave. The door behind us squeaks open as Madison slips through it and into the courtroom. It takes me a second to recognize her with the new haircut. She's dressed for court in a pink blouse and black skirt, which makes her seem even less like herself. Her arms are wrapped around a file folder that she clings tightly to her chest. The defense attorney begins to address Arden and my eyes return back to the front of the room.

"I have only one question for you," he begins. "Can you tell the court how Henri Boguet came to be bitten?"

"Your laws didn't apply at the time," Arden says, skirting the direct answer. "He killed my father."

"Please answer the question."

Arden huffs and after a pause replies, "I bit him."

There's renewed clamor as Arden is allowed to step down from the witness stand. This is what Boguet was talking about when he said more heads would roll than his. It's not enough that he effectively ended Arden's life, but now Boguet will see to it that he's tried as well for what happened over four hundred years ago. I glance to Roul for reassurance but my eyes slip back to Madison as she rushes to the front of the courtroom to call the attention of Mister Smith. She says something urgently to him over the cacophony, pointing fiercely at the file folder to emphasize her words. What is she up to now? Breber bangs his gavel to regain control of the courtroom.

As the voices subside, Mister Smith says, "Your Honor, new testimony has just come to our attention. We would ask for a brief recess before proceeding."

So she's going to take the stand too. I would actually like to finally hear her side of the story before we speak again. It might go a long way in helping me not dig myself deeper into the pit that is Madison's wrath. Breber looks to the defense attorney like he expects an objection for the last-minute addition but gets none. Instead he instructs the court to take an hour recess. It gets louder as the crowd moves and discusses what they've heard. Roul continues to be unfazed and merely turns to walk out of the courtroom. Unsure of what to do, I get up and follow his security detail. Arden waits outside the doors. As the rest of the crowd pours out of the courtroom a gap is left for the Luparii to move about without any contact. The leader glaces over to me and then over to Daniel, who exchanges a look with her. Something isn't right. I can't help but feel they recognize each other. When the Luparii leader nods at him it gives me a sinking feeling in my gut. Something's up. Something bad, I'm sure of it. My inner wolf senses a trap. I should be far away from here. I pick up my pace to keep on the heels of my pack.

"Hey," Daniel calls out and I know he's talking to me when he hisses, "*Perro.*"

Dog. There are worse things to be called but I'm guessing this tops the list of curse words. I can feel him on my heels. Ignoring him is hard to do and I feel his hand pushing between my shoulder blades, shoving me, egging me on. I try to keep walking but before I know it he deftly slips his foot between mine and I trip over it, falling flat to the floor. Ahead of me, Roul and his entourage stop to turn around, their attention finally drawn to what's going on behind them. My heart pounds, pumping unwanted adrenaline throughout my body and feeding the wolf within who wants to come out. My brain struggles between two states, flashing the images around me like a strobe light. Daniel isn't done. He grins treacherously and I brace myself for a kick to the ribs, all the while trying to take control of the wolf. Instead of pummeling me while I'm down as I expect, he reaches down as though to help me to my feet, making it look like he wasn't the one to trip me up in the first place.

"Are you okay?" he asks loud enough for the bystanders to hear, but as he reaches down he whispers low enough that only I can hear what follows. "I know you're too weak to fight your own battles, but now you have your little bitch testifying too?"

I let out a snarl that isn't quite human and I can feel my control slipping away with anger. Just as the color fades from my vision Daniel is pulled violently away from me by the back of his shirt collar. The surprise of it snaps everything back into focus. He spins around with lightning-flash reflexes to retaliate against my unknown ally, pushing him back slightly with one arm as he does. The look in Arden's eyes as he stumbles back half a step is the look of a man with nothing left to lose and I bet Daniel immediately regrets that shove. A deadly smile crosses Arden's lips. He's just been given all the reason he needs for payback.

"You dare touch me?" he yells, moving to grab onto Daniel's shirt with both fists.

As I rise to my feet I see Daniel has his hands up in surrender, his eyes darting around the circling crowd to see if anyone witnessed him touching the 'untouchable.' Something seems to have snapped in Arden. He shoves the kid back hard against a wall, pinning him there with both hands. Daniel is completely disarmed. Fight back against his attacker and he breaks one of the foremost rules of the Hounds. One with certain and terrible consequences.

Some of the bystanders begin whispering as others looking on in stunned attraction. Even the Luparii watch with bated breath, uncertain of how they should react. Daniel is shaking at this point. Fear gleams in his eyes. The entire corridor hushes with anticipation.

"*This*," Arden says, loud enough for the crowd to hear. "This is how it feels like to be one of *them*."

His voice breaks at the last word as he points to us, the pack.

"You rule in tyranny in a way that only humans are arrogant enough to do," he continues steadily. "But it's my curse now to live as such a monster."

Immobilized, Daniel looks to the crowd for help but Arden won't have it. He grips his chin and forces him to face him.

"What fate do I administer?" Arden snarls. "Do I take a hand? Is that what I'm owed?"

Releasing his grip on Daniel's shirt, he pulls out a switchblade from his pocket and flicks it open between their faces. I edge forward. He's going too far and someone has to stop him. How, though?

"That's what you'd call a fair punishment," he starts calmly, his eyes going to the courtroom door where Breber stands watching in silence, "but I still live by my honor."

Arden draws back, setting Daniel free. The kid scrambles away but he doesn't make it far before the Luparii leader stops him. She grabs his arm, looking between Daniel and the pack, but says nothing. Breber steps toward the crowd.

"There has been no harm done," he says in his even but theatrical voice. "Heaven's Hand does not apply the law so blindly that we cannot see the forest for the trees. We must evolve with the times and find forgiveness in our hearts for the indiscretions of youth."

The Luparii woman grimaces then releases her hold on Daniel.

"How times have changed," Arden growls.

He seems to make a move to leave but veers instead toward Amara, who stares at him with wide eyes.

"But I welcome your change of heart," he says to Breber before wrapping an arm around her waist and pulling her against him for what will go down in my books as the longest, most intimate kiss and public display of affection ever. She keeps her fists clenched to her sides and Breber has no choice but to say nothing. To add insult to injury, he's even forced to move out of their way as they return to their seats in the courtroom to await the outcome of the rest of the trial.

G. VERSCHLIMMBESSERUNG

Verschlimmbesserung: *noun*. Making something worse by trying to make it better.

I feel like puking.

My testimony will change everything, not just in this trial but in whatever history books there are in this messed-up world. Here's where the true power of words comes into play. All those printed letters and numbers in the file folder will mean something at the end of the day. Something that will put Boguet away for a very long time if not see him hang.

Mister Smith explains to me that he expected Boguet's lawyer to object. Usually defense attorneys want to actually see the evidence well in advance so they can know what they're up against and prepare a case. It's called discovery, he tells me, as if I've never watched a law show on TV before.

I sit in a private room listening to Mister Boring yawn on about legal procedure and the questions he'll ask when I hear a commotion out in the hallway. Before long the court is finally called back into session. I take the stand and sit tight. Boguet doesn't know yet that he was betrayed by Boadicea. She handed Connor all his dirty little secrets, from the antivenin right down to the chemical makeup of the cure. With Trajan's help I was able to dig up the more condemning information.

"Miss Dallaire, will you please answer the question?" Breber presses.

"Can you repeat it?" I ask, but there's an edge in my voice that he told me to keep a lid on so I follow up with a saccharine, "Please?"

After like five seconds of brain-stuttering, Mister Smith pulls it together enough to repeat himself. "How did you come into possession of the files in question?"

I explain about Boadicea, skipping the part about shooting her, knowing full well that there's no such thing as immunity from the consequences of what I did. Walking away from it and just plain walking are two totally different things.

The more questions I answer, the more documents are entered into evidence. When I see the Ziploc bag with the spring-loaded auto-injector syringe and little vial filled with the cure, a knot of regret twists in my heart. Trajan gave it to me as more than just a finder's fee and here I am turning it in to a court of law. Even though I knew what it was as soon as he handed the package to me, it was too unreal to process. He said, "*Think of it as your glass slipper, Cinderella.*" As if happily ever after could come so easily.

"Exhibit 26 is hereby moved into evidence."

Mister Smith hands me the document. "Miss Dallaire, can you please describe to the court the contents of this document?"

"It's an email between Henri Boguet and his financial backers," I answer blankly before looking over at Breber to make sure the next punch lands appropriately. "It outlines their intent to weaponize Wolf's Bane against the will of the recipients and with force if necessary."

A murmur rises from the crowd as the words sink into their thick skulls, but they're too enthralled by the show to get carried away.

"Can you please read for the court the name of the other party that has funded this research?"

Before answering, I scan the crowd. All those bitten people sitting on the edges of their seats, waiting to pass judgment. It's what they're good at. Even if Boguet's co-conspirator deserves to be fed to the wolves, it doesn't give me any satisfaction to say the name.

"The Luparii."

A shocked silence follows. Boguet's attorney stands like he's finally going to object. But he doesn't. Following his lead, Severine and the other Luparii rise to stand in a line behind the prosecution. With military precision, they each pull out two guns from inside their blazers and in a matter of seconds they unleash chaos.

It's showdown at high noon. Gunshots ring, a bad memory echoing between my ears. The Heaven's Guard bailiff doesn't know what's hit him before he collapses to the floor. This was not part of my bargain. I need to get the hell out of Dodge before being caught in the crossfire.

My heart pounds so fiercely that it hurts my chest,

thrumming against my breath until I almost suffocate. Then a numbness washes over my hands. I can't breathe. Even though I have a sensation that it's happening, there's nothing my brain can do to stop me from crumpling into the well of the witness stand. Everything fades to black.

15. WRETCHES AND KINGS

Before the first shot is even fired, the pack is on the move. In front of us, Arden agilely leaps across the length of his pew, flipping it and using it as a protective barrier. I see Madison collapse in the witness box and I'm sick with the thought that she might have been shot. The first bullet takes down the bailiff and chaos ensues. I crouch down with Roul and Amara, thinking of a way to get to Madison as the two bodyguards stack our pew up against Arden's, doubling the barrier. Within seconds the room has changed from a civilized court of law to a madhouse of pandemonium filled with writhing agony as the Hounds change as quickly as they can into their more fearsome form.

The humans are armed with two pistols each, but they might as well have brought knives to a gunfight. The Luparii only number about a half dozen but they move with stealthy precision amidst the hulking beasts that surround them. More shots are fired and I'm still reeling from the surprise of it all. Trajan dives toward us and instinctively my hand reaches for my gun but Roul reaches out and pulls him to safety. The animal inside me is fired up at the chaos. As guns are discharged, my inner wolf trembles but the others have stayed in human form, so I fight to do the same. There are screams too, from both the wounded and the attackers. And the air is thick with the smell of fear mixed with blood and a chemical scent that I don't recognize.

Somebody rushes past me, brushing by my shoulder as they charge the exit, and the contact startles me. I pull out my gun, the cool feel of the metal in my hand a very clear reminder of my human form. The two bodyguards transform and with a nod from Roul leap gracefully over our barricade, while at the same time Amara and Arden run headlong around the far side. I have no idea what's going on and can only watch through a slot between the bench backs. I can't see Arden or Amara from this angle but the male bodyguard zeroes in on Boguet, who is now the hulking beast that's haunted my dreams since that night at Père Lachaise Cemetery. The wolf lunges but Boguet catches him in his hideous claws, pulling him close and clamping down on the thick fur of his neck with venomous teeth. Boguet tries to keep a grip, but the wolf seems not to have pain receptors. He merely pushes his paws against the scientist's chest and attempts to shake off the attack even as flesh tears and blood gushes into Boguet's distorted face. Without warning the Cleopatra-haired Luparii leader steps in and calmly unloads two bullets into the bodyguard. It strikes me suddenly that I never asked his name.

Two of the court guards lie obviously dead near the judge's bench but three others who were shot collapse, rolling on the floor and morphing back to their human forms. It's clear that some of these aren't regular bullets. They're using bio-weapons based on Boguet's research. Weaponized cures. Still in human form, Breber jumps up from behind his bench and tries to escape back to his chambers but instead narrowly escapes a bullet that tears into the wood next to his face. He's forced to dodge back down again, trapped behind his bench. As far as I know Madison is still in the witness box next to him. I duck down and try to compose my thoughts amidst the gunfire. She's clear across the other side of the room, near the leader of the Hounds, who is currently target practice for the Luparii. There's no easy path to get to her.

I ready myself to move. In my periphery I see Amara still in human form going head-to-head with Boguet's lawyer. Next to her Arden takes a punch and falls. With only a second's hesitation to make eye contact with me before he does, Roul leaps over the barrier with his gun drawn. A bizarre sequence of events unfolds next that will determine so much more than I can completely comprehend in the heat of the moment. First, Amara spins around instinctively to come to Arden's aid. Clear as still water, I see the gun being raised toward her. Roul shouts at her, catching the Luparii marksman's attention, but there's another Luparii behind the pack leader raising a gun. Arden is back on his feet in an instant, equidistant to Roul and Amara, and with only a fragment of time on his side. As he leaps he catches a bullet in his shoulder but succeeds in pushing Roul out of the line of fire. Amara shifts at the same time that the other Luparii fires. The bullet flies by, nicking the fur of her neckline. Roul rolls into a firing position on the floor and discharges three bullets, taking out the other shooter. They're safe for the moment. It shocks me out of my inaction. Head down, I lunge around the barricade and run along the far right wall of the courtroom toward the front, where more benches have been overturned. Glancing back briefly, I spy Amara now standing protectively over Arden and clasping a hand over his wound. The gold chain with the ring dangles from her neck, almost touching him. The others in our group advance toward the front on the left hand side.

Breber roars ferociously from his judge's stand, which calls full attention back to him. He's clearly not in control of his senses and is filled with the kind of rage that's mostly seen in movies. In werewolf form now he leaps across his bench and into the battle, where the remaining Luparii move in to surround him. Josh and Brother Christopher come to his defense. This gives me the distraction that I need to make my way to Madison. The judge and the monk seem to be able fighters and, guns or not, the humans are no match for them. Boguet, his lawyer and the Luparii leader have disappeared, however, somehow making their escape. They're not my priority right now. I'll leave that to more capable hands. I've almost reached my goal but it appears that Daniel isn't done with me and has decided to use this lull in fighting to make up for his earlier embarrassment. He charges at me, catching me off guard, and I scramble with the gun Roul gave me. Before I can aim it, he swats the weapon to the floor and then swings clumsily at me with his other hand. The brute force of his blow causes me to fly back against the wall and next to a fallen Luparii. As I try to pull myself up into a defensive stance before the next attack, my hand comes up on the Luparii weapon. I pick the gun up and fire at Daniel as he leaps at me. The bullet catches him in the chest. Only instead of a bullet, a little blue tail fin like a tranquilizer dart sticks out of Daniel's torn shirt. We both stare at it and I can see that he's trying to process what just happened before he drops unconscious to the floor and morphs back to his human self.

With a path finally clear to the witness stand, I put what I just did out of my mind and run to find Josh crouched outside of it, just staring in. He hasn't shifted back, but I can see the anguish in his eyes. There's one more gunshot and then the noise within the courtroom slowly subsides as many flee the room in pursuit of Boguet and the others. Or maybe I just tune it all out. I'm too afraid to look and see what Josh sees. What else can I do? Filled with dread, I move past him and turn to peer into the stand. In my heart I was prepared for the worst. But the scenario that ran through my thoughts was much different than the one unfolding in front of me now. Madison is curled up in the corner, eyes squeezed shut and covering her ears with the palms of her hands. She doesn't seem injured in any physical way. Relieved, I step into the stand, bend down and place my hands on her shoulders. Instantly she screams, a soul-crushing screech that causes me to stumble back into the cramped corner across from her. Her eyes open, filled with a mix of surprise and terror as she glances between me and Josh. Tears stream down her face. Behind me, he lets out a sound that has no human equivalent.

Breathless, she holds me in her gaze and her expression softens as fresh tears flow along the tracks of the old ones. I grab her again and pull her close. The instant I do, she completely breaks down and weeps into my chest. The dampness seeps through my dress shirt as her fists clutch at whatever fabric she can get a hold of. All I care about is that she's safe, that she's alive, even if she's barely clinging on to rational thought. It's like the minor panic attack that she had in my apartment kitchen in Paris months ago. And like that time before, I don't say a word while she pulls the fragmented pieces of her world back together. The scars that I saw on her the other night, they run deep. Beneath the surface of her confident exterior is a wall that holds back her innermost fears. From time to time, like tectonic plates, certain triggers cause rifts that allow those fears to break through and rise to the surface. I have no Richter scale for the moments that shake Madison, no way of ebbing the inevitable tide of tears. In a way it's utterly useless for me to be holding her. I can't fix her. It's not for me to do. But she's walked alone along a lonely road for too long. I get that now.

I hear movement around the room again. The others have returned and are checking the dead or helping out the wounded. Outside the witness stand, Josh's presence is obvious. He whispers in a rasp to himself, unintelligible words that are like a chant. Like my leather necklace, I imagine his meditative repetition of words is meant to bring his human self to the surface.

"What happened?" I hear Roul ask.

"I'm afraid Boguet's barrister failed to take the bait," the prosecutor, Mister Smith, answers.

"This was their plan from the start," Roul says. "They had no intention of seeing this trial through to the end."

The voices bring Madison back around. As she gains control of her breath, her grip on me loosens. I resist the instinct to cling to her, and she pulls away, wiping dampness from her face. Her makeup is smudged around her eyes and tear-tracks haphazardly pattern her cheeks. I smile as I realize even dressed up and with this new look of hers — or old one, whatever the case may be — she kept her eyebrow ring and I look down at the four-leaf clover. Never in my life have I wanted to kiss a girl more. The feeling of Madison slipping away surges in me so I lean forward and gently press my lips upon her brow, brushing against the clover. She goes very still and I can count on one hand all the times we've been here before, standing at the precipice of *almost* and staring down into the abyss of *what-if*. It's like she comes more into focus whenever she stops moving. Ever so slowly Madison tilts her face up toward mine. For the briefest of moments I fool myself into thinking I can make the blind leap, but it only takes a second for her eyes to flicker away, to extinguish my chance.

Josh reclaims his human form behind me and his chanted words become clear. "*Mea culpa, mea culpa, mea maxima culpa...*"

Madison turns cold. She rises rigidly to her feet. As I stand up next to her I can see that Josh is in rough shape, slumped now against a wall. His eyes are as sharp as glass cutting through us. From the swelling along his left cheek-bone it looks like he took some blows to the face, whereas I came out completely unscratched. Boguet had said I would live or die by his command, and I wonder how much was pure luck and how much was intended. Madison takes a deep breath beside me. She steps out of the witness stand, walks right past Josh without so much as a second glance in his direction and marches out the doors of the courtroom. He doesn't move a muscle except for his eyes that follow her path as though somehow he can see her contrails. His whole existence revolves around a girl who left his orbit, and he was the one who spun her off her axis. Even if things were different, Josh needs her more than the reverse. And what he's asking for is far more than she has left in her to give.

"That chant," I start to shake him out of it, "what do the words mean?"

Exhausted, he shuts his eyes and leans his head against the wall. There's a lingering rasp in his voice when he speaks. "Through my fault, through my fault, through my most grievous fault."

A prayer for forgiveness for the absolution of sins. He keeps his eyes closed and I know he has no other words for me, so I step down and walk away down a path that's riddled with the injured and the dead to leave him to his misery. Some of the remaining nuns and monks treat the survivors for gunshot wounds amid the clutter of overturned pews, their white robes speckled with blood. Many of those hit with Wolf's Bane are waking up now, in shock, dazed and disoriented. In the middle of it all, Breber stands assessing

the chaos in his black velvet robes like some dog-headed
deity that wrought all this carnage upon them.

I leave this scene and walk out to the hallway, where Roul
and the others form a semi-circle around Arden. He's holding his shirt in his hand and pressing the fabric against his
bleeding wound. Amara's face is creased with worry, a rare
display of emotion for her. He still wears the vambrace on
his forearm to cover his tattoo, but anyone who knows him
at all knows he'll never be anything but a pack werewolf.
When he leapt into battle without a second's hesitation he
was willing to lay down his life for those who had turned
their back on him only a month ago. Now the pack clusters
around him, unsure of how to go about treating his human
injury.

Trajan steps forward from the sidelines and says to
Arden, "Hand me your knife."

The image these words conjure makes me woozy. I'm no
medical expert but I'm fairly certain a lot of things could go
wrong trying to remove a bullet without proper tools and
sterilization. With his free hand, Arden digs into his pants
pocket then tosses his switchblade. Folding out the blade,
Trajan stands by his injured side.

"You're gonna wanna bite down on something."

Arden glares at him as he pulls his bloodied shirt from
the wound. "Just do it."

As the blade goes in, I avert my gaze but not before I see
Arden grit his teeth. Those canines and his snarling face
wrenched in pain are impossibly wolf-like. Madison reap-
pears at the end of the hallway. She's thrown on a sweater

and jeans and washed off her makeup, and I notice she has her rucksack slung over her shoulder as she walks toward us. It's clear that she's leaving this place. Whether it's alone or with us remains to be seen. A roar of anguish echoes throughout the corridor, recapturing my attention. Trajan casually tosses a bloody ball of metal aside and fishes a tube from his blazer pocket. He's about to pour the contents of the bottle into the wound when Arden grabs his wrist.

"It's a chemical hemostat," Trajan explains. "A clotting agent. To stop the bleeding."

Arden glances over at Roul, who nods his approval. After a second of hesitation Arden lets go so Trajan can finish his job. The female bodyguard hands over the shirt of her fallen comrade for him to put on just as Breber emerges from the courtroom behind me.

"Rodolfus de Aquila," Breber says, straightening out his torn silk cravat. "Am I to understand you had foreknowledge of this attack on Heaven's Hand?"

"An educated guess. As I'm sure you're well aware, we've danced with the Luparii before. I knew they were backing Boguet's research into the antivenin and then the cure. It was only a matter of time before they used Wolf's Bane to this end. The Luparii wasn't about to allow you to unceremoniously put an end to their investment in Boguet."

Roul told me the Luparii were dangerous but I had no idea they were this level of dangerous. Bio-weapons or not, they were outnumbered and out-muscled in every way. It was no small miracle that Boguet and the leader got out alive.

"The Hounds have been in bed with the enemy for centuries," Amara adds from Arden's side. "You had every chance to see this betrayal coming."

"They served their purpose," Breber finally says.

"I have no doubt," Roul retorts. "Whatever power you held as magistrate, the deals you made against us and against your own kind, it was only a matter of time before they saw you as you are: a small man with a thirst for power. They used you, and you allowed yourself to be misused."

Roul makes to leave and motions for the pack to follow. It should be so easy.

"Do not think you can walk away," Breber says. "Your pack's well-being still falls under the governance of Heaven's Hand."

There's silence for a moment as tension between them escalates through tiny flexes of muscle and changes in their stances.

"My parting gift to you was saving your life, Breber," Roul answers.

"And for that I extend my personal gratitude and also offer the protection of Heaven's Hand. We still have an entire army at our disposal."

"For how much longer do you suppose that will stand true? Word will spread quickly about the cure. How many among your kind wouldn't trade their lives in for a human one again?"

"We are selfless servants of a higher power," Breber says. "And our work on this Earth is not yet complete. This unpleasantness is but a temporary setback. I can assure you, our allies will be rewarded. And our enemies crushed."

Roul shakes his head. "These are promises I've heard before."

"Don't you trust me?" Breber asks me directly. "Heaven's Hand will bring back justice to the strong, the brave and the free who join us."

Nothing about his words is a comfort to me. It must hold true for Roul also because he again makes to leave. And again he's stopped.

"There is still the matter of who bit Connor Lewis," Breber says, grasping for control. "It is not a question that can go unanswered."

Roul spins around on his heel and takes a forceful step toward Breber, meeting his gaze. "There's a war coming. Enough blood has been spilled for one day. You'll have your fill before this is over."

He doesn't say anything further, just leads us down the corridor toward the staircase and out of this place. Arden is barely conscious through the pain, propped up by Amara and Trajan on either side. Madison lingers momentarily by the courtroom doors, scanning inside, probably looking to either say goodbye to Josh or ask him to come with us. When she sees that he's already gone, she releases the strap of her rucksack on her shoulder and just gives a little wave to the room. Like she's bidding adieu to a life she'll never see again.

H. MEA CULPA

Mea culpa: *exclamation.* Used as an acknowledgment of one's fault or error.

I had no idea what I was going to say to Josh. Everything he's become is so mixed up with the Hounds that I can't know for sure what he really believes anymore. Everybody clings to something to pull them out of the dark, and he went to his faith. I never got that about him. Now that the truth is all out in the open I wanted to give him a way out. At least for a while he'd be safe with the pack. Aquila promised me that much.

What happened in the courtroom, the casualties, that was just skeet shooting for the Luparii. War is coming, like he said, and it's going to get even messier. It's the kind of war that will never hit newspaper headlines.

After hundreds of years of working together, the Hounds and the Luparii have turned on each other. The pack werewolves probably don't stand a chance on their own. Without organization they'll be picked off easily.

All I want is to disappear. And I can now. I've paid my dues to both sides. There's nothing stopping me from leaving right this second. As we step outside into the courtyard, I look out toward the horizon and consider just taking off. While I'm pausing to think about it Connor's hand brushes against mine. I don't know if it's on purpose. I never know with him.

"This is all way too *Sound of Music* for me," I say, abandoning ideas of escape for now.

He shoves his hand into his pants pocket and looks away. A cold wind howls as we head toward the archway out of here. Nobody's talking. It's like we just came back from a funeral. Or are going to one.

"Madison?"

At the sound of my name, I turn. Josh stands outside the abbey doors. It hollows me out to see him like this, devastated.

I don't know why, but I'm suddenly reminded of how long his hair used to be. That brings back memories of running my fingers through the thick locks and getting lost in those sky-blue eyes.

Sometimes we would laugh about the dumbest things until we could barely breathe. And just as we were winding down because we forgot why we were laughing in the first place, we'd look at each other and it would spark a new fit.

I don't remember the last time I heard him laugh. What the sound would even be anymore. I'm not the only one who changed after the accident.

He approaches me the way someone would a stray dog, concerned but cautious. His eyes search mine, looking for some kind of answer. In his expression I can see the hurt. Like I wasn't going to say goodbye. But I was. I did. He just wasn't there to see it.

Josh stops just a few steps away from me. No closer than Connor is to me, but no further away either. I wait for him to say something and can see his brain stuttering the way it does when he's about to deliver bad news.

"I know you don't owe me anything," he starts, trying to keep an even tone.

"Don't—"

"No, Maddy," he continues forcefully. "For once, just let me finish a sentence, alright?"

Pressing my lips sealed, I stare up at him. This moment right here could be the last time we see each other. Maybe I should just suck it up and tell him what he wants to hear so he can be free from the night that destroyed everything. But I know forgiveness doesn't work like magic. I can't just wave a wand and *obliviate* the memory away like some Harry Potter character.

"What I did to you ... I can't let you leave without making things right."

I barely have time to register the movement of his hand before Connor bodychecks me out of the way. Something flashes in the sunlight as Josh stabs downward. My jaw drops but no sound comes out as I hit the cobblestones on my side, my right forearm taking the brunt of the fall. What the hell? He tried to stab me? Josh merely raises his hands in surrender and tries to back away as the pack surrounds him.

Confused, I sit up and watch as Connor pulls something from his chest. Shaking, he drops the weapon onto the path and it breaks into pieces, shattering the once-protected fragile vial like the glass slipper that it was. A syringe. The vial from the evidence bag. Wolf's Bane.

Even though I haven't known Aquila long, I've never seen him lose his cool. He does now for just a second.

"No!" he howls with a ferocious snarl.

I lunge at Josh, punching at his torso and screaming. He just lets me as he stares at Connor in disbelief. It makes me even madder to know I'm not getting through to him. Josh takes hold of my wrists, but his expression changes as his eyes are drawn to something behind me. The body language of the entire pack alters also as they edge forward. Pulling myself out of Josh's grip, I spin around and gape in disbelief.

Where Connor was standing a second before is now a wolf wearing a suit.

Literally.

Deliriously, I laugh at the spectacle of it.

Then Connor switches back, just like that. Head bowed, he casts a wolfish grin as he peers at me with warm brown eyes. He never ceases to surprise me.

"No freaking way." Trajan murmurs what all of us are thinking.

Roul glances over at him before turning away and putting a hand on Connor's shoulder. It's like the universe just exhaled a sigh of relief.

"You just wasted your way out of this mess," I tell

Josh.

"I didn't want you to have to live this life anymore. I had to make it right."

"You're too late."

"What do you mean?"

I hadn't planned on saying anything until the time was right, but Josh just forced me to push ahead the publication date on this information. "Connor bit me too."

"What are you talking about?" Josh asks, clenching his fists.

"I did not," Connor pipes up.

"At Fontainebleau."

"That was barely a nick," he insists.

"It was enough."

The way Josh straightens up, it's like he's preparing for a physical blow. "Enough to do what?"

I can't look either of them in the eye. "To heal me."

"You mean to cure you?" Josh asks.

"Not in the way that you think," I say, shaking my head. "His bite ... it changed me ... I'm not like you anymore. Watch."

Painlessly and effortlessly, like Connor did a moment ago, I shift into my new wolf form.

16. THE ONLY HOPE FOR ME IS YOU

"You son of a bitch!"

I try to wrap my head around this revelation as Josh punches me in the jaw. Madison switched back from a pretty brown wolf to human in just seconds. My head reels as much from the punch as from the discovery. How could that tiny bite amount to so much? Is there *nothing* normal about me? Regardless, this news could change everything. If Boguet could create a cure and weaponize it, maybe Roul has the resources at his pharmaceutical company to engineer the reverse. Or at least find a way of reproducing my venom. There's too much to process and as I stumble back from the surprise attack, a stinging ache rings across my teeth. Before the fight can escalate any further Roul intervenes to keep us apart. I work to calm myself. Josh is livid and I'm concerned he'll transform again. Or I will. Madison acts quickly, grabbing a hold of his clenched hand and speaking in a language I don't understand until the very end.

"*Confiteor Deo omnipotenti et vobis, fratres / quia peccavi nimis cogitatione, verbo, opere et omissione: / mea culpa, mea culpa, mea maxima culpa.*"

Although I'm sure he's said and heard the words many times before since being bitten, the shock of the chant coming from her lips is clear on his face. As he relaxes, there's something deeply melancholic about Josh as he stands in this ancient courtyard. His poise reminds me of the way an archangel would be depicted in a Renaissance painting in the moments before dispatching a beast. And I suppose that's fitting given the inevitable direction this conversation has to take.

"One hour," he says. "That's all I owe you before I let them know."

From behind him, Arden exchanges a glance with Amara. A single nod is all it would take to communicate an end to Josh as a threat. I see the chain of events unfolding in my head: Amara leaping from Arden's side, pulling the hair on back of Josh's head with one hand, reaching around to grab his jaw and snapping his neck.

"No!" I order.

Only then realizing the danger he's in, Josh spins around. Madison is equally afraid. Whatever her feelings for him, this is not what any of us bargained for: friends turning on each other, allies becoming enemies.

Roul shakes his head. "An hour it is."

He moves posthaste, the pack following suit and breaking away from Josh. Only Madison lingers by his side. For the first time since we met she seems unsure of what to say or do next. From afar I watch the scene unfold between them as he tenderly cups her cheek in the palm of his hand. He leans in to whisper something to her. Maybe a final plea to stay, or maybe just goodbye. I turn away and run on the heels of my pack. Stay or go, the decision is hers, and I don't look back, too afraid of what I might see. Nothing good ever comes of looking back. She said so herself. Eventually I hear her footfalls behind me, racing along the cobblestone path. When she reaches my side, Madison slips her hand into mine and keeps pace with me.

We catch up to the others as Roul talks strategy. We're going to part ways in three groups. Each party will take different modes of transportation back to Paris in order to mitigate losses should anything happen along the way. Arden and Amara will lie low, traveling through the mountains. With a little help from one of Roul's wonder drugs, Arden will be healed and at full speed within a couple of days. Trajan and the surviving bodyguard plan to drive to the Frankfurt office of Fenrir Pharmaceuticals, where he'll conduct more research based on what he's just learned about my freak DNA. There's enough security there to keep him safe for now. Roul and I will return to Paris right away to warn our allies before it's too late.

Madison folds her arms across her chest. "And where exactly does that leave me?"

"You're free to do as you choose," Roul says. "That boy won't turn on you."

"In case you forgot, I'm one of you now."

"You don't want that," he answers. "Go with Trajan. He can reproduce Wolf's Bane for you back at Fenrir."

"Not an option," she says flatly, staring at Trajan.

"Out with it," Roul orders. "We haven't much time."

"Alright, well," Trajan stammers. "We now know that the effects of the cure developed from Connor's DNA at Boguet Biotech are permanent." He pauses to glance over at Arden. "The cure has no effect on Connor. Generations of passing along the gene seems to have integrated the marker more smoothly into his DNA. It can't be isolated or switched off. Now that Connor's a werewolf he has his own unique brand of venom. When he bit Madison it changed her old Neanderthal marker and rewrote it like a software update. In theory, Madison might not be curable."

"Connor bit me too," Arden interjects. "It almost killed me."

"You had already been cured," Trajan explains without hesitation. "Your Neanderthal marker was already switched off, permanently, before he bit you."

My mind tries to keep up. Madison can't be cured because of my bite. I've done the same to her as Josh did. At the same time, maybe if I'd bitten Arden before the fight in the cemetery he might still be a wolf. I don't even know where to start feeling guilty. Another thought occurs to me. If his theory holds up, I could potentially create other werewolves who can't be cured. It makes me downright anxious.

"Who else knows about this?" I break in. "The Hounds? The Luparii? Are they both going to come after me?"

"As far as I know, only Boguet," Trajan answers. "Maybe the Luparii, depending on how much he shared with them. For now, everything else is just a hypothesis."

"Well, how do we find out if it's true?"

He shrugs. "Like all hypotheses, we test it."

"They'll come for Connor," Roul says. "I can't be assured that you'll both be safe at the lab if it comes to that."

Trajan smiles slightly. "Madison will do."

"When did this become about me?" she counters.

"Nobody will be looking for you yet," Trajan says. "You're the only one he's bitten. You and your venom may have the same properties as Connor's now. The fastest way for us to find out is to test out the cure on you."

"And what if I don't want to be cured?"

We all go quiet, unprepared for this reaction. Although if I'd been asked to predict it I might have known. It's not out of character for Madison to dig in her heels like this, even if it is completely irrational.

"It's not going to take long for Boguet's team to figure it out," Trajan says. "Once Prince Charming back there tells the Hounds what he saw, it's only a matter of time before they figure it out too."

"Figure what out, exactly?" I ask.

"That you're the next step in the evolutionary chain for werewolves. Your kids will carry the mutation, so will their kids." Trajan flashes me a smile. "Natural selection likes a winner. It won't take long for your mutation to take over and all these dinosaurs will be a thing of the past."

I feel like a big target just got painted on my back. Not to mention that we're in some kind of evolutionary arms race and Madison has raised an iron curtain. I don't understand her stick-to-itiveness.

We've made it to Hell so I say, "Look, can you all leave us for a second?"

By the way Roul holds me in his stare, I know he's not going to give me a lot of time. If I can't convince Madison to help us, I'm not sure what will happen. His code of honor won't force Madison's hand, but if he lets her walk away, we'll lose our best chance at testing out the one thing that could give us a fighting chance against Boguet. He nods briefly, and he and the others walk ahead.

"Five minutes," he tells me, heading into the house to get our bags.

"The cure means you get to walk away," I start. "You get back all the things that were taken from you, be the person you were meant to be. Isn't that what you wanted?"

She rolls her eyes. "Boguet's cure doesn't set everything to factory default settings, Connor. We're people. People change. I have nothing that I want to go back to. And after everything that I've seen? There's no being normal after all of this."

"It might be the only thing that saves them."

She crosses her arms across her chest. Although her expression is stern, she won't meet my eyes. I reach out and hold her by the elbows. It brings back memories of Club Cin-Cin, which feels like a lifetime ago. The simple contact brought a smile to her face that I haven't seen since. Accidental happiness. I lean down, pressing our foreheads together.

I murmur softly, "What happened at Fontainebleau..."

She shuts her eyes. "That's not how I wanted to tell you."

"I don't know what to say, Madison." My voice quavers.

"I know sorry doesn't cut it."

"Sorry?" She pulls away, glaring up at me. "God, Connor, for someone who's so smart you're sometimes a complete idiot."

The silence goes on for an eternity. She deserves to be free of the cruelties that she was dealt, to walk away from it all and be the free spirit that I know is longing for a way out. She's finally free of her curse and I'm asking her to potentially give up everything she's gained. If the cure were to work, she couldn't walk away from this life any more than I could. Madison unfurls her arms and grabs a hold of my tie, and I think for a second that she's going to try and throttle me with it. She yanks suddenly, pulling my face to meet hers. Standing on her toes she presses her lips against mine. It's a sweet kiss — even her lip gloss tastes of vanilla — but it ends too soon. Roul clears his throat behind us to announce his return. When Madison pulls away her eyes are wet.

"Okay," she says, the moisture carrying to her voice. "I'll go with Trajan."

It was me she didn't want to walk away from. For just a flash of a moment, I have a selfish thought that she should stay with me. Even in that second, I hate myself for it. I wish we could just forget the world. But it's not that easy. If my venom does turn out to be permanent, it could not only heal the bitten but it could save the born from the cure. It's too important. An SUV pulls around front of the house, Trajan at the wheel. He glares over at us impatiently with the female bodyguard looking on from shotgun.

I want to say something meaningful but all I get out is,

"Madison—"

She flings her arms around me in an embrace. "Shut up, Connor."

I wrap my arms around her and gently kiss the top of her head. She feels so small in my arms and yet somehow she fills up so much space in my thoughts. How will I remember this moment when so much of the future is at stake? I try to swallow this unformed memory whole: the familiar scent of her, the little pills of wool on her well-worn sweater. I've already been missing the cherry-red of her hair. I wonder what eyebrow ring she'll wear tomorrow or the next day. When she steps out of my embrace she looks to Roul like she's firing off a warning shot. He owes her. We all do.

17. SO FAR FROM YOUR WEAPON

A chauffeur who I never see beyond the Plexiglas divider drives Roul and me to Magdeburg-Cochstedt Airport. On the drive I stare out at the bleak winter landscape and think of the war ahead.

"*Para bellum*, right?" I offer.

Those are the words inscribed over the door at La Pleine Lune, a werewolf stronghold in the city below the city of Paris. Amara told me it was Latin and meant "prepare for war." Fitting words given our current situation.

"No, it's: *si vis pacem, para bellum*," he corrects. "*If you want peace, prepare for war*. Don't ever lose sight of that first part."

"Who are all these allies you talked about before?"

"The other packs," he replies but holds back from saying more.

He means to bring together the other packs against our common enemies. Strength in numbers has always been his game plan.

I lean forward in my seat. "You're going to unite them?"

"It hasn't been done before. Unifying the packs." He

shakes his head in wonder at the thought of it. "Not on this continent. But we've never faced a threat like this."

Hope is slim, fleeting even, yet I have to think that if anyone is capable of pulling this off, it's Roul. He knows both sides, has lived his entire life on the blade's edge between humans and werewolves. We arrive at a private hanger where a Learjet with a generic-looking blue and white Fenrir Pharmaceuticals logo on the tail waits for us. It's mid-morning and the chill of winter is in the air. I stare out at the airstrip and the stretch of green grass around us, thoughts of running playing through my mind. I follow Roul up the steps of the plane. Inside, a crew member greets us silently before he closes the hatch door and heads to the cockpit with the pilot. Wide leather seats face each other and I slump down into one in the middle. At the back is a stocked bar with an array of expensive-looking bottles of champagne and cognac arranged alongside crystal glasses. Roul takes two lowball tumblers and pours each of us a glass of sparkling water from a mini fridge. He hands me a glass before taking the seat across from me. Finally a chance to rest.

The hum of the plane's engines starts as he leans back in the leather chair and loosens his tie with one hand. It's the first time that I get a sense of his age — I mean, his real age. He's not just in his mid-thirties. Roul has seen things in his life that I haven't even begun to cover in all my history classes put together. It must be exhausting being him. To carry so much weight on his shoulders. The future of the pack, *his* pack, is all on him. If he fails to convince the others to band together, the very existence of all werewolves could be at stake. His gaze meets mine and I'm suddenly aware that he's been watching me, watching him. So I take a sip of water and look away.

In a worn voice he says, "What is it that you want to ask me?"

I hate that I've been so obvious. At the same time, what *don't* I want to ask him? Everything I've learned about being a werewolf so far has been condensed in a crash course. Where do I start? At the beginning, I guess.

"Why did you look for me in the first place?"

He tilts his head back, angling his profile toward the window so all I see is his close-shaven human face. The sun beams in through the window as the plane breaks through clouds, highlighting his lightly tanned skin and rugged features. By the look of him he's as tired as I feel. His hair is neatly combed and he's as well-dressed as ever, but there are dark patches beneath his eyes and for once he slouches.

"You're likely not old enough to understand," he says softly.

"Try me."

Roul swirls his drink around so the bubbles fizzle and he looks down into the glass as though he can read something from it. "Youth is spent looking ahead," he starts, "toward the future, toward the life you want to build for yourself and the ones you come to love. Everything is new and you rush through the years, the decades, as though the end will never come. But when you've lived long enough, you begin to look back at the things that you did ... or didn't do. Sometimes it fills you with a regret for never having stopped to appreciate everything you had during those halcyon days."

I stare at him in wonder and he grimaces.

"As I said, you're too young to understand."

He closes his eyes, basking in the warm glow of sunshine, and soon dozes off. I spend the rest of the short flight thinking about his words. He's built what I'm assuming is a multi-billion-dollar pharmaceutical company from scratch. He's led his pack into the modern age, surviving centuries of pitchfork-wielding and gun-slinging angry villagers. To me it's always seemed like he has everything. But all that wealth and prestige aside, what does he really have? Once, he had twin sons with a human girl he thought he loved. He was forcefully separated from the girl. One son never knew him, growing up and dying without ever discovering the secret that he would pass on to generations ahead of him. The other son, Arden, would live for centuries right under Roul's nose, all that time believing that he was another man's son, never to know his real father so that he'd be protected from the dishonor of half-human blood. In the end, I'm all that's left of his legacy. That's why he found me.

Before I know it, the jet lands at a small business airport on the outskirts of Paris. When Roul wakes, I can't bring myself to say anything. Another limo waits for us in the hanger to take us to Roul's house in the 16th arrondissement, which is clearly the most fashionable and sought-after districts in the city. Madison pokes fun of me for living a posh life, but she has no idea. The neighborhood is called

Passy on the Right Bank. It's sort of like the Upper East Side only distinctly French. We drive by boutiques and cafés brimming with stylish patrons. Festive lights are strung up on the trees that line the wide streets of Champs-Élysées and Avenue Foch. People are out Christmas shopping, completely oblivious to a war about to be waged.

Eventually we turn down a quieter residential street where the chauffeur pulls over in front of a stately stone building wrapped within a wrought iron fence. I sit in the car for a moment to stare up at the place. This is home now. All the windows are barred with elegant metal detailing. When Roul shuts the front gate behind us, I get a momentary sense of being caged. I brush off the feeling, realizing that I should have slept on the plane because all I want now is to lay my head down and rest. I follow on Roul's heels toward the ornate front door. As he twists a key into the lock I glance up toward the clear blue sky and catch the sun, too bright, in my eyes. My vision is momentarily dotted with colors. Spots of blue, violet and a bright red one make me dizzy. Roul turns to say something before he opens the door, but the expression on his face changes suddenly. With lightning speed he grabs me in a crushing bear hug and swings me around like he would a child. As I spin I catch a streak of red light again. He says something into my ear but I don't have the wherewithal to process any of the words.

The thick smell of blood hits me as he pulls away. It gushes from a horrible wound in his neck and his life flows from it. Still, he draws a gun from the holster beneath his left arm and my mind switches gear mechanically, scanning the streets and the rooftops. I see a flash in a second-story window across the way as a marksman scrambles back into darkness. Airy drapes billow ghostlike in his wake. Roul continues to stand, gun outstretched, for a long and terrible moment. He's statue-still except for the blood pulsing from his throat. All of his concentration is spent just simply standing there, carefully surveilling the area. After what feels like an eternity of not breathing, he collapses in front of me — just falls to his knees like he's hollow inside and some force has crushed him like a pop can. The gun slips from his fingers and clatters next to him. I grab a hold of Roul and lay him gently down on the wide entranceway of his home.

Pressing his hands onto the wound, he chokes on his own slick breath. He sounds like he's liable to drown on his own blood. He briefly pulls his fingers away to stare at a bloody palm while the other hand continues to apply pressure on his throat. Roul merely smiles sadly at the sight. I take my phone out to dial for help but I don't know whom to contact.

"Who should I call?" I ask desperately.

He puts his free hand over mine, gripping it so that smears of red coat the screen and my skin, and he shakes his head weakly. I slump down by his side, acknowledging at last what I knew all along but pushed down to the back of my brain. It's what I knew when I stopped just short of really biting Madison at Fontainebleau Forest. There are a handful of major arteries in the body that would constitute a sure kill. The sniper aimed at the carotid, in the neck, for a reason. There's no hope, no possibility that he'll survive. All I can do is watch helplessly as Rodolfus de Aquila's life slips away in front of me.

For whatever reason I still cling to his arm where I caught him. Like if I hold on to him, I can keep him here. My vision blurs with tears. I have so many questions left unasked. His gunmetal-gray eyes start to glaze over as he watches my face. With his tattoo uniting man and beast, I wonder if he laments not leaving this Earth in the form of a wolf. That he'll die clothed in this inelegant form. Releasing his grip on my hand, he urgently marks the space between us, using his blood as ink. With a shiver of his hand, he stops. His eyes turn to the sky and he smiles again, staring out at the clear blue. With a slow and final exhale, he leaves his body. He leaves me. I follow his dead gaze up and catch sight of a bird's silhouette circling the sky, free from the heavy burdens of this world.

A sting of pain on my neck focuses my attention. The bullet must have grazed me upon exiting his throat. A scratch, but a close scratch. Behind me, the dull metal shimmers from where the bullet lodged in the stone. The copper pennies I had taken from Arden's near-death experience are in my pocket where I've been carrying them with me ever since. I pull the coins out, staring at the mismatched pair. Shakily I shut Roul's eyes then gently place them over his lids. Resting back against the wall, my brain churns into motion and rewinds back everything that just happened to the brief fragment of time before Roul was shot. He died because of a bullet that had my name on it. His last act was to shield me from a Luparii marksman, cradling me protectively in his arms, and speaking in my ear. I heard everything he said but only now is my brain allowing me to process his last words.

"Lead the packs."

Kat Kruger is a freelance writer and social media consultant with a degree in public relations from Mount Saint Vincent University. Her first novel, *The Night Has Teeth*, won the 34th Atlantic Writing Competition. She splits her time between Toronto and Halifax with her husband.

Photo © Edmund Lewis

Made in the USA
Charleston, SC
31 March 2014